THE GRANBURY MURDERS

A Mark and Lori Novel

DR. CHARLES SOMERVILL

ISBN: 1522888527
ISBN 13: 9781522888529

ACKNOWLEDGEMENTS

I owe thanks to a large number of people. First of all a bouquet to my spouse and favorite librarian, Linda, who carefully analyzed my many rewrites. A shout-out certainly goes to my reading volunteers, ranging from law officials to ranch owners, who read and re-read chapter after chapter, often making suggestions for each. Their enthusiasm for the book kept me going, so thank you to Brenda Gay, Brenda Kay, Christy, Dutch, Emily, Jack, Jane, Jo, Les, Ruth, Sandy, Sonny and to my character namesakes, Mark, a former Asst. DA from Alabama and his vivacious spouse, Lori. I acknowledge the wonderful town of Granbury, always a delight for visitors and for those of us who live here. I love the churches in Granbury, and especially appreciate First Presbyterian for the cover picture and allowing me to have fun inventing fictional members. (No members were harmed or killed in this book.) I am grateful for my editor and coach, Timothy Staveteig, who provided professional guidance, and for the evaluation and suggestions of The Granbury Writers' Bloc. Everyone has made this book a fun and exciting work to produce. Thank you!

CHAPTER 1

A cat jumped up on the wooden porch carrying a dead mouse in its mouth. "Well, hello kitty cat," the man said. "Are you doing your job and keeping the rats down? Come over here if you want your petting." The cat dropped the mouse at the man's feet and jumped up on his lap, purring. "Yeah, you're proud of your kill, aren't you?"

"You're like me, kitty. Your mission is to kill things so that they don't get out of hand." He paused. "Well, there is one difference. You seem to enjoy it. I can't say that's true with me. I kill for maintenance reasons. I can take or leave the killing part, but sometimes it needs doing when the mission is at stake." He petted the cat behind its ears.

"It's just like it should be, no one here but you and me, kitty. Nothing but wide open country, wild critters, a glorious sunset, and a few distant lights over the hills from Granbury. Ah, would you listen to that! The coyotes are speaking up. God's greatness!"

"Thanks for the gift of your fresh kill, kitty. It's been a few years since the last one for me. With all this land it's hard to remember the exact spot where I buried them. No matter. The mission's the thing, isn't it? Oh, how I wish God would give me a clearer idea of what I'm supposed to do!"

The cat stretched, jumped down to the porch, and sharpened its claws on the wooden post. The man walked back to the house, finished his beer and yawned. Getting sleepy, time to go to bed. He adjusted his pillow and pulled the sheet over him. Every night I dream of the angel you promised me, God.

I don't mean to be faithless--I am your warrior--but it gets old year after year waiting for my orders. I know that a single day is like a thousand years to you, but I'm begging. Send me a sign. Send me something.

Wait--there's a bright light, blinding in the mist--something's moving. Is it my angel? Please let me see you, please! Speak to me!

God has heard your pleadings. Your mission will soon become clear. You will know the angel when you see her. The time has come.

Where? Tell me where! I've waited so long. --What is that sound? A bell! I know that sound! I've heard it before--but where?

Patience, my warrior, patience. The future winds its way even now. Everything will be revealed to you.

I can't stand it! Show me the place! Please don't leave me. Don't go.

The vision faded and the dream ended. That Sunday morning he drove into town and heard the bell. There it is, he smiled, and there's the church.

$$\blacktriangle$$

Seventy miles from Granbury, two Dallas detectives answered a call. "Over here, officers," the farmer said. "The brush is pretty heavy this fall. You might watch out for snakes. You from Homicide?"

"Yeah. Dispatch said that you saw what happened." Detective Mark Travis and his partner Gary Haltom made their way through the tumbleweeds.

"I saw Consuela Sutton pushed out of a truck that looked like her hus-band's-- Henry Sutton," the farmer answered.

"So you know the victim?" Mark bent down on one knee to check for signs of life.

"Not personally. I know her when I see her."

"She's a pretty woman--or was," Mark's partner, Gary Moreno, moved closer to the little figure curled in a fetal position. "It looks like her throat was cut but her head slumped down and stopped the blood flow."

"She has a pulse!" Mark jumped up and used his cell phone. "I need an experienced team of paramedics immediately--nine miles west on farm road 2280. The victim sustained a six inch laceration--front side of her neck. Extreme care is needed for moving."

Gary turned to the farmer. "Was it Henry Sutton who threw her out of the truck?"

"Can't say for sure. I was over a hundred yards away when it happened. I saw her thrown out, and I ran over."

"How long ago was that?" Mark asked.

"Thirty minutes maybe. Then I waited for you detectives."

"Look at the arms of this little lady," Gary said, "--bruises, some of them older."

"Her husband is a mean one," the farmer took off his baseball cap and swatted a wasp. "His last wife went back to Mexico--at least that's what Henry said. He abused her too."

"Can you identify the truck as Henry's?" Mark asked.

"White pickup, same size as Henry's. Of course, there are other trucks around here like that."

"Where does this Henry live?" Gary took out a notepad.

"On his ranch about five miles west from here. You'll see the sign on the left, 'Sutton Ranch.'"

Gary turned to Mark. "The truck's got to have some blood in it."

"Yeah, I'll call in an APB," Mark said. "We need to stay with the scene."

Henry Sutton was apprehended within the next hour, but claimed self-defense. "Consuela came at me with a knife," he said during his interrogation, "so I pushed her out of the truck. She must have cut herself as she fell. I didn't want her coming at me again so I left her there."

With the blood evidence inside the truck and his wife forcibly tossed out into the weeds, Henry's story didn't wash. Consuela recovered and gave her statement two days after that, identifying her husband as the assailant. The case looked open and shut.

⁂

One week later, Mark Travis stormed into the office of his precinct and tossed his badge on his partner's desk. "I'm sick of this insanity," he said. "Gary, I'm through with all of it."

"Aw you've been quitting for the last eight years," Gary replied. "What now?"

"I mean it this time," Mark held up a memo. "We work our butts off and this shi--uh, stuff happens."

"Stuff indeed! You know--you've really cleaned up your language since you married that preacher lady."

"Shut up."

"Can't blame you, a looker like Lori. Let me see that memo."

Mark pushed the memo across Gary's desk. Gary picked it up and noted the name on the prisoner release form. "Henry Sutton's been released?!"

"Yeah," Mark sat down on the edge of Gary's desk. "Consuela changed her story, dropped the charges, and went back to Sutton. --I'm serious about quitting, Gary."

Gary ignored Mark's last comment and threw the memo in the trash. "We need to forget this. The woman's suicidal."

"Yeah," Mark agreed, "Next time he'll kill her for sure."

"And if that happens and we go out there, I hope he backs away just a little bit—give me any excuse." Gary fingered his holster.

Over the years, the two partners had backed each other up in more than one gun fight. Pulling the trigger didn't seem to bother Gary. Mark was sickened by the killings. He remembered his conversation with the departmental psychologist who had the job of clearing officers after a shooting.

"Your feelings are entirely normal," she told him. "Half of the detectives I've talked to feel the same way. Killing someone was by far the worst thing they ever experienced; they wished it never happened."

"It doesn't get any easier the second or the third time," Mark said.

"I'm surprised that most of you stay with the job," she observed.

"What about the other half--how do they cope?"

"They pass it off as part of their job--maybe a defense mechanism that comes in handy," the counselor said.

"I don't have that option. I don't have an off and on switch. All I see is the carnage and the dark side of people."

Mark did not want to become like Gary whose handgun had become a part of his anatomy. He was fed up and wanted out. The time had come to break the news to Lori.

⚓

Mark drummed his fingers on the steering wheel as he drove home. I'm lucky to have someone like Lori I can talk to. Otherwise, I would go nuts.--But I'm not sure how she'll feel about my quitting. It'll affect our life style--have to get another job somewhere. Mark drove up to his driveway and saw Lori getting out of her car struggling with a grocery bag.

"Let me help you with that." Mark treasured Lori. He first remembered her as a smoking hot redhead working in the DA's office as a trial attorney in Arlington. Then came the shocker--something that was not a part of his plans.

Mark thought about it as he loaded up his arms with two sacks of produce. Here I am helping a Presbyterian minister with her groceries and actually liking it! Not at first, of course. Everything seemed like it was slipping away, my sexy DA becoming a holy Jo. Then I saw the contrast between her world and mine. What a difference it makes to come home from another sad and gloomy day to Lori's world of hope and light! I love my "preacher wife" and the life she's given me. I hope she still loves me after we've talked about another career change--only this time it's mine.

Lori and Mark put up their groceries and dined on the meal they had fixed together. Mark was on the verge of making his announcement when Lori put down her fork and rubbed her hands together, a familiar sign that something was up.

"I have something to tell you," she said.

"You're running off with the head pastor?" Mark smiled.

"No, it's worse than that," Lori replied. "I had a phone interview with a church in Granbury."

"Granbury?!" Mark exclaimed. "Hmm. I went fishing there about twelve years ago. As I remember, it's fifty miles southwest of here and has a really cool town square."

"It's grown since then," Lori said. "The Hood County area has about 60,000 people, but the locals still call Granbury a small town. The church has doubled during the last fifteen years to 400 members."

"So you think you might be interested?"

"Maybe. The members are mostly retired and semi-retired, but more young people are moving in. I think it's one of the most promising churches in our region."

"That would be quite a change from an associate at First Church!" Mark said. "Are you sure you want to look at this? You'll have to preach each and every Sunday. Your cell phone will never stop ringing."

"I think I would love it," Lori hesitated a few seconds. "One other thing. I'm not sure the timing is right for this, but do you remember Rob Galloway?"

"Yeah, isn't he the DA at Granbury? We worked on a case together four years ago. Nice guy. What's your point?"

"It might be something or it might not. Rob is on the pastor's search committee and he told me that he's looking for an investigative officer--and he remembers *you*."

"So now you're job hunting for me!" Mark smiled.

"I'm sorry," Lori took her empty plate to the dishwasher. "Let's just forget the whole thing. It's not a big deal."

Mark remained at the table. "Yes it is, or you wouldn't have pursued it. You're worried that I'll be giving up my job for you. Well, it's not that way. I hate my job and I was just going to tell you that I'm thinking about resigning."

"I don't believe that, and it's not going to work if one of us is unhappy. If you went to Granbury, you would be bored silly."

"The Lord moves in strange and mysterious ways," Mark replied. "I'd like to get the hell out of Dodge and take a look at Granbury. If I got the job as an investigative officer with the DA, it's actually a step up--with my own office and responsibilities for the entire county. The DA's office is independent from the police and the sheriff's departments. I'd be working less with dead bodies and more with broader types of investigation. --Sounds good to me. When's your next interview?"

"They want to meet with me Saturday for a face-to-face."

Mark stood up. *I need to make it clear that I'm supporting her.* "Hey, I can help you with that interview."

"Right, you have a master's in communication, and you won't let me forget it."

"--And I taught an interview class at TCU."

"I know."

"Let's role play."

"Uh, let's not."

Mark continued undaunted. "Here's one question that interviewers often ask of managers. How would you define leadership?"

"Oh, alright. Pastoral leadership is a matter of vision."

"Hmm," Mark frowned. "Just what do you mean by *vision?*"

"For me, it's a vision of the talents or gifts that members can develop," Lori said. "The pastor seeks to encourage the ways in which people can participate."

"Those Granbury people are not going to buy that preacher vision stuff," Mark said. "They'll want to know how you get things done--how you get people to do what you want them to do."

Lori folded her arms. "So how do I do that?"

"Well, they're volunteers so you can't dock their pay. What you need to do is cultivate a network of friends and focus on the values you share with them. That way they'll come to trust you and do what you want. It's really just interpersonal leadership."

"I see. Let's take a look at that. So you define leadership as getting people to do what you want them to do," Lori walked toward Mark as she would an opposing attorney. "That definition won't work in churches. They want a leader with vision, not someone who manipulates. I had enough of that stuff in the DA's office."

"You're headed in the wrong direction," Mark said.

"No I'm not," Lori swatted him with a wet towel.

"It's about getting things done," Mark insisted.

"It's vision," Lori said.

"You want the last word?"

"Yes," Lori laughed.

"You can't have it," Mark leaned over, kissing her on the back of the neck.

Just then the phone rang. Mark answered and sat down. "When? You're joking. Aw, man! Wow--wow! Hey, Gary, thanks. Thanks very much for the call."

"What?" Lori asked

--Henry Sutton," Mark shook his head. "His wife just shot him dead. It's been a good day after all."

Chapter 2

The members of the pastor's search committee had heard Lori preach on an earlier visit. "Lori is by far the most attractive of our candidates," John Summers said as they drove to meet her at Fort Worth. "We don't need an interview. We need a closing! Let's wrap this thing up."

She's uh, well--gorgeous. Do you think our women are ready for someone like that?" Joe Michaels asked.

"That's not what I mean by *attractive*," John Summers protested.

"If she comes, I'd like to see her fatten up on our pot-luck suppers." Belle Ashton patted her ample tummy. "Do you think she has any other qualities beside good looks?"

"I love her sense of humor," Thelma Hill said. "She's got great people skills and what a preacher!"

"She's got a beautiful, vibrant voice," John Summers added. "People will feel honored just from a phone call."

"We may have to build a bigger church," Joe Michaels laughed.

"Now let's not get carried away," Rob said. "Let's see how she does in this interview."

By prior arrangement, to avoid curious onlookers at First Church, the six member committee met with Lori in a classroom at Westminster Church. Lori was dressed in a well tailored suit which she wore during her time as an Assistant DA. Belle Ashton was quick to notice.

"Do you always look this good?" Belle sucked in her mid-section. "That's a fancy suit."

Lori returned Belle's stare. "I only wear this suit when I'm trying to impress people I respect. It's one of the few I have."

"--a tactful answer," Belle smirked.

Lori felt a twinge. *I can't let this twit push my buttons but if she keeps it up …*

"Lori, we were very impressed with your sermon," Rob Galloway began. "We'd like to start this interview by asking how you see yourself as a pastor?"

"I like the title of 'teaching elder' as described in our Book of Order. Presbyterian pastors are trained as teaching preachers. I have a great enjoyment in my calling as pastor, but I don't think my calling is higher than anyone else. We have different gifts but we are all called to be Christian followers."

"How humble," Belle said.

Lori turned away from Belle. *I've put up with worse from defense attorneys. I can handle this.*

"Lori, how would you define leadership?" John Summers asked.

"What?" Lori remembered her discussion with Mark.

"Leadership. How do you see it?" Joe Michaels joined in.

"A leader must have a vision of what the church can become," Lori paused. "My vision is of a shared ministry where our gifts may be used for God's glory. My role as a leader is to promote an environment where these gifts will be encouraged and developed."

"Poetry, sheer poetry," Belle said facetiously, "a guru who makes house calls to release the gifts within us."

Lori could feel her blood pressure rising and was about to respond to Belle when the DA, Rob Galloway, spoke up. "I agree that the church should be a place where gifts are put to work," Rob said, "but could you be a little more specific as to how you would function as a leader?"

"Lori, here's my problem with your answer," John Summers chimed in. "We've interviewed eight other ministers and the 'gifts' answer was the same for each. I think they're reading the same book. With your background I was hoping for something uh,--well, something more in terms of practice."

"Yes, tell us how you would function," Joe Michaels said.

"You want to know how I would get things done," Lori could see Mark laughing and wanted to slap him.

"Right," Rob said.

Lori paused. Okay, what was it that Mark said? "In order for a church leader to get things done, a leader must develop trust relationships--cultivating friendships, sharing Christian values."

"Tell us how you would cultivate friendships," Joe asked.

"Oh, I don't know," Lori wanted the interview over. "Let's do lunch, get together at Bible study, parties, sports, birthday celebrations, office conversations…

"Goodness gracious!" Belle exclaimed as she took a swallow of coffee. "So now you're going to charm us!"

Something primeval came over Lori as she slowly turned to Belle. "Yes, dammit! I'm gonna charm you--you and your little dog too!"

Coffee sprayed from Belle's mouth. To Lori's surprise, Belle laughed convulsively. "Ha! Ha!" Belle got up from the table and ran over to Lori. "That did it! That did it! I'm voting for Lori!" Belle embraced Lori with a firm hug.

"Well now!" Rob slapped Joe on the back. "That's what I call leadership!"

"She gets it done and doesn't back down," Joe agreed.

The rest of the time was spent in laughter and small talk with Mark invited to share dinner at a restaurant. Lori would never tell him about her answer on leadership. However, she wasn't entirely satisfied with her interview. Something's missing from those answers, she told herself, from both my vision comments and Mark's interpersonal stuff. I can't put my finger on it just yet, but it's important, something to do with my identity. I'll work on it later.

⚔

Lori's final interview came the first week of December. Lori and Mark arrived in Granbury early to explore the town square.

"I'd heard about their tour of lights," Lori said, but I didn't expect this!"

Granbury was a blaze of lights and activities with horse drawn carriages carrying people on a "tour of lights" featuring historic homes and buildings. "Check it out," Lori said. "The buildings all have red candles along their pathways with volunteers dressed up in 19th century costumes."

"I don't think I've ever seen a town with this many historic markers," Mark said as they walked around the square.

"It's like the town square is personally greeting us," Lori said. "Look at all those little elegant shops lit up for Christmas--each one trying to outdo the other."

"No one going out of business here," Mark observed. "Wow, they have two live theaters!"

"Bistros and cafes on every side, lights spreading like a spider web from the tower of the old courthouse to the shops. Christmas trees on every corner," Lori said.

"Big trees loaded down with packages," Mark observed. "Those packages wouldn't last two seconds in Dallas! I don't think we're in a high crime area."

"I can't believe this place," Lori pulled Mark into a little shop called the Panhandle.

"Hey, where are we going? You only have one hour before your interview."

"Kitchen gadgets! You like to cook."

"It smells good," Mark inhaled the aroma. "Oh, I see--gourmet coffee samples. Maybe we could stay for just a second."

"May I help you?" Jennifer Olson asked.

"Just looking. We're visitors," Lori replied.

"I like how your shops are built with those large artistic lime stones," Mark said. "Expensive stuff!"

"Just the opposite of what you might think," Jennifer smiled. "Those 'artistic' lime stones were the poorest materials available in the late eighteen hundreds. Later on, other more prosperous towns were embarrassed by their lime stones and covered up their shops with facades. Granbury couldn't afford to do that so everything you see is original. Now we're a big attraction--all because we were poor!"

Mark and Lori briefly visited two more shops and then went for a drive in the neighborhood around the square.

"Look at that library!" Lori exclaimed. "If this is a poor town, I'd like to see a rich one!"

"Yeah, it's beautiful--modern but built with lime stones, matching the old art museum next to it."

"And if that's not enough, what a lovely surrounding park with a walking path, street lanterns and bridges all lit up for Christmas."

"You're going to be late for your interview."

"No problem. The church is right around the corner from the library."

The interview consisted of escorting Mark and Lori around the church grounds, ending up at the hundred year old sanctuary. The building was on the "tour of lights," with visitors coming and going. One *visitor* sat alone on the back row, aware of the rumors of a possible new pastor, carefully looking at Lori as she came into the sanctuary.

"That's her. It has to be--even more beautiful than they say. Look at the people mulling around her. Yeah, they know she's something special, but they have no idea how special. Look at the way she walks-- graceful, confident, with a purpose. She has a message for me. I can feel it. She's the one! That big guy must be her husband. Huh! Now that I look at him, he's about my size, tough looking dude. I may have to take him out to my ranch. Ha! --show him my layaway plan."

Lori stood admiring the sanctuary. "I get this feeling of peace here, something warm and friendly."

"A lot of us feel that," Belle Ashton, whom Lori had won over, whispered to Lori, "If you take the job as my pastor, can I bring my little dog to church?"

"This is like the church in <u>High Noon</u>," Mark was intrigued by the New England styled architecture. "Are these floors original?"

"Yes," John Summers replied. "We sanded them down, but those are something you rarely see, four-inch red pine."

"Beautiful," Mark said. "What about those large tin tiles on the ceiling?"

"The square decorated ones? --Also original and so is the bell in the tower; it still works. You can hear it out in the countryside."

"This building is sensational," Mark surveyed the tall ceiling and the crystal chandeliers, "but how do you get 400 people in here?"

"Two services," Rob Galloway, the DA, pulled Mark aside. "Does Lori know you interviewed at my office?"

"Not yet."

"You got the job, but I need an answer in one week," Rob whispered. "I can't wait longer."

Lori was occupied by other members of the search committee.

"We're ready to negotiate," Belle said. "You're the one we want. You've seen our financial reports and know what we paid the last pastor. We don't expect to get you on the cheap. Are you ready to talk about it?"

"Whoa! Coming here is a big decision. Can I think about it? Give me a couple of weeks."

"One week would be better for us," Rob said.

"Two weeks," Lori said politely. "You're not the one making this move!"

Mark looked at Rob, smiled and held up two fingers.

"Alright," Rob laughed. "We'll make that work for everybody."

Driving back to Dallas, Mark suspected that Lori was already leaning toward Granbury. She was uncharacteristically quiet, humming to herself with a little smile.

"I think you've made up your mind," Mark said.

"Now what gave you that idea?" Lori laughed.

Mark could see that the change was coming. When he returned to his office, he discussed his plans with his partner. Gary invited Mark to lunch the next day.

"Go ahead and order a T-bone," Gary said as they sat across the table from each other. "I'm picking up the tab. If you're leaving, I want to do this right. Mind if I ask you a few questions?"

"Depends on the questions."

"You and Lori have both been offered jobs in Granbury, right?"

"Right."

"Who got the first job offer."

"I did."

"Really?" Gary took a healthy swallow of his Shiner Bock beer. "I can believe that, but who had the first interview?"

"I guess she did, but what's your point?"

Just then their captain, Henry Mason, joined the table.

"I'm sorry I'm late," Captain Mason said, "but I never turn down a free lunch. What are we celebrating, Gary?"

"I don't think it's a celebration," Mark suspected an ambush.

"Well, I think Mark is following his wife out to Granbury and taking a new job."

"Damn," Mason said, "and he just made lieutenant? What's going on here, Mark?"

"I think he's pussy whipped," Gary said.

"How would you like my foot up your ass!" Mark said loudly.

"Boys, please!" Mason reacted. "This a public place."

"Sorry, Captain," Gary said, "but this guy needs a come-to-Jesus-moment."

Mark started to get up from his chair to confront Gary, but Mason restrained him.

"Gary, exit-interviews are my job, not yours," Mason said. "I want you to pick up your damned hamburger and get the hell out of here!"

"Well, I'm not going to welsh out on lunch," Gary got up and put forty dollars on the table. "That should cover it."

"Just go!"

"I'm gone!" Gary nearly knocked over his chair heading for the door.

"Thank you for lunch, asshole," Mark shouted after him.

"Now Mark," Mason put his hand on Mark's arm, "I want you to calm down. Gary's upset because he doesn't want to lose his partner. Since you're married to a minister, you should become more sensitive to shit like that."

"I suppose."

"And I'm not happy either," Mason said, "--losing our best detective! Would you please fill me in on the details and it better be good."

"I'm just tired of dead bodies. I barely get through one case and there's two more, all in the same week. I like being a detective, but I'm sick of the carnage," Mark filled in the details about Granbury. "Lori just happened to be thinking of leaving when I was."

"You love your wife, don't you?" Mason said quietly. "It's natural that you would want to follow her."

"Look, Captain," Mark said, "that's not it. I thought about this and prayed long and hard. I used to not take much stock in prayer. Now I do. Maybe you don't."

"Well, I don't tell many people this," Mason smiled, "but my Daddy was a Baptist preacher. I'm not much of a churchgoer myself but I'm not going to argue with a God thing. If you've prayed about it and you think that's the answer, then God bless you. I'm not even going to suggest a counter offer."

"You don't have the budget for a counter offer," Mark laughed. "Beside that, I don't think I'm worth much right now--bad language and all."

"Got the same problem. Old habits are hard to break," Mason said. "Gary pushed your button and you stripped gears. Maybe you'll have better companions in Granbury."

"No, I couldn't have better friends than you and Gary," Mark said. "I'll miss you both."

"You've done a lot of good for this department," Mason said. "It won't be the same without you." Captain Mason shook Mark's hand, then pulled him in for a hug. "God bless you boy!"

CHAPTER 3

L ovely day for a walk, just lovely. And here comes Bullet, my faithful dog, to join me. Bullet arched his head for a petting and the man scratched him behind his ears.

Good boy, good boy. Glad to have you with me. I need to check on one of my ranch residents to see if last week's rains exposed his grave. Can't have that. Oh well, maintenance is always a problem on a ranch.

On a much bigger issue, I need to make some plans, Bullet. As you know, I have a wonderful mind for planning. I think we are about to be blessed with a gorgeous angel to guide my mission. I was beginning to think it was all a dream, but here she is. Now I need to prepare.

The dog ran ahead and splashed into the pond. Have fun, boy! I never could figure out why people out here call it a 'tank' instead of a pond. Us Texans have peculiar ways sometimes. Okay, the time has come to sit down and dictate a planning outline on my cell phone. Here's a good rock for stretching out and thinking it through, somewhere near the place of burial.

First off, I can't spook her. She's obviously in human form and may take a while to discover our mission. So how do I go about this specifically? Communication's impossible if I stay an outsider. No, I'll have to join the church and become active as an insider with direct contact.

Bullet charged up the hill from the pond and shook himself vigorously. Well, thanks for the soaking, stupid. Now scat, I'm trying to think. Where was I? Oh yeah--joining the church, but maybe not immediately. Due deliberation, careful consideration. That's how it needs to look, nothing too eager, nothing impulsive. I'm a thinking man, calm and rational about my decisions.

The man frowned and pulled himself up from the rock. Rats! Is that a hand poking up? Yeah, it is. That's what happens with the rain. I guess it's time to buy that new excavator I've been thinking about. Need to plant this guy further up the hill and do the job right. I'm lucky the coyotes didn't dig him up.

Maybe next in line is that rugged looking guy who's sleeping with my angel. I hate the thought of that, even if she is married to him. She deserves better, much better.

I have 3000 acres, plenty of room for the big guy--well, no bigger than me really. Hang on, just hold it. I need to stop thinking like this. It's not wise right now--he's too high a profile and I don't want her upset.

She is amazing really, a powerful sensual quality. I didn't count on that. A sexy angel doesn't make much sense. Why would God jeopardize the mission by giving me such thoughts? It's distracting, to say the least. Maybe it's a test. Here I am out in this wilderness wrestling with temptation. Am I up to the challenge? Of course I am. I can think of her as uh, art appreciation. She's too beautiful to be real and guess what? She's beyond real, an angel sent with a message special for me. That's it. That's my focal point, a special messenger.

The man walked back to his ranch house with a smile of satisfaction, a thinking man, a careful planner.

⚔

January came and then February. By the end of March Lori and Mark were settled in the country-style house they had purchased across the street from the Granbury library. They sat outside on their patio having their morning cup of coffee.

"Are you experiencing buyer's remorse?" Mark looked up at the high pitch of the roof. "Changing light bulbs is going to require a ten foot ladder."

"Those lights are LEDs," Lori replied. "They're supposed to last at least ten years."

"I like having two bathrooms and two walk-in closets," Mark said.

"It's a good design," Lori said, "no hallways, just a great room up front with a island separating the kitchen. Oh, and I love that office going out from the second bedroom. It's an elegant little home, easy for you to clean."

"And a laundry room leading into a two car garage with an attic to store our junk," Mark added. "Uh, did you say 'for me to clean?'"

"You need to get rid of some of that junk," Lori said. "It's a good time to start over doing things right."

"Yeah, yeah," Mark put down his coffee and changed the subject. "So how are things going with you at church?"

"Well, as you know, I'm finishing up a new members' class tonight--all of them young adult singles."

"Rob Galloway credits you for that," Mark observed. "He says that because of you the sea of gray is receding on Sunday mornings. --not sure how it happened so quickly."

"Sally Lawton has been recruiting," Lori replied.

"That cute little blonde?" Mark asked.

"So you noticed," Lori gave Mark a playful kick.

"Everyone seems to love you," Mark said.

"It's the first year, the honeymoon year. They warned us about that in seminary," Lori said. "The second year won't be so easy."

"You can handle it," Mark finished his bagel.

"I'm glad you understand that," Lori draped her arms around Mark's neck. "I certainly don't want you defending me."

"You're like Joan of Arc," Mark grinned, "a minister with vision."

"Yes and I can get the job done too. I'm a functional leader."

"You function very well. All your parts are working."

"Glad you appreciate me," Lori took the coffee cups into the kitchen. "Time to go to work."

⟡

That evening, Lori concluded her new members' class of young adults.

Sally Lawton stood up, her petite shapely body twitching in anticipation of the proposal she was about to make. "Lori is a wonderful teacher and I for one want to learn more from her. What say we continue these classes? Do I have an Amen?"

"If we do," Mike Garland said, "we need to keep it small, maybe just for this bunch so that we could have a good discussion."

"I suppose we could continue for a while longer," Lori replied. "Where should we meet?"

"Let's meet in our homes," Sally replied. "We could each bring some snacks."

"I'd like to volunteer my place for the first meeting," Billy Ray offered. "I have a log-styled ranch house that I think you'll like."

"How far out?" asked Zeb Mallory.

"Well, it's about seven miles to the turn off, then another mile to the ranch," Billy Ray replied. "The road is newly paved. I'll make sure you get there."

"Sounds like an adventure," Betty Jones said. "All in favor say Aye!"

"Aye!" Everyone agreed.

"Oh my," Lori laughed. "You're going to make me earn my keep. Alright, how about calling it the Seekers' Class with anything goes. All questions are welcome."

"May I suggest a topic for our first meeting?" Sally seemed eager to do just that.

"Sure."

"Presbyterians are sometimes accused of being cool and aloof, but that's not you Lori. You are on fire in the pulpit! People who are spiritually aware are drawn to you."

"Well, I don't claim to--"

"Let me make my point! I'm not content with just the history and creeds of our church. I want to know how God has touched the members of this class. I know there are some wonderful experiences with the Lord in this room. I can feel them, and I want to know about the gifts that the Holy Spirit has given us. "

Lori fumbled for a response. God help me. Where is this woman coming from and where is she going with this?

Sally turned to the rest of the class. "I don't want to impose, but would that topic be agreeable to the rest of you."

Everyone nodded, some reluctantly.

"Good! Then it's agreed. And Lori, why don't you choose some scripture to go along with it."

"Thank you so much, Sally," Lori said. "I'll see what I can do."

When Lori came back home, she groaned and tossed her Bible onto the table.

"Tough day at the New Members' class?" Mark asked.

"Yes and it may get tougher. They want to continue the class and the topic has already been assigned to me--spiritual experiences and gifts."

"So why are you groaning?"

"I don't want to kill their enthusiasm but it's this business of focusing on spiritual gifts. The Apostle Paul had that problem with the Corinthians. That's why he came up with the 'more excellent way' in I Corinthians 13."

"The one about 'if I have not love, I am nothing?'"

"Right. The problem comes when a gift is claimed to be better than others or when someone uses it to get their own way."

"I've heard you say that ministers are not more spiritually blessed than others. --But doesn't your three years of seminary make you better?"

"Better trained maybe, but not better in compassion or caring for others."

"Not morally better?"

"No, and as soon as you start thinking of yourself as morally superior to others you get into trouble. It's one thing to be confident of your training. It's another to think that you are a better person than others."

"I don't think you're guilty of that."

"Of course not--and as Richard the Third said, 'I thank God for my humility.'"

"Amen," Mark laughed.

"I guess what I'm saying is that spiritual gifts can become an ego trip. It can take over a church, sort of like pride in a family bloodline--my family is better than yours' stuff."

"So my gift is no better than yours," Mark concluded.

"And it's okay for you not to have a special one," Lori said. "A loving, forgiving person is gifted enough."

"Do you think Sally Lawton is headed in the wrong direction?" Mark asked.

"I don't know. Maybe she's fine. We'll see."

CHAPTER 4

At the Seekers' Class, eleven members showed up at Billy Ray's ranch. Lori began the meeting.

"From 1 Corinthians 12:14-16 we can see that gifts are like parts of the body. They all work together and the foot does not claim to be greater than the hand or vice versa. We can also see in 1 Corinthians 13 that love is the greatest way--greater than any spiritual experience we might have."

"I agree," Sally Lawton said. "We have to go beyond our spiritual experiences, but we shouldn't discount them. They can be life changing. I'm glad we agreed to share these with one another tonight. I'm so excited! I think it will be a blessing. Lori, would you begin with yours? From what I've read, you were a very successful lawyer. You were even featured on the cover of a law review magazine! What led you to give up such a promising career and become a minister?"

"Alright," Lori remembered her testimony at a Presbytery meeting. "There was no bolt of lightning. I guess the change came when I started thinking about the people I prosecuted in murder trials. Some got the death penalty. That bothered me. It's one thing to defend yourself at home in fear for your family's life. It's another after capture and imprisonment, to strap the person down and deliver a lethal injection."

"You mean like Dexter?" Mike Garland said, referring to the TV character.

"Exactly. Dexter is judge and jury of the guilty. Then he injects his victims and binds them up for their final execution. The State is carrying out the same type of killing. In my opinion, it's sanctioned murder."

"I don't agree," Zeb Mallory said. "Some people are better off dead."

"Well, Dexter and the state of Texas would agree with you," Lori replied.

"So how did the Spirit lead you to become a minister?" Sally persisted.

"I began to wonder what sort of vocation might give me a sense of joy--something that I could wake up to in the mornings and really enjoy going to work. Of course, there's nothing wrong with being an attorney. I believe that some people have a calling to do that too, but not me--not anymore. After a lot of thought and prayer, I found my joy in becoming a minister."

"Did you feel the Spirit?" Sally asked.

"I think that's the way the Spirit led me. It wasn't all of a sudden."

"Thank you, Lori." Sally frowned, not quite getting the spirit-filled answer she wanted. "Next, I would like to hear from Billy Ray."

"Why me?" Billy Ray protested. "There's nothing special about me."

"Oh yes there is, Billy!" Sally said. "You don't remember me because I was three years younger than you in school. But I remember you--our star quarterback and that wonderful game you won against Cleburne. You were magnificent! God has big plans for you, Billy, and I want to hear how you've grown since then spiritually."

Sally looked moon-eyed at Billy Ray. Lori began to wonder if Sally was hoping for this moment.

"I don't know about *spiritually*," Billy Ray replied. "Eight years ago my father disappeared, and I was left on the ranch by myself. I finished college at Tarleton and now I work in the sheriff's department as a deputy. I read about Lori and started attending church. That's about it."

Billy Ray looked at the floor and shuffled his feet. His admiration for Lori had indeed begun as a spiritual experience, but he was not about to share this event with anyone. There Lori stood at Communion, a light shinning around her, her face glowing in a soft golden circle. God's messenger, but only for those who have eyes to see.

Sally leaned toward Billy Ray. "You have come so far, Billy. You lost both parents and have practically raised yourself. And now here you are seeking God's blessings. I think that's wonderful!"

"Would anyone else want to talk about their journey?" Lori addressed the group.

"In a minute maybe," Mike Garland said. "First of all I'd like to point out that something unusual has happened here. Those of us who showed up are all single and yet we didn't come here for that purpose."

"Hey, what would it take to start a Singles' Group?" Betty Jones asked.

"We already have an older one," Lori replied.

"How about a young one?" Mike asked. "Make this one a regular class."

"We're getting off the subject," Sally objected.

"If enough of you want it, we'll start a Young Singles' Group," Lori said. "Let's go back to Mike's journey."

"My journey nearly ended with my divorce," Mike said. "I thought about suicide. Then I read an article Lori wrote about loss of faith in the local paper. I'm still searching and I hope this Seekers' Class will be a place where I can rediscover my faith. I haven't had any spiritual experiences."

"--But something brought you here," Sally said. "I would call that a spiritual experience. You might see it that way later on."

"I'm not an enthusiast like you, Sally. I'm not ready to roll down the aisles."

"I'm not trying to make holy rollers out of anyone!"

"Sally, I think you're really sweet," Betty Jones smiled. "We could use a little spiritual enthusiasm in our straight-laced Presbyterian tradition."

"Do I sound straight-laced?" Lori asked. "Presbyterians may not roll down the aisles but we find joy in our worship and our outreach to others. I'm very proud of how we help the poor in our community. We are a compassionate people."

"You're more than a Presbyterian," Billy Ray said. "You are very special, Lori."

"Amen," Sally said. "Lori is a spiritual dynamo."

"I give up," Lori said quietly.

"I want this class to continue," Billy Ray said. "I have a big room here so let's meet again next week."

"How about next month--if that's what you want to do," Lori thought about her other meetings and obligations.

"I like next week!" Sally said.

"Next month is fine," Mike replied. "Let's not gang up on Lori. All in favor of next month, raise your hands."

The class agreed and the meeting was set at Billy Ray's. After the class finished, Lori returned home and talked about the meeting with Mark.

"I like their enthusiasm, but something is bothering me that I can't put my finger on."

"How so?"

"I don't know. I get uneasy when people love me more than I think they should."

"Now that's a new one. I haven't heard you complain about that."

"It was a little over the top with Sally and Billy Ray."

"Sexual?"

"No, it was more like, well--hero worship."

"In what way?"

"I'm not sure. I felt like I was being installed as some sort of cult leader."

"You do have charisma."

"Yeah, I'm great--just great. How was your day?"

"Looking at cold cases--stuff we wouldn't even bother with in Dallas."

"How old?"

"Four or five years back--two county residents who can't be found."

"Suspicious circumstances?"

"No evidence of anything. They just disappeared with no forwarding address."

"Why would the DA look at that? There's nothing to build a case on?"

"Pressure from family and city council members."

"So you're interviewing people with lapsed memories," Lori concluded. "It doesn't sound worthwhile. Are you sure you like this job?"

"It's small town stuff. I enjoy getting out into the countryside interviewing people and looking for meth labs. The salary's right and it beats giving death notifications."

"I hope you don't get bored."

"Not a bit. I like working with Rob. How about you?"

"This church is very active," Lori said, "never a dull moment. I'm glad we came."

"Me too," Mark agreed, "so let's just enjoy it."

CHAPTER 5

Autumn came and put an end to the infernal heat of a Texas summer. Mark wondered whether the church's honeymoon with Lori might also be drawing to a close. He observed how some of the older women suddenly grew quiet when he walked by during fellowship time. He couldn't resist a jibe or two.

"Good morning, ladies," Mark said with a Clint Eastwood smile. "I hope I didn't interrupt your conversation. Was it something I said or did? Or maybe it's just that people get quiet when they see a detective coming. If you're hiding something, it'll go better for you if you confess up now. I'm watching you."

The women responded with nervous laughter, then each went their separate ways. Mark looked after them shaking his head and wagging his finger in mock consternation. I wonder what they might have in store for Lori. Oh well, Lori can take care of that bunch. At least they know that I'm aware of their shenanigans.

At his office the next day, Mark was flipping through some papers when Rob Galloway walked in.

"We've got trouble," Rob announced. "The hospital helicopter spotted what looks like a drug exchange in Culler's Bend. A deputy sheriff is on his way here to go out with you. I think it's a good idea to go armed. It's a rough crowd out there."

The door opened, and the DA's administrative assistant leaned in. "Mr. Galloway, the deputy sheriff is here."

"Tell him to come in."

Billy Ray quietly opened the door. He was about the same height and weight as Mark. The two men together presented an imposing presence.

"Mark, meet Billy Ray," Rob said. "You may know him. In fact, he joined our church last Sunday."

"Well, a good looking lad like this is hard to miss." Mark noticed the Colt 44 and the smooth leather holster suspended on Billy Ray's right side.

"I'm glad to meet you, sir," Billy Ray shook Mark's hand with a firmness that felt more like a challenge than a handshake. "I very much admire your wife. She's an angel."

"Angels don't have her red hair, but she'll do." Mark retrieved his hand.

"Well, you guys may be going where angels fear to tread," Rob said. "Culler's Bend has quite a history. The last sheriff refused to go there by himself. That's why I'm sending you both."

"I've been there before," Billy Ray replied. "We can handle it."

"Be careful," Rob said as the two left for their assignment.

On their drive out, Mark was curious about the matter-of-fact coolness of Billy Ray. It seemed oddly robotic.

"How did you get into this business?" Mark asked as Billy Ray drove.

"After my father left me, I entered the Criminal Justice Program at Tarleton University. They said that enforcement was a good fit for my personality; I agreed."

"So you're part time?"

"No, full time for the last four years. I finished up my master's last summer. I don't need the money, just the opportunity."

"You're a true believer."

"You might say that," Billy Ray replied.

"You seem uh, absolutely confident."

"Yes sir, I am. God has laid his hand on me."

"Yeah--well uh, yeah, we may need that."

"We're coming to the spot where the lab was reported," Billy Ray unstrapped his pistol. "Are you ready?"

"I hope so. Let's see if we can do this peacefully."

The two exited from the patrol car and ran toward the door of a metal Quonset building. Shots came at them from behind.

"They flanked us!" Mark said as they retreated to a grove of trees.

"I'll go after the one on the left," Billy Ray whipped out his 44 as he took off in that direction.

"Wait! We need back-up," Mark yelled, but Billy Ray was already zigzagging in and out toward his target. The assailant was caught off-guard and his assault rifle fired in the wrong direction. Billy Ray fired one lethal shot to the head and the man collapsed in a heap.

"Damn!" Mark said as he engaged his assailant on the right. The door of the metal building opened and two other combatants came out with AK 47s. Billy Ray walked out in plain sight and immediately shot one. The other retreated back into the building.

Mark wounded his assailant and the man threw down his gun. Billy Ray headed toward the building.

"No! Don't go in there!" Mark shouted. "Wait for back-up."

"There isn't time. They could destroy evidence," Billy Ray effortlessly kicked in the door. Mark had no choice but to follow.

Three men were waiting behind overturned tables.

"Throw your guns down, you're surrounded!" Mark crouched down but Billy Ray walked toward the men firing. One man went down, and the other two stood up with their hands raised.

"Billy Ray, you're nuts!" Mark said as he handcuffed the remaining bad guys.

The drugs lay in white powdered packages around the room. It was a major bust that would make the headlines of the surrounding area, not only of Granbury, but Fort Worth and Dallas. Mark knew one thing for sure. He did not want to go out again with Billy Ray.

Chapter 6

Lori and Mark regularly worked out at the YMCA in Dallas so they transferred their membership to the one in Granbury. Lori especially loved racquetball; she was well suited for it with her agility and coordination. Mark had taken up the sport three years prior, but Lori had been playing since her teens and had won tournaments in her division. Mark was reluctant to play with her as they entered the Y in Granbury.

"Why don't you pick on someone your own size," Mark complained. "I get a drubbing every time we play. It lowers my self-esteem."

"You only learn when you play with the best," Lori laughed. "You might do better if you concentrate on where the other player is. You can't just hit it hard."

"I know where you are. You're right there where the ball ends up regardless of where I hit it. I can't get it past you."

"You do better every time we play. C'mon!"

At the Y, heads turned as Mark and Lori entered the racquetball court. Three church members immediately approached them.

"Hey Mark, are you going to beat up on our pastor?" Ethan Snider asked.

"My money's on the woman in red shorts," Belle Ashton looked at Lori.

"Can we watch?" John Summers put down his jumping rope.

"No!" Mark said.

"We're going to anyway," Belle said.

"You don't understand," Mark objected. "Lori's a tournament player; I'm not. You don't want to watch this. It won't be pretty."

The three church members pulled up chairs at the glass wall to watch them play. As predicted, Mark's points were few and far between. Lori gracefully moved around the court owning every shot.

"Holy cow!" Ethan's eyes were wide with amazement. "She's a pro. Mark never had a chance!"

A tall statuesque black woman greeted Mark and Lori as they came out of the court.

"You play very well," the woman said to Lori. "How about some cut-throat. My partner had to cancel."

"Cut-throat! Two against one?" Mark looked suspiciously at the slender Amazon who was challenging them. "I imagine you're pretty good."

"My name's Celesta." They shook hands.

"I'm Lori. This is Mark. Let's play!"

As they played, a larger group pulled up chairs to watch.

"Wow. Now this is *my* fantasy team," Ken Mayfield said as he watched Lori and Celesta take the serve away from Mark.

"Pig." Belle turned her head toward Ken.

"No ma'am," Ken replied. "I'm an admirer of athletic ability."

"Right."

Mark grimaced as he came out of the court. "That did it. You two play each other. I'll watch."

"For shame, detective," Ethan said in pretended disbelief.

"You go in and play those two."

"I got better sense than that."

"Yeah. Well at least Lori found someone that can give her a game."

Indeed after that, Lori and Celesta became friends and happily played each other on alternate days of the week. And several of the older men in Lori's congregation happily watched.

The time came as Lori was working with Junie Barrows, the record keeper of the elders, when three older women walked unannounced into Lori's office. Junie looked up and smiled as they came in. She remembered how these women were helpful during the time of her mother's death.

"Good afternoon," Lori stood up behind her desk. "How can I help you?"

"We would like a word with you," Judy Snider said.

"Certainly. Do you mind if Junie stays? We were just completing some records."

"Hmm, we hadn't planned on it, but I suppose that would be okay." Virginia Mitchell said. The women nodded in agreement. "Junie might represent our younger women in what we have to say."

A twinge of queasiness tugged at Junie's stomach. She started to get up. "Maybe I should leave."

"No, stay," Lori said.

"Then let's begin," Margaret Henshaw said as the three women sat down on the long sofa in the office. "We want you to know that we are interested in your success because when you succeed, we all do."

"We're not saying that you are a failure," Judy Snider interrupted. "There are just a few things that we would like to suggest."

"Junie, why don't you write down their suggestions?" Lori said.

"If that's alright with them."

"Yes dear, go ahead and make us all a copy," Margaret replied.

"This all has to do with the manner in which you represent this congregation more than anything else," Virginia Mitchell leaned forward. "Some of it is fairly simple--the way you dress for example."

"How is that?" Lori asked.

"You have very tailored clothes but they fit a little tightly."

"Really?"

"And you may have noticed men staring at you when you play racquetball at the Y."

"No, I've been looking at the ball."

"You must be aware that you and your new racquetball friend are the talk of this town," Margaret said.

"Uh, strike that!" Judy Snider turned toward Junie who was scribbling a note. "What Margaret meant to say was that when two very attractive women are moving all around in their shorts--"

"Don't write that down either," Virginia raised her hand. "We're not saying this very well. It's just that we want you to be known as our pastor, not as some--

"Someone admired for other qualities," Margaret said with the others nodding.

"Please don't take this personally. We're only thinking of our church and we do so want you to be a wonderful success."

"Junie, do you have anything to add?" Virginia asked.

"No," Junie kept her head down and pretended to continue her writing.

"Then that's all we have to say," the women left with little half smiles.

After they were out of hearing range, Lori sighed and approached Junie.

"That put you in an awkward position."

"I know. I know, and maybe I should have spoken up. They're in another world, another generation."

"You don't think they were jealous?" Lori asked.

"I saw some of that, yes."

"I saw a lot of that and I don't excuse their behavior. I'm not putting up with it, Junie. I have other opportunities and I can go elsewhere. For a town of 60,000, this small-town cornball is out of line."

"They were here before the town grew. Please Lori, give us a chance. You've done wonderful things with this congregation and you're very well admired. Well, by that I mean--"

"I know what you mean," Lori stood up and started pacing. "The problem is that there may be more than the three of them in the congregation thinking this way."

"No, I really doubt that. They're not speaking for other members." Junie paused. "Listen, Lori, I know them very well. I can talk to them. Please let me try. I can stop this. I won't let them scare you away, Lori."

"I'm not scared. I'm pissed."

"You have every right to be, but this incident does not represent the rest of us. We love you, Lori, and we intend for you to stay here and enjoy your pastorate. I'm going to see to it. I can do this."

"I'm uneasy in asking you to do that, Junie. I don't know what to say to them, but I know what I'd like to say."

"These ladies are no match for you, Lori," Junie said. "With your skills, you could cut them down and humiliate them, but please don't do it. Believe it or not, they're not bad people. They just got off on the wrong the track."

"Junie, you're too good to be true, but I can't let it go much longer. Right now, they're feeding off of each other. It's like building a case for a jury. They'll start with one thing and then add other stuff to it until they get a conviction. I know how that works."

"Give me one week," Junie gave Lori a hug. "That's all I ask."

"Well, okay. I admire your confidence." Lori walked Junie to the parking lot and they both headed home.

CHAPTER 7

When Lori arrived home, she was still caught up in the confrontation at her office and barely noticed Mark who reached out unsuccessfully for a hug.

What do I do with these old biddies? I can't just give in to them. I really don't want to leave, but what are my options? Do I honestly think that Junie can make a difference? What could she possibly say? ...Okay, think it through. There's some unfinished business here, but I can deal with it later. I've had tougher times in court.

After her second glass of Pinot Grigio, Lori observed Mark more closely. Hmm, so now he's walking out on the back porch, watching the sunset. Neither of us has spoken for fifteen minutes. She joined him on the patio. "What's going on with you, mister?"

"Haven't you read the papers," Mark replied, "--about the great shoot-out with Billy Ray at Culler's Bend?"

"That was two days ago," Lori said, "and it's not your first shoot-out. What happened to my cool-headed detective?"

"I never saw anything like Billy Ray. For some strange reason, he gave me some of the credit that came out in the paper today. Now they want us to work together."

"So?"

"He's crazy, Lori. He's doesn't care about his life or anybody else's. I don't want to go out on another job with him."

"The paper says you're both heroes."

"He was all over the place, refusing to take cover--blazing away. He was in his own world. I don't understand the guy."

"He's had a hard life," Lori said. "His mother died right after he was born and then his father disappeared when he was a teenager. I think his father may have blamed him for his mother's death. Billy Ray has this shell around him. At our Singles' group, Sally is trying to break through it, but I don't think she'll succeed. That shell's his protection."

"Yeah, that makes sense in a weird way. From what Billy Ray told me, he thinks that God has given him that shell--his own special shield. He's either bullet proof or suicidal."

Mark paused and took a closer look at Lori. "Now it's your turn. How was your day? And don't tell me that it was just fine. I can see otherwise."

"Alright, here's the story." Lori recalled the comments of the three women.

"My, my," Mark responded. "Those sweet little old ladies. Well, Lori, what did you expect? They lost their figures years ago and now they have to put up with yours. It's not fair."

"Well, I'm not putting up with *them*. What do they want me to do--wear overalls on the racquetball court? Avoid their husbands?"

"Let's see. What's the communication principle here? Hmm. Nope, can't think of one. Worse yet, it's hard to take back what they said publicly with each other. If they had come in individually, it would be easier to later apologize."

"Wonderful. I'm glad I married you for your communication expertise."

"No need to get snippy. So really, what are you going to do?"

"Go back to Dallas," Lori shrugged. "At least that way you won't have to partner up with Billy Ray."

"I like it here and I can handle Billy Ray. We won't have that many cases to work together."

"Well--okay. I wasn't serious about Dallas."

"Didn't think so."

Lori and Mark went to bed, comforted by each other's ability to listen without overreacting. However, each remained concerned about the other and wondered what the outcome might be.

⚓

Junie Barrows did not have to wait long for a contact with the women who confronted Lori. They called her that evening and arranged a lunch meeting the next day in order to get her on board. Junie carefully rehearsed what she might say, but so did the three women. After their meals were served at the Bistro on the square, Virginia Mitchell spoke first.

"One of my fondest memories is of your mother, Junie, and I know that she would have agreed with what we said to Lori yesterday."

"Yes ma'am," Junie said, "but in all due respect, I don't."

"Why not?"

"You three and my mother are in a different generation from me. My generation believes that both men and women have every right to wear shorts at the Y. We also like our clothes to fit tighter than yours."

The women looked at each other wondering what to say next. After they took a few bites of their food, Margaret Henshaw spoke.

"We're not talking about you. We're talking about our pastor and that's a different situation."

"Oh, she's suppose to look differently from the rest of us at the Y?"

"Don't be disrespectful, Junie. We are a good bit older than you." Judy Snider said.

"That's exactly my point! I really do respect you, but I also respect what Lori has done for the congregation. For years now, you have complained about having no young people at church. Well, thanks to Lori, now we do. Don't expect Lori to conform to your generation. If you make her kowtow to your way of doing things, she would lose the respect of our younger members. Do you really want that to happen? Don't you enjoy us young people and want to see us grow?"

The women looked at each other again and then ordered more tea. It was time for Plan B which they had carefully rehearsed with Virginia Mitchell taking the lead.

"Lori is an accomplished attorney and very smart," Virginia began. "She's old enough to know the importance of working with older members in the congregation. I feel very much left out by Lori. Mary Beth was in the hospital last Monday and I didn't hear about it until Friday."

"Didn't you get your email?" Junie was puzzled. "Lori always reports her hospital visits at least by the day afterwards. I remember reading about Mary Beth."

"I don't expect to *read* about it. I expect a phone call from my pastor. Mary Beth is a personal friend of mine."

"Don't you have a computer?"

"Yes, my grandson gave me one but I don't use it."

"Why not?"

"Because that's not the way I communicate," Virginia stated.

"But you do know how to use email?"

"No and I don't want to learn."

"Virginia, most of our older people do use email," Junie pointed out.

"That doesn't make them more deserving than myself. I think I have a right to the same information they get."

Junie turned to the other two women. "Do you expect phone calls from the pastor whenever someone is in the hospital?"

"If Lori really cared, she would call," Margaret Henshaw and Judy Snider nodded in agreement.

"I don't know how to reply to that," Junie buried her head in her hands in disbelief. Was Lori supposed to know all the friendship connections and make personal calls for each event?

"We don't envy the difficult job that Lori has," Virginia said, "but her failure to communicate is not the only problem she has. It's her manner. She's much too assertive. At times, she seems bossy and arrogant. She needs to know when to hold her tongue and show some respect for the opinions of others."

"I disagree with you entirely. Like other successful young women today, Lori is politely assertive. You've been taught to be quiet around men and authority figures and let them have their way. That isn't Lori. She'll listen, but she doesn't put up with nonsense. You know where you stand with her."

"Yes, we certainly do. Lori opens her mouth and says things without giving a second thought to it," Judy leaned away from Junie. "I've been embarrassed on her behalf on more than one occasion. If it continues, Ethan and I will have no choice but to transfer our membership."

"You want to turn Lori into a passive aggressive little relic of the past," Junie was out of patience. "If you continue this nonsense, yes--yes, you may succeed in driving her out of our congregation. But if you do, I'll be here to give you all the credit. Your names will be written up large. Here are the notes I took at yesterday's meeting, every word. And that's just for openers. If you turn what you are doing into a campaign, then I will personally oppose you with the elders. I won't let you do this to Lori."

"Please dear," Margaret Henshaw raised up her hand. "You are overreacting and becoming emotional. Our intentions are good and we wish no harm to Lori or our congregation. We just want to see some progress in Lori's behavior."

"Yes, I'm sure you have purely good intentions, but you are purely wrong. You've said what you wanted to say to Lori and to me. Now let that be the last of it. I'm not asking you. I'm telling you as politely as I know how, please shut up!"

At that point, Junie abruptly left the table with Margaret Henshaw's mouth wide open. These women weren't prepared for a full scale conflict, and Junie felt sure that the subject would become mute.

However, when Junie gave more thought to what she had said, there was one nagging exception to her feeling of satisfaction. With a rapidly changing technology, Junie understood that thirty five year-olds such as herself might become just as likely an old fogey as those in their seventies. Even now she might be thought of as a relic of the past by savvy students starting out in college. She regretted some of her comments to her older friends but thought to herself in her school teacher fashion. If we want to stay connected with others, none of us have a real choice of refusing to accept a widely used means of communication. That was true of the telephone and it's true of today's technology. On balance, she felt justified in her comments and reported to Lori in an email:

"Dear Lori,

Sometimes members in our congregation are surprisingly good and sometimes disappointingly awful. Despite their remarks, I don't look at my older friends as particularly bad. Like the rest of us they sometimes act one way and sometimes the other. And sometimes they can't help themselves and just need to be told to shut up. I told them that in just those words today, and I doubt that they will trouble us much further. Love, Junie."

Lori wrote back "Thanks, Junie. We'll see what happens. If they get out of line again, I may choose to reinforce what you said with words of my own. I hope and pray you serve a second term as our record keeper. You are wonderful. Love, Lori."

After a few moments of reflection, Lori pressed the delete key. Then she called Junie and suggested she do the same.

CHAPTER 8

When Mark returned to his office, he found Rob Galloway waiting for him. Rob had some file folders in his hand and put them on Mark's desk.

"I thought these might be helpful for your investigation of our missing persons," Rob said. "There's not much here--just some profiles of the two missing men."

"Yeah, I know," Mark opened the files. "This one right here--missing for four years--Marshall Evans, a retired psychology professor from Tarleton University. Everybody I've interviewed says the same thing about him. No enemies, great guy with his loving wife Alice who's still working as an RN, and two older children living out of state. His students liked him and so did his peers. If there was foul play, I haven't found it."

"There's no reason for him to leave home. His absence makes no sense," Rob noted.

"I'm at a dead end. I've interviewed everyone you suggested including friends, neighbors, professors and former students."

"Okay, write up what you've got so at least we can show what we've done. We'll tell the relatives that we're keeping the case open. How are you coming on the other missing person, Hank Casey, from five or was it six years ago?

"That's the oil rancher living outside of Thorp Springs," Mark thumbed through the file. "Two wells came in twenty years ago, producing over a million dollars each. Since then, Hank claimed some fame as a western artist."

"He's good--or was. I have one of his sculptures in my office, the cowboy roping a steer," Rob said.

"Well, I can't get a rope around this case. He has two sons, Hiram and Wynn, living with his ex-wife in the Appalachia mountains. Hank's neighbors are spread out on other ranches; they didn't have much to do with him," Mark sat back in his chair.

"You might get a start on this case by looking at your own communication thesis," Rob suggested.

"My research on Opinion Leaders? I'm surprised you read it."

"I read some of it. You said that there are Opinion Leaders whom others go to for specific information about what's going on in the community."

"Right, Opinion Leaders have knowledge in a particular area, maybe it's farming, country music, local politics or even something simpler. It might be some good old boy who can tell you where to go fishing. Depending on their area of knowledge, they may be rich or poor, and may or may not have a high IQ. The people in the community usually know who to go to. Opinion Leaders are well known."

"Okay, so they have knowledge in a specific area," Rob continued. "But, if I read your stuff correctly, the one thing Opinion Leaders have in common is their social behavior--a lot of talking, a lot of friends, and an eagerness to share their special information, right?"

"Yes, what are you getting at?"

"Well, with that sort of inclination, would there be Opinion Leaders who specialize in just gossip--people who have grown up in the area with information on the private lives of community members?" Rob asked.

"Hmm, gossip Opinion Leaders?" Mark pushed away from his desk. "By golly, you're right, and they could be a good source for questions on our missing persons. I think I know some old biddies who might fit that bill."

"But how much stock should we put in gossip?" Rob wondered.

"From the research I've read, gossip and rumors are more reliable than some people think. It's a starting place--not evidence but better than nothing."

Mark made a phone call to Margaret Henshaw who eagerly agreed to meet when he explained that she might be of help. When he entered her house, he was not surprised to see Judy Snider and Virginia Mitchell there also.

"If you're asking about someone in the community," Margaret said, "we want to make sure you get the best information available."

"I'm most grateful," Mark sat down at the kitchen table with coffee and cookies already served to him.

"Well, now let's see," Mark opened one of his folders. "I'm looking into a missing person's case."

"There's really three of them," Virginia Mitchell said.

"Three?"

"Yes, Professor Marshall Evans, Hank Casey, and Eddie Larson."

"Eddie Larson?"

"Billy Ray's father. He just up and left eight years ago--left Billy Ray to fend for himself. "

"Oh right, Billy Ray's father, Eddie Larson."

"Hank Casey and Eddie used to go hunting together," Judy said.

"When they weren't drinking," Margaret laughed.

"No one misses either one of them," Judy continued. "You can ask anybody--bad tempered, smelly old goats with lots of money.

"Worse than that," Virginia added, "Eddie Larson beat Billy Ray and left scars with his belt buckle."

"Do you know that for sure?" Mark asked.

"I know a teacher who saw the scars on Billy Ray, but Billy Ray wouldn't own up to it. Billy Ray had a memorial service for Eddie five years ago, but it was only last year before Eddie could be declared legally dead--good riddance."

"Hank Casey was just as bad," Margaret chimed in. "After Eddie disappeared, Hank bragged to his drinking buddies about his ongoing affair with Barbara, Billy Ray's momma."

"Hank got around," Judy added. "Maybe women were attracted to his sculpture work."

"Wow," Mark exclaimed. "I wonder if Eddie knew about his wife's affair with Hank?"

"I doubt if it would have made any difference. Eddie never had much liking for Barbara."

"After Barbara died having Billy Ray, Eddie changed his tune," Judy said. "He talked about her as if she were the best wife on earth."

"Billy Ray grew up thinking just that," Margaret said. "No one had the heart to tell him any different."

"What was Barbara like?" Mark asked.

"Just ordinary and stupid for marrying Eddie," Judy replied, "not really mean like her husband. Eddie had poor Billy Ray believing that it was his fault for his mom's death."

"We really feel sorry for Billy Ray," Virginia said. "We were very pleased to see him join the church. Lori gets credit for that."

Mark wondered, could Lori survive these three? Maybe all churches have such a trio. They aren't mean-spirited--just spoons that stir things up and love to talk about others.

"You ladies have been very helpful." Mark started to leave.

"Wait," Judy motioned him to sit back down. "You haven't asked us about Professor Evans."

"Marshall Evans, yes. What can you tell me about him?"

"Wonderful man. He was by far the best loved professor at Tarleton," Virginia said.

"He made a difference in the life of every student he taught," Judy said. "I think it was a turning point for Billy Ray."

"How so?"

"As you know, Billy Ray had this terrible guilt about his mother," Judy continued. "Dr. Evans helped him work through that."

"Dr. Evans was a psychology professor," Mark remembered.

"And a Christian," Judy said. "He lived his faith."

"We were so sad when he disappeared," Margaret reached out to touch Mark's arm. "It was like losing a member of our family."

"Looking at the three of you," Mark smiled as he stood up again to leave, "you have a strong family right here."

"That's such a sweet thing to say," Judy replied.

"Yes, and please say hello to your lovely wife," Margaret said. "We've so much enjoyed her as our pastor."

"Thank you again for your help. We're fortunate to have you lovely ladies in our community." Mark steadied his balance as the three women rushed to give him a parting hug.

Mark tried not to laugh as he thought about their confrontation with Lori. On the other hand, they seemed sincere. They honestly wanted to love and be loved. Hmm--maybe Lori can enlist them as volunteers for hospital visits. They'd be good at that if the patients don't mind a detailed medical report given to the community.

CHAPTER 9

When Mark came home, Lori greeted him with her hands on her hips. "I can't believe what I just heard," she said. "Tell me it's not true."

"Let me guess. Margaret Henshaw called you."

"--All honey and sweetness as if she were never a moment of trouble. She raved about this handsome detective who interviewed Judy, Virginia and herself. What in the world did you say to them?"

"I asked for some help in my investigations. I thought they might know something about my missing persons."

"I'll bet you got an ear full."

"They were helpful."

"Well guess what? We've been invited to dinner this Friday, and all three of your new best friends will be there."

"Am I going to be the only man? What about Judy's husband?"

"Ethan's off hunting in Montana."

"That's where I ought to be."

"Not a chance. You brought this on yourself. How about telling me the details of this interview, or do I have to hear it from them?"

"Why spoil their fun. I'll let them tell it."

That night Mark sat alone reading in his easy chair. --Wait, I may have unleashed some unintended consequences. Those women are going to blab the details of our interview all over the neighborhood. If Billy Ray is involved, I don't want him to know my interest in him. I can't control their talking, but maybe I can influence how they present it. These women are sympathetic to Billy Ray. I need to come across the same way if I don't want to arouse suspicion.

⬥

On Friday, when Mark and Lori arrived at Margaret Henshaw's home, they were greeted warmly with hugs from all three women. During dinner they talked non-stop.

Judy stared at Mark with big, soft brown eyes. A smile broke out on her face. "You and Lori must be so proud of each other," she said, "You are such a God-send for us in Granbury."

"Yes we are, and I take all the credit for it," Mark replied. "I even review Lori's sermons and select her outfits during the week."

"You are joking, aren't you?" Virginia's eyebrows raised up a notch.

"No, I'm very serious. Lori gets no credit at all."

The three women looked at each other and then laughed.

"Don't worry, Lori," Judy said. "Mark is wonderful but so are you."

Lori folded her arms. Any more of this sticky sweetness and I can skip dessert.

"Mark, have you given any more thought to our interview with you? Virginia asked. "Are you working on a--what do you call it--?

"A lead," Lori said blankly.

"Right," Mark said. "Well, I've been reviewing what you ladies said. I am certainly sympathetic to Billy Ray and all the trouble he's endured."

"Oh he *has* endured so much," Judy agreed. "We're glad that both of you understand that. We have such high hopes for Billy."

"His father must have been a nightmare," Mark said.

"Yes, Eddie Larson won't be missed," Margaret dabbed some gravy from her mouth. "It's just as well you didn't have him on your missing persons' list."

"Yeah, I'm glad I won't have to investigate Eddie's disappearance. Good riddance to bad rubbish."

"You put that so well, Mark. Good riddance to bad rubbish," Virginia said.

Lori stared in disbelief. What's going on here? Mark doesn't even like Billy Ray.

"It's a wonder that Billy turned out as well as he did," Judy said.

"Amen," Mark replied. "I understand him so much better after our interview. What a remarkable young man."

An hour later, Lori tossed her napkin on the table and stood up. "It's been a delightful evening--and a simply delicious dinner. It was so good of you to invite us. I'm afraid I have some sermon preparation for tomorrow."

On their way home, Lori studied Mark while he was driving.

"Is this the husband I married?" Lori asked.

"As far as I know. Why do you ask?"

"Are you suddenly a fan of Billy Ray's?"

"Oh that. No, I'm not. I think he's nuts."

"Then why--"

"I have my reasons. Don't worry about it."

"I think you better tell me. I'll find out anyway." Lori moved over and snuggled against Mark's shoulder.

Mark told Lori about his suspicions, and why he didn't want the women to know about it.

"Your suspicions are really thin," Lori said. "I can't picture Billy Ray's involvement."

"You may be right. I'll be careful."

The next day, Mark typed up his interview notes for Rob Galloway. Rob was still reading them when he walked into Mark's office. "I assume you deleted these notes from your computer."

"No, but I will." Mark shifted in his chair. Hmm, Rob may not be with me on this.

"What do you plan to do next?" Rob asked.

"I called Alice Evans and asked if I could see Dr. Evans' client files."

"And?"

"No dice. Alice said her husband would never allow it. She still has hopes he's alive, even after four years."

"What are you after?" Rob started pacing.

"Billy Ray had close connections with all three of the missing men. He was in counseling with Marshall Evans who disappeared about the same time Billy Ray began his job as deputy sheriff."

"I'm not sure I follow. What specifically are you looking for with Dr. Evans?"

"--just a hunch. Billy Ray was probably required to provide a psychological evaluation at the sheriff's office. I'm thinking it might connect him with Dr. Evans."

"I don't know what you expect to find. It's highly likely that his psychological profile is going to be okay, or Billy Ray wouldn't be working with the sheriff." Rob paused. "--But if you want to see it, I probably could get it for you."

"How?"

"Well, you two will be working together, so I'll ask the sheriff to trade Billy Ray's profile for yours. I'll make it sound routine."

"Good plan. --Wait a minute. You have us working together again?" Mark asked.

"You'll be thrilled to know that Billy Ray has asked to go on a case with you tomorrow. Are you up to it?"

"Oh no. Well, maybe. I might learn more about him."

Rob stopped at the door on his way out. "There's something else you need to know."

"What?"

"The sheriff's retiring a year from now."

"So?"

"Rumor has it that he's backing Billy Ray for the election." Rob said.

"For sheriff! How is that possible? Billy Ray's only been in the department four years."

"Yeah, but he has a master's degree in Criminal Justice, and with all that publicity on the drug shoot-out, he's a hero. And then too, people remember him as the high school quarterback. He may have a good shot at it with the sheriff's backing."

"This can't be happening!" Mark sunk back into his chair.

"You have to be careful, Mark, really careful. Right now all you have is suspicions. We don't want those suspicions to get out into the campaign--if Billy Ray runs."

Mark studied Rob's face. "You have some real doubts about my suspicions."

"I have a hard time picturing Billy Ray killing those three men."

"Would you want him dating your daughter?"

"Well, no. --Go ahead with your investigation but tread lightly. Don't discuss your suspicions with anyone, not even Lori."

"Lori and I have already discussed it. She wasn't impressed."

"Sometimes I forget that she was one of us. I'm sure she'll be discreet. --So how are you going to investigate without Billy Ray finding out?" Rob asked.

"Billy Ray will hear nothing bad from me. If anything, I'll be sympathetic for the loss of his parents."

"Good enough--that way, we keep the door open in case you're wrong," Rob took a step back into Mark's office. "God, I hope you're wrong. I really do."

CHAPTER 10

Early the next morning, Billy Ray walked into Mark's office dressed neatly in his dark brown uniform with his badge and shoes well polished. Man alive--He looks like a poster boy for law enforcement. He's got his campaign in high gear.

"Here's my file," Billy Ray handed a folder to Mark.

"Leave it in Rob's office," Mark replied. "I think he's already delivered mine to the sheriff's office."

"I know, I read it--and you're welcome to read mine. I guess it's a way of getting better acquainted."

"I guess so."

"I don't see you wearing a gun," Billy Ray said.

"We're going out to see Elton Moody. He's a drunk and a wife abuser. He's big and mean, but I don't think he's a killer."

"We're serving him a warrant and putting him under arrest. His rap sheet says that he picks fights in bars and doesn't take long to end them. We need to be armed."

A knock came at Mark's door and then Rob entered without invitation.

"Mark, why aren't you armed? Or were you just going to pack a picnic for your pal here?" Rob enjoyed alliterations. "I think you need your weapon for this one."

Mark normally wore a gun, but with Billy Ray he wanted to lower the potential for violence. He was hoping Rob would understand that.

"If you think it's necessary," Mark reached into his desk drawer for his Glock.

"Listen, Mark. This guy is six foot five and three hundred pounds of pure meanness. He left his wife in bad shape and he could do the same to you."

As Billy Ray drove with Mark out into the countryside, spring blue bonnets spread over the fields with their deepening color of blue as if to compete with the sky. Mark spent the time observing Billy Ray, wondering about the outcome of the arrest. Hmm, he's cool as ice, but it's not just an absence of fear. He's intent, focused on a mission--like a religious fanatic going after the infidels.

"Let's don't be too eager to pull our guns," Mark said.

"I won't, unless he pulls his or resists. Are you familiar with Oak Bend?"

"It looks like a pleasant place to live." Mark replied.

"Not in the area we're going. The meth labs have been a problem in the old trailer section."

"I haven't heard of any shootouts." Mark said.

"There was one."

"You were there?"

"Yes."

Oak Bend was blessed with beautiful live oak trees and shared part of Granbury's thirty-three mile lake. It was hard to imagine a drug problem after traveling through the well kept neighborhoods of the valley, but three miles later came the hills. Run-down trailers were widely separated by groves of hackberry and mesquite trees interspersed with old refrigerators, tires and other used up items.

"Get ready," Billy Ray said as he drove into a large grove with trash strewn about a dilapidated shack. "I think we're in for real trouble. God has given me the gift of discernment for situations like this."

"Huh?"

Billy Ray jumped from the car. "Elton Moody! We have a warrant for your arrest! Come out with your hands up!"

Mark ran over to Billy Ray's side. "Hey, tone it down. Are you trying to start something?"

"Just following procedures." Billy Ray seemed to regain his composure as his blue eyes fixed on the door of the shack.

Elton Moody came staggering out pointing a gun in the air. He caught himself as the wooden steps buckled under his weight. "Hey, don't worry. I'm just a little uh--well, er, I'm drunk and this gun, uh, hey, she ain't loaded. I carry it for show."

"Put the gun down," Billy Ray jerked his Colt 44 from his hard leather holster.

"Go easy," Mark said. "He's not pointing at us."

"Final warning!" Billy Ray shifted positions to get a better angle. "Put it down!"

"Aw, you're taking the fun out of this," Elton waved his gun wildly and pulled the trigger. To his surprise, it exploded. "Oops."

"Wait!" Mark lunged at Billy Ray as his Colt fired. Elton's brains splattered over the door of his shack. The rest of his enormous body fell with a thud.

Mark sat down and buried his head in his hands. Lord have mercy. I left Dallas for this! Waves of nausea swept over him.

After Elton Moody's body was taken by the coroner, Billy Ray carefully observed Mark. "Uh, how do we report this? I don't want your story to be different from mine."

Mark shook his head and then replied, "Oh well, he was drunk, waving his gun. You gave him two warnings. His gun went off and then you fired."

"Is that it?"

"That's it. You followed procedures."

"But you aren't happy."

"I've seen enough dead bodies. I was hoping this time would be different."

"Have you ever killed someone?" Billy Ray asked.

"Yes," Mark replied.

"More than one?"

"Yes, what are you getting at?"

"I thought you acted slowly on this one."

"I've handled drunks with guns before, but I never killed one. I did taser a drunk one time when he wouldn't put down his gun."

"That's what you think I should have done."

"I would have preferred it, but that's not going into my report. You followed procedures and that's all I'm going to say."

"Mark, you kept your gun in your holster. That put us both at risk. -- But I'm not going to put that in my report."

"Go ahead. Put it in. Put it in."

"Uh, no, I'm sorry. I shouldn't have said that. I meant no disrespect. Our reports are the same. You have a great record with your own way of doing things and that's fine. I just hope you respect mine."

"Let it go, Billy, let it go."

"I still look forward to going on assignments with you."

"Fine, but I'll take the lead on the next one." Mark gazed out the window as Billy Ray started the car. God knows I hate going with him, but I need to stay close.

"OK, you lead." Billy Ray glanced back at the shack as they drove out of the grove. "That dead son of a bitch is not going to hurt anyone, not any more--not ever."

Mark did not respond but thought he saw a connection. He's killing his father all over again. Moody had no chance. His future had already been decided by Billy Ray's father. I can't let you go on killing people like that, Billy Ray. I just can't.

Chapter 11

When Billy Ray returned to his office he felt uncomfortable. He wasn't sure that Mark would give the same account of the killing. After The Hood County News called, Billy Ray gave the following account in his interview: "My partner, Mark Travis, gave Elton Moody every chance to put down the gun. But when Elton started waving the gun at us, immediate action was required. I was in a position to provide it. It was either him or us." The paper took Billy Ray's picture sitting behind the sheriff's desk.

That night, Billy Ray turned on the TV and watched an old re-run of "Have Gun, Will Travel." He stretched out drowsily in his father's leather chair. The title music drifted over him, "A knight without armor in a savage land ..." That's me, God's warrior bringing justice wherever I'm called.

Smoke came from the fireplace. Billy Ray got up to adjust the vent, but an apparition of his father, Eddie Larson, slowly emerged. Am I dreaming or being haunted? It doesn't matter. I've seen it before, and the outcome is always the same. He's not in control--I am.

"Looking for your booze, old fool?" Billy Ray sneered at the ghostly image.

The apparition pointed to the back bedroom. "Show me again, Billy Ray."

"You probably don't remember what happened to you, do you? Follow me. We'll go through it one more time."

The scene came into view like a movie with Billy Ray setting the stage. "There I am asleep. I needed that sleep real bad. I took exams all day and was up the night before. You came in next, but before you do, let me show you something you missed. Look back into the hallway. Do you see that open safe? You don't trust banks, do you? You have a ton of money in there from the oil leases."

The ghost laughed. "I don't trust you either, Billy Ray."

"No, but I saw the combination. Later on, I traced your signature for a joint bank account to continue getting the oil checks. --Uh oh, here comes the big scene."

Right on cue, Eddie came at Billy Ray with a cattle prod. "What are you doing sleeping, boy? We've got cows to feed!"

"Just let me have another hour's sleep. I'm worn out."

"Hell no! You get your lazy butt out of bed," Eddie staggered closer to Billy Ray. "You either earn your keep or I'm going to throw you out of here."

"You're drunk. The cows were fed eight hours ago. Leave me alone you old fool!"

"I'll teach you to disrespect your father." Eddie pushed the button of the cattle prod and placed the prongs on Billy Ray's neck.

Billy Ray cramped with convulsions. "Ohh, God!" Eddie came at him again but Billy Ray rolled out of bed and moved to the side to shake off the effects.

Billy Ray narrated the scene again. "Now it gets interesting. I'm an eighteen year old college freshman with dreams. And you're in the way, old man."

Billy Ray gave a single high kick that knocked his father across the room. The old man's head made a crunching sound as it hit the wall behind him. His body slumped to the ground, blood coming out of his nostrils.

Billy Ray pointed to his father's body. "This part's easy, just watch. You're already half dead so I pick up a pillow and smother you. You don't even fight back. Next, I bury your body under that live oak tree you like so much. You got your favorite resting place and I got your money, a fair trade."

The ghost howled. "You haven't heard the last of me, Billy Ray."

"It's my dream, you old sot! Now go away."

The apparition disappeared and Billy Ray resumed his sleep. After a while, he dreamed of Lori Travis, dressed in her beautiful blue robe preaching words of comfort just for him. Be of good peace, she said. God understands what you did. You are the arm of the Lord, Billy Ray--under God's own protection, anointed for God's own purpose. She bent down to bless him, gently kissing his forehead. Sleep now, rest.

Billy Ray wanted to embrace Lori, but he pulled back. No, I must not. I cannot allow myself to be drawn to her. Lori is sacred, sent to reveal my warrior's mission. I am your knight, Lori, your obedient servant. He knelt down before her. --But then as he rose to his feet, Lori reached out for him and …

A knock on the door silenced the dream. Billy Ray angrily stomped over to answer it. As he opened the door, the moonlight fell on Sally Lawton in a softly flowing summer dress perfectly accenting the curves of her body. Her pale blue eyes sparkled as she looked up at Billy Ray. Oh my God, she's turning me on! I've never seen anyone so--so utterly voluptuous.

"Hi Billy Ray," Sally said in her gentle North Carolina accent. "I got to thinking about you and thought you might enjoy some of my casserole. Would you like me to--"

"Come in," Billy Ray took the casserole and put it in the refrigerator of his kitchen.

"I know it's a little late. Have you already eaten?" Sally stood close to Billy Ray.

"I like that dress." He reached out to touch her shoulders.

"I thought you might."

The scent of her perfume was intoxicating. Billy Ray pulled her closer. "Are you sure you know what you're doing, little girl?"

"I'm a big girl, Billy Ray. I know what I'm doing and I know what I want."

Billy Ray's arousal escalated. "Damn it, I've taken all I can take." He kissed her full on the mouth, then picked her up and carried her to his bedroom. He half expected her to wiggle free and run for the door, but she didn't. The next few hours were the most intense of Billy Ray's life. Sally's moaning and groanings filled him with a passion that satisfied every part of his warrior longings. Her movements heightened his senses to the point of forgetting everything and everyone else. Lori Travis became a distant memory.

Later as they drifted off to sleep, Billy Ray held Sally gently in his arms. She is a Godsend. She has released me from all the impure thoughts of my mission. I can now focus on the warrior I was meant to be.

In the morning Sally fixed Billy Ray breakfast and started to laugh. "I have a little secret, Billy Ray." She curled up on his lap. "Guess what my middle name is?"

"Tell me."

"It's Mae--I'm Sally Mae. We're Sally Mae and Billy Ray. God has a sense of humor, don't you think? I think it's all part of His plan."

For some reason Sally Mae was a little less attractive when she talked about God. Even so, Sally Mae had roused him like no other, and their relationship continued.In the next few months, people remarked on the changes they saw in Billy Ray. He seemed less wooden, less prone to take an aggressive stance. On assignments with Mark, Billy Ray kept his colt in his holster and spoke calmly in a matter-of-fact manner to suspects. Even Mark began to doubt his own suspicions. The private world of Billy Ray was still there but thanks to Sally Mae, it was carefully concealed.

CHAPTER 12

Advent came again with Christmas soon to follow. Lori greeted Mark with a surprise when he came into the door.

"What have you got there!" Mark looked at the little creature curled up in Lori's arms.

"It's my new friend. Isn't he cute."

"That little friend is a Siamese cat! They're crazy! Why didn't you get a dog?"

"He was out in our back yard. Someone must have dropped him off. He hasn't been fed and I want him!" Laura looked pleadingly at Mark. "I don't think he's a pure Siamese. See his face, it's a little more rounded. I checked in the neighborhood. No one knows about him. And thanks to our last owners, our house is already constructed with two cat doors. Of course he does have to go through both in order to get into the house--through the garage and then a right turn through the laundry room.--But I think he's smart enough to figure that out. Look at those bright eyes!"

"That cat looks 100% Siamese to me, blue eyes and all. He's going to be trouble." The kitten jumped from Lori's arms and started chasing Mark's shoe laces.

"My cat is *not* going to be any trouble and you better treat him right," Lori laughed as the cat grabbed Mark's shoe laces. "What should we call him?"

"With those cold blue eyes, I'm going to call him Billy Ray."

"What is it with you and Billy Ray? I thought you had eased up on him."

"I have--a little maybe," Mark picked up the cat and held it. "I guess a dog would be too much of a problem with both of us working. He is kind of cute. I hope he can figure out those cat doors. I'm going to call him BR. That could stand for Billy Ray or we could give him a religious name, like Brother Cat, your choice. "

"Brother Cat? No, not BC, so I guess BR will do. --Hey Mark, you need to get rid of that five o'clock shadow and start the grill."

"What's going on?"

"You don't remember, do you?" Lori said with an exaggerated sigh and slumped shoulders. "Celesta is coming over with her husband, Rex Barkley. You need to get the ribs on."

"Sounds good. Is there some special occasion?"

"Well, yes. You missed it because you go to the first worship service. They joined the church at the second one."

"Really! Rex will have to sit on the back row. Otherwise, no one will be able to see over him," Mark moved his hand six inches above his head.

"Did you know that he was a star basketball player at OU?" Lori started preparing the vegetables.

"No, but I can believe it."

Rex and Celesta arrived and after dinner, sat around the table for some small talk.

"So you played for Oklahoma," Mark said to Rex. "What do you do now?"

"I'm a high school counselor and part time coach," Rex replied. "Counseling is what I enjoy most. I finished up my doctorate at Texas Tech two month's ago."

"So what are your plans now that you've completed your PhD?"

"Maybe private practice. I'm not sure. I like what I'm doing now."

"I'll tell you a secret," Lori said to Rex. "I hate counseling. Counseling too often leaves people at odds with you. You have something on them, but they don't have anything on you. It doesn't make for mutual relationships."

"I think you're right, Lori," Rex said. "The role of counseling may not be compatible with that of pastor. You sometimes uncover stuff that the client doesn't want to face. A counselor is more of a facilitator than a friend."

"As a pastor, I think it's more important to remain as a friend," Lori said. "I'll leave the counseling to someone else."

"I'll tell you what," Rex said. "If you run into something where a member needs counseling, I'll offer my services as a part of my church giving."

Lori put her hand on Rex's arm. "I didn't mean to put you on the spot, but that's wonderful! Thank you! I'll take you up on your offer."

The rest of the evening went by with laughing and chatter as each one interrupted the other eager to tell the next story. One story in particular, told by Rex, caught Lori's attention.

"Fifteen years ago, we knew we had the best team," Rex said. "There was no doubt about it. We were a big item on the news; no one could beat us--no one! Then came the final eight."

"The Elite Eight?" Lori asked.

"Yes--eight teams in the play-offs. The loser goes home. As luck would have it, we got the Cinderella team from some little college no one ever heard of. We knew they couldn't win and we were already looking ahead toward playing one of the big teams in the Final Four."

"I think I know what's coming," Mark said.

"It was unbelievable," Rex said. "Some little guy, about five foot eight, was fast as a jack rabbit. He would the take the corners on offense and sink those three pointers every time he touched the ball. --I mean, nothing but net! Of course, three point shooters are commonplace now, but back then there weren't so many. We fought back with everything we had but with two seconds to go, that little squirt finished us off with a final three pointer. And then they went on to the Final Four and lost by only point!"

"I think I know the team," Mark said.

"Please don't mention the name," Rex said. "I know pride goes before a fall, but for us it was a time when we had come to faith. No other team had our confidence and ability. At least, that's what we thought."

ᚠ

Later at bedtime, Lori propped herself up on her pillow. "Mark, don't go to sleep yet. I have an idea for a sermon and I'm afraid I'll lose it if I don't talk about it now."

Mark's eyes were half shut. "I'm all ears."

"OK, here's what I'm thinking. It's about what Rex said."

Mark rolled over to face Lori. "Uh, do your think Rex was giving you a story for a sermon?"

"Well, sort of. You're still asleep, aren't you?"

"Thoughtless of me. Go ahead with your thought."

"Rex had a wonderful team with a proud history of doing things a certain way. Our churches are pretty much the same in their denominations--Baptists, Methodists, whatever. We say that we are all Christians but we're proud of our own history and way of doing things. I don't think we're really prepared to learn from each other."

"Got it! We need to respect the traditions of each other. Now I can go back to sleep."

"No, that's not what I'm saying."

"Rats."

"I'm not talking about respect. Respect is too easy--it's a good way to ignore the other person with a 'live and let live" attitude. You go your way and I'll go mine. I'm talking about a willingness to listen and learn from the other."

"So how does that fit in with what Rex said?"

"His team was a closed system. They were so proud of doing things their way that they weren't opened to others."

"Okay, I think I can wrap this up. They weren't prepared to defend against the three point guy. So we should guard against pride."

"Yes, but there's more to it than that."

"Dang."

"It's not just our denominational pride, although that's a big part of it. It's how we come to faith in defining own spiritual experiences--how we interpret our discoveries. My way of coming to faith may have blinders that define how I look at the spirituality of others. We end up looking for experiences that match our own and discounting others."

"Give me a for instance."

"Well, different perspectives have different blinders. A spiritual journey might start from an emotional experience after the death of a parent or the birth of a baby. Or it could be an intellectual discovery after listening to a scholarly theologian."

"Or a nature lover might look at spirituality in the awe of the universe," Mark said. "People come to faith in different ways."

"Yes, and that's true with denominational histories too. So here's what I'm thinking. It's good to celebrate my coming to faith, but *not* if it excludes other experiences and ways of coming to faith."

"Lori, I'm constantly amazed at what triggers your sermons. The basketball comparison is a little strange, but I think I've got it. --If I can just go back to sleep."

"Are you ready for my sermon? I can do it quickly by taking you from Point A to B?"

"Sure."

"Well, point A starts with the three point shooter--an unexpected experience that made a big difference. Then comes Point B, our unexpected experiences with Jesus. I'm thinking of the seventh chapter in Luke where John the Baptist was in prison and sent his friends to Jesus asking 'Are you the one who is to come, or should we wait for another?' I think John's idea of a spiritual person may have differed from Jesus--at least at this point."

"What did Jesus say?"

"Tell John what you have seen and heard--the blind receive their sight, the lame walk, the lepers are cleansed, and the poor have good news preached to them ... And blessed is anyone who takes no offense at me."

"Do you think John got the point?"

"The scripture doesn't say. What's more important is that *we* get the point. It's the same Jesus, but coming to faith may be from different places--a thief on the cross, a woman at the well or John the Baptist in prison. We all have to seek, ask, and knock--and if we listen, we might learn from each other's perspective if we don't take offense."

"Thank you for the sermon," Mark said. "Now I won't have to go to church."

"Yes you do," Lori snuggled up to Mark who immediately dozed off.

Lori had a feeling of discovery, something she had learned about herself. I'm not so much a doorway to the truth as I am a fellow seeker who knows some things, but not everything. Maybe I should listen more and learn from the different experiences of others making their own discoveries. I'm a traveler with other travelers. I can enjoy the process and leave the final product to God. That's a very comforting thought, Lori. There may be more coming, but for now, get some sleep.

CHAPTER 13

Once again the Seekers' Class met at Billy Ray's. Sally sat close to Billy Ray who seemed oblivious to her squeezing his hand. Zeb Mallory whispered to Betty Jones after returning from Billy Ray's bathroom. "Guess what's hanging up in Billy Ray's shower?"

"Something personal?" Betty replied.

"Female undies."

"Really?"

"Small size."

Betty glanced over at Sally. "Oh my, that's amazing."

Lori called the class together and began. "Since we have fifteen members in class tonight, let's divide up into three groups. I've selected some passages and discussion questions for each group. We know that King Saul didn't turn out too well. So let's move on to David's reign in II Samuel."

Billy Ray was puzzled. What's going on with Lori? She isn't teaching us like she did before. Why are we in groups? I don't want to hear what other people think--their regurgitated pap. Lori is God's chosen.

The groups reported on David's reign, but began to argue about David's morality.

"David had no right to remain king," Zeb said. "If he'd been in Texas, he would have received a lethal injection! The killing of Bathsheba's husband, Uriah, was premeditated and cold blooded. Look at David's instructions to his commander in II Samuel 10:15: 'Set Uriah in the forefront of the hardest fighting, and then draw back from him, so that he may be struck down and die.'"

"David was God's anointed," Billy Ray raised his voice, "sealed with God's covenant. God's blessings shielded him, even from his own sins. He was not subject to the death penalty. Uriah was a major obstacle that threatened David's rule."

"It was still murder and David was punished," Betty countered. "The prophet Nathan told him that 'the sword would never leave his house.' His family was in constant turmoil."

"Do you think his punishment fit the crime?" Mike asked. "It seems to me that it was his family that got punished. David got off light."

"Up until that time, David had been a great king," Sally Mae pointed out.

"It's not always about faith, hope and love," Billy Ray said emphatically. "The mission comes first. There are special considerations for God's warriors."

"So if I've been a good little warrior, it's alright if I go out and commit adultery and murder?" Zeb smirked.

"No, it's not alright, but there is forgiveness. We've come a long way in our understanding with Jesus," Mike said.

"Maybe Jesus has come a long way," Betty said, "but I'm not so sure about us--the crusades, the inquisition, the Salem witch trials, and now pre-emptive war that can be started by one man."

"So what's the alternative, Betty," Zeb shot back. "Are we just going to lay down and let the bad guys take over."

Billy Ray stood straight up from his chair unaware that he was now standing. "No, God appoints leaders and warriors. Those of us who know God's will are going to prevail against the major obstacles that threaten to undo us."

"You're scaring me, Billy Ray," Betty said.

"So you know God's will?" Mike looked at Billy Ray.

"Don't you!?" Billy Ray waved his Bible.

"No, I'm just a seeker," Mike sat down his coffee cup.

Billy Ray awkwardly regained his seat. "We need to hear from Lori."

"Well, I tend to agree with Mike," Lori replied. "Only we're not just individual seekers left on our own. The church is a community of seekers discovering God's will together--and we know in part, not fully. We always have more to learn. None of us can claim to know God's will perfectly."

"Tell us what you think about David." Billy Ray was certain that Lori would speak God's truth and vindicate him.

"Okay, here's one thought. If David could be forgiven for everything he did, I like the chances for my own forgiveness," Lori said. "I'm also less inclined to judge others."

"And that's it?" Billy Ray frowned. "That's all you have to say?"

"I really enjoyed listening to all of you. You've raised some good questions. We can talk about this some more the next time."

"You didn't talk much at all," Billy Ray said.

"I get to talk on Sundays," Lori answered. "I need to hear how you come to faith and wrestle with questions. It helps me with mine."

Billy Ray hung his head. "Lori, I--I don't know. Something has changed in you. You don't seem as certain. I thought you knew God's will."

"I like what we did tonight," Betty said. "I feel more a part of this group and more alert to what we're studying." Others agreed with Betty but they wanted more from Lori.

As Lori drove home, she worried about Billy Ray's sense of certainty. There's no searching or coming to faith in Billy Ray. He's already there and expects the rest of us to be there too. He seems to be modeling on some sort of warrior image, like the one he has of King David. There's nothing flexible; he's wrapped up in his own bubble. I wonder what would happen if that bubble ever broke? I'm not sure I would want to be there when it happens.

A

Six months passed and BR had grown from a playful kitten to a stealthy cat. He still liked to wrestle and tumble with Mark, but he was getting too fast and Mark was getting the worse of it. At bedtime, BR jumped up on Mark and challenged him to their usual contest of cat attacks.

"No, BR," Mark scolded. "I'm tired of getting scratched. You win. I give up."

BR scurried around the bed then charged at Mark's outstretched hand.

"No, I mean it!" Mark got up and put BR outside. "You're not playing, you're practicing. Go pick on another cat or chase a bird. I'm not going to be your target."

"He's just trying to please you," Lori said.

"I'm pleased that he's outside," Mark replied.

"What about your suspicions of that other BR?"

"Billy Ray? Nothing to go on," Mark said.

"Maybe you should do a little more investigating."

"Huh! I thought you wanted me to ease up on Billy Ray?"

"I've had a chance to observe Billy Ray during the last eight months of our Singles' Bible study."

"What did you see?"

"He gets into strenuous arguments with the others, making his case for God's anointed to deliver justice--on the violent side. Mercy is not a part of his vocabulary. Finally, the others caught on to that and gave him a hard time--made fun of him."

"Looks like he would stop coming," Mark said.

"He doesn't come as regularly as he used to, but Sally Mae brings him back and pats his hand the whole time. He just sits there with a look of disap-proval, waiting to make his case."

Mark closed his book. "And that's the reason you want me to continue my investigation?"

"It's just a hunch--like the ones you get," Lori replied. "When Billy Ray hears something he dislikes, he focuses on his opposition like BR looking at a bird. It gives me the willies."

Just then there was a clatter coming from the laundry room. Mark rolled out of bed to investigate.

"Oh, I forgot to tell you," Lori said. "BR figured out how to get into the laundry room. The cat door closes with a magnet and makes a clatter."

"Wow, that cat managed two doors and a right turn," Mark observed. "smart kitty."

Lori walked over to greet BR. "Especially when you offer tuna on the other side of the door. Wait a minute--what's that in his mouth!"

"I think it's a snake," Mark said.

"Oh no! Get that thing out of here!"

"He's just trying to please you," Mark laughed. "It's a little garter snake, not poisonous."

"We've got to train him not to do that!"

"That'll be your job," Mark took the snake and tossed it out in the backyard.

Lori picked up the cat and gently shook him. "Look at me BR!--No! NO! Bad kitty!"

Mark laughed and went back to bed. "I'm sure that'll work just fine."

"I'll be dreaming of snakes all night long!" Lori took BR outside, and closed the door to the laundry room to prevent BR's entry to the bedroom. "Mark, first thing in the morning, I want you to check our laundry room."

Mark started to laugh, but thought better of it. "It's what cats do, and he's so *cute*."

"I think BR may be a good name for him after all," Lori said and spooned Mark as she went to sleep.

CHAPTER 14

Mark was in his office when Dr. Marshall Evans' wife, Alice, came to see him. She was still in her nurse's uniform and her eyes were red with bags underneath.

"I've given up hope for his being alive," she began. "Marshall and I were very close and I would have heard something by now. It's been almost four years since he disappeared. I know Marshall would not approve of my grieving this long, but I go to bed every night thinking of him. Is there any way you can find out what happened?"

Mark moved from behind his desk, seated himself beside Alice, and took her hand. "Do you remember my asking permission to look at his files? That's the only place I know to begin."

Alice moved her hand from Mark's. "I don't think I should do that. Marshall was very respectful of his client's confidentiality."

"I understand your concern," Mark said. "--Maybe we could limit our search without looking at every client."

"Well, I'm still not--"

"What if you looked for me?" Mark broke in. "You don't have to look through all of them--only the ones six months before Dr. Evans disappeared. Look for something unusual."

"What do mean by unusual?"

"Something out of the ordinary--an angry letter, a disgruntled client or something out of place. If it catches your attention, I want to know about it."

Alice leaned down to pick up her purse. "Disgruntled clients are not that unusual."

"Well, look for something out of the ordinary," Mark replied. "I won't look at anything unless you ask me to."

Alice paused as she walked to the door. "So you're leaving it up to me? I don't know. Let me think about it."

Mark went to the door with her. "I know it's not easy, but there's no place else to go. Let me know what you decide. I appreciate your coming in."

Later that afternoon, Rob Galloway came into Mark's office and sat down.

"We have a visitor on his way to see us," Rob said, "and we need to talk about it."

"Who?"

"Billy Ray. He's definitely running for sheriff and I think he wants our endorsements."

"That's tricky," Mark said.

"So what do we do?"

"Can we just stay neutral and tell him we'll support whoever's elected?"

"Are you still uncomfortable with Billy Ray?" Rob asked.

"Yes, and even Lori has doubts."

"Just doubts--nothing else?"

"She's had a chance to observe Billy Ray close up." Mark replied, "There's something about his behavior that bothers her, and Lori usually gives others the benefit of the doubt."

Rob placed his hand on Mark's shoulder. "I'll tell you what let's do. I'll call the other candidate, Earl Blanton, and tell him that we've decided to remain neutral."

"Good. That way we can say the same thing to Billy Ray." Mark followed Rob into his office as the call was made to Earl.

A few minutes afterwards, Billy Ray walked into the office and studied his reception. Something's going on. They're not smiling and they look uncomfortable."

"Have a seat, Billy Ray," Rob said. "What can we do for you?"

"I think you may know," Billy Ray sat down. "I need your endorsements."

"We're in a difficult situation politically," Rob said. "We're good friends with both you and Earl so we've decided to remain neutral and not endorse either one of you."

"Have you told Earl this?" Billy Ray asked.

"As a matter of fact, we called Earl right before you came," Rob said.

"I'm sorry to hear that," Billy Ray said. "May I at least have your vote? We've done a lot of work together."

Mark leaned back in his chair. "We can't promise that either. We have to keep faith with you both."

Billy Ray summed up the response. I'm not buying this. Rob has endorsed other candidates. And Mark was caught off guard by my question. They have no intention of supporting or voting for me.

"We can promise you one thing," Rob said. "If you're elected, you will have our full support. We enjoy working with you and we look forward to the prospect of your election."

Billy Ray left without further comment. If Mark is against me, then Lori will be of no use either. How can Lori be God's messenger? Could I be wrong? Maybe my warrior's mission lies elsewhere--perhaps as the new sheriff.

Billy Ray drove back to his office and reported his disappointment to Sheriff Lyle Richards. The sheriff was looking forward to retirement and had agreed to act as Billy Ray's campaign manager.

"Are you sure you're not just feeling paranoid?" Lyle asked.

"I'm sure," Billy Ray said. "Mark doesn't approve of the way I handled some of the cases we worked on. There's not much I can do about that now, but it messes things up with his wife Lori. She's the pastor of my church."

Lyle drummed his fingers on his desk. "You need the support of your church."

"I doubt Lori will give it."

Lyle walked around his desk and sat next to Billy Ray. "Maybe you don't need her support, at least not by itself."

"What do you mean?"

"Last year, I spoke to an adult group in your church about law enforcement. The pastor didn't even know I was coming--and that's the key. Mildred

Hopkins, the program chair, lines up the speakers. They meet in a restaurant once a month, about fifty in attendance."

"I don't know Mildred."

"I do--real well. She'll be delighted to hear from me. I really wowed them. Did you take public speaking in college?"

"Yes, but I wasn't that good."

"You will be with me as your coach. The main thing is to personally engage your audience. Don't memorize your speech. Just walk out into the audience and tell a few stories to show how you handle things. Talk a little about what you learned in your criminal justice classes--and the practical experience you have in working with me. Hell, you can do that right now! All you need is a few index cards to keep you on track. --But we'll practice so that you can go in strong."

Lyle talked to Mildred who had no problem in setting a time for Billy Ray to speak. "After all," Mildred said, "Billy Ray is a member of our church. We certainly want to hear from him."

Lyle's confidence was contagious, and Billy Ray proved an apt pupil in their coaching sessions. He learned which questions to anticipate and how to rephrase the more difficult ones without claiming too much. Finally, Lyle gave Billy Ray a hug and said, "You're ready, boy. You're ready!"

Billy Ray continued to work on his presentation over and over. His time came sooner than expected. One of Mildred Hopkins' speakers cancelled four days before her presentation and Billy Ray was called in to fill the gap. Lori had no idea of Billy Ray's speaking engagement and was caught completely off guard at the dinner. There was nothing she could do but grin and bear it.

Lori listened intently as Billy Ray spoke. I can't believe this. Billy Ray is speaking without notes like a real pro. He's relaxed and smiling--got them eating out of his hand. It's not what I expected and certainly not what I wanted.

Half way through the speech, Lori's cell phone buzzed and she left the room to answer it. Then she walked back in and whispered to Mildred

Hopkins, "I'm sorry. I've got to leave. Alice Schuman just passed away and the family's asking for me." Mildred nodded understandingly and refocused on Billy Ray who had raised his voice slightly to counter the distraction of Lori's leaving.

After another ten minutes, Billy Ray moved toward his conclusion. "So you know my training, and I'm grateful to Tarleton University for my master's degree and their excellent criminal justice program. If you want to know my practical experience, I can give it to you in two words: Lyle Richards. With Lyle as my mentor, the last four years have opened my eyes to superb law enforcement. I want to continue Lyle's legacy and build on it. I want to be your sheriff. Will you help me?"

The crowd's loud round of applause took Billy Ray by surprise. "Thank you! Thank you! I have one more thing, and then I'll be open for questions. I just happen to have some signs in my truck with my name on them. If you don't mind, I'd like you to pick up a couple--one for yourself and one for that other Presbyterian who missed out on this meeting. Do you know anybody who would enjoy waking up tomorrow with my sign in their yard?"

"Yeah!" Joe Michaels hollered. "The preacher lady! Give me four of those signs. I'll stick two of them in her yard tonight."

"Good idea," Belle Ashton agreed. "She'll appreciate that."

The meeting broke up with lots of handshaking and congratulations to the candidate. The next night, Joe Michaels came home from his late shift at the nuclear power plant in nearby Glen Rose. He quietly planted one sign by Lori and Mark's driveway and the other on their front side.

When the sun came up the next morning, Lori was roused out of her sleep to hear something like cursing coming from their front porch. She walked out in her robe and pajamas to see Mark tearing up Billy Ray's campaign signs.

"Who in the hell put these things up!?" Mark shouted.

"I have no idea," Lori replied. "but the neighbors are going to come after us if you don't calm down."

"I'm sorry. It--well, it caught me off guard."

"Billy Ray has started early," Lori said sleepily, "ten months from the election."

Mark took a deep breath. "Alright, alright. I can take them down as quickly as they put them up."

Lori punched Mark on his arm. "Yes you can. Thanks for the wake-up call, loud mouth. Your turn to make coffee."

⚓

Later that day, Joe Michaels drove by Mark and Lori's house and saw that the signs had been taken down.

Joe frowned. Vandals, or maybe the opposition. That won't stop me!

Joe then went by the sheriff's office, picked up six more signs just in case, and laughed as he replanted two of them. I can put them up just as fast as they take them down. Should I tell Lori? Nah, I know she'll appreciate it, and I don't need to be patted on the back. I'll be the silent Good Samaritan.

When Mark came home, he tore up the signs again. The next day Joe put up two more, and Mark again ripped them apart. This pattern was repeated each day for three weeks until Lyle Richards talked with Joe. "We're about to run out of signs. You've taken over forty of them. What's going on?"

"Sheriff, I'm glad you asked," Joe said proudly. "I'm putting them up on our pastor's front lawn, but the opposition keeps taking them down."

"I see," Lyle said knowingly, "I'll take care of it. In the meantime, don't put any more signs up."

When Joe left, the sheriff chuckled. No use in provoking it further, but I would love to have seen Mark's face. That'd been worth the cost of the signs, every bit of it.

CHAPTER 15

Two weeks later, Alice Evans again met with Mark in his office. She was carrying a folder from the files of Dr. Marshall Evans.

"I'm probably wasting your time," Alice said, "but you asked me to look through Marshall's files for anything unusual. I did find one file that was different from the others." She pulled out a letter from her file folder and handed it to Mark. It was a copy of Billy Ray's evaluation.

"I've already seen this," Mark said. "What's unusual about it?"

"There are two things," Alice replied. "The other files have my husband's notes going back to the client's first visit. Billy Ray's file has only this letter--nothing else."

"That is odd," Mark raised an eyebrow. "Would Dr. Evans have some reason to dispose of the notes?"

"None that I could think of."

"What else was unusual?"

"The way the letter was written," Alice said. "Marshall sometimes dictated his letters to me, so I know how they were written."

"What was different in Billy Ray's evaluation?"

"Marshall tailored his evaluations. The sentences and comments are rarely the same."

Mark poured a glass of water for Alice. "Let me see if I have this straight. Each client was given an individual description. No two sentences are alike?"

"Not exactly alike. In fact, I never heard him dictate the same sentence twice."

Mark paused. "So what did you find in Billy Ray's?"

Alice examined her copy of the evaluation. "It was the similarities that bothered me. I checked the files for evaluations written for other clients and compared them to Billy Ray's. Some of the sentences are almost alike."

Mark folded his arms. "So you have Billy Ray's file with missing notes and some odd similarities to other evaluations. Anything else?"

Alice hesitated. "I want you to examine something and please keep it confidential. It's a comparison with the evaluation of another client. I've blacked out the name," Alice took the evaluation from her folder and placed it beside Billy Ray's. "Compare the last paragraphs of the two."

"Hmm," Mark looked at the two evaluations, "--practically the same, word for word. May I make a copy of this?"

"Well, I'm a little uncomfortable with that, but go ahead. What do you think? Where does this leave us?" Alice asked.

"I still have one question," Mark said. "Looking at these two letters, Dr. Evans's signature is the same on both. It doesn't appear forged."

"Look a little closer," Alice replied. "The signature is not just the same, it's identical. That's because Marshall used a stamp."

Mark studied the signatures and then leaned back in his chair. "Huh! Both are carefully done with no smudges. Alice, I appreciate your coming, and I want you to keep quiet about what you found. I wouldn't want the wrong person to hear about it."

Alice's eyes widened. "You mean the killer."

"Maybe. All we have are suspicions, but we need to be careful," Mark said. "If anyone asks why you came here--just to be on the safe side, tell them you wanted advice on a security system. In fact, security is a good thing to consider. For starters, do you have a dog?"

"No."

"Then get one that has a loud bark. For your own comfort, you might also put up a camera and a motion detector; I know someone who can do that for you. Also, I'll give you my cell phone; put it on speed dial and don't hesitate to call."

A heavy sigh escaped from Alice, and Mark gave her a hug. "I didn't mean to scare you," Mark said. "--just precautions. Nothing's going to happen to you, you'll be fine. I'll keep a lookout for you. You've given us some important information--not enough for a jury, but a step closer."

⚔

Deputy Billy Ray was doing paper work in his office when Sheriff Lyle Richards walked in unannounced. He pulled up a wooden chair to get closer to Billy Ray and sat down with a thump.

"I've got a little matter to discuss with you, son," Lyle said. "She goes by the name of Sally Lawton."

"What's Sally got to do with anything?" Billy Ray asked.

"You've been sleeping with her for about a year now, and everybody knows it."

"It's none of their business."

"If you're running for the Sheriff of Hood County, it's definitely their business," Lyle shot back, "--unless you don't want to be elected."

"So what would you suggest?"

"Well, she's a pretty little filly--long blonde hair, blue eyes, good figure, nice personality. You obviously enjoy being with her. What's wrong with marrying her?" Lyle asked.

"I could just dump her," Billy Ray replied.

"You'd do that to such a sweet thing? People don't like a hard-hearted sheriff."

"I don't like being put in this position," Billy Ray protested.

"You put yourself in it," Lyle replied. "If you want to get elected, marriage is a sign of stability and family values. Sleeping around won't get it."

"I could just shoot her." Billy Ray's mouth was smiling, but not his eyes.

Lyle laughed. "Too messy and a waste of a pretty lady. A lot of guys would give their eye teeth to be in your position. Sally would be a trophy wife for anybody."

"I don't need a trophy. Can I think about this?"

Lyle grabbed Billy Ray's arm. "No you cannot. The word is out and you need to make an honest woman out of her. I think you and Sally might hit it off in the long run. She could be good company."

"I prefer it when she doesn't talk," Billy Ray said, "but the sex is good."

"It'll work. Now you go and propose. Let me talk to Sally about how to break the news. I've got an idea on how to keep things rolling--especially at your church."

"Church?"

"Indeed yes, we want to make sure your pastor is on board."

Billy Ray mulled it over. Hmm, Lyle may be right. A happily married man's more likely to be elected than a single guy. Sally could testify as to my character. This could come out on the plus side.

"There's just one problem," Billy Ray said. "I'm not sure Lori will do the wedding."

Lyle stopped at the door on his way out. "Yes she will. You leave that to me and Sally."

CHAPTER 16

The next Sunday was Mother's Day and the church was full. During the prelude, Lori enjoyed looking out over the congregation to see who was there. There's my friend Celesta, with her six-foot-ten husband Rex Barkley. He's helping me out with the counseling--thank God. There's my husband, the second tallest man in the congregation, sitting next to them.

Lori shifted her gaze to the other side of the aisle. There's Rob Galloway with the other members of my old pulpit nominating committee--Joe Michaels, John Summers, Belle Ashton, Thelma Hill. It's funny how they still stick together even when the job is done. I guess they got to liking each other during their committee work.

And there's some of the singles on the back rows--Zeb Mallory, Mike Garland, Betty Jones--with some visitors. And sitting in the middle are the three amigas who fell in love with Mark, Virginia Mitchell, Margaret Henshaw, Judy Snider. --And my advocate, Junie Barrows sitting right next to the old trouble makers. God bless her."

Wait a minute, what's this? --Billy Ray and Sally Mae seated next to Sheriff Lyle Richards? That's interesting. Sheriff Richards never misses a Sunday at First Baptist, or so I'm told. And just look at Sally--all smiles this morning.

The organ prelude ended, and the elder in charge, Mildred Hopkins, came to the pulpit. She welcomed the visitors, read the announcements in the bulletin and then looked out over the congregation. "Are there any other announcements or celebrations you would like to mention?"

Sally Lawton shot up like a rocket and began bouncing up and down. "I have one! I have one! I want everyone to know that Billy Ray and I are engaged! And we want everyone to come to the wedding! And uh--what was the other thing I was going to say?"

Sally looked at Sheriff Richards who muttered something with his hand over his mouth. "Oh, oh--of course--we want Lori to do the wedding, and we'll work out a date that's convenient for everyone! I'm so excited!"

The congregation responded with a sustained applause. Mildred Hopkins waited for the excitement to subside and then turned to Lori.

"Lori, I can't think of a better announcement for Mother's Day, can you?"

Lori was in shock and sheepishly grinned without comment. She looked over at Mark who had his head buried in his hands. The rest of the service would be a blur with Lori struggling to get through her sermon. To make matters worse Mildred Hopkins invited Lori and Mark to lunch. Lori accepted and learned too late that Billy Ray and Sally were also invited.

⚔

Lori took a deep breath and glanced at the menu. Easy girl, think of a way to buy some time--maybe the 'minimax principle.' How can I minimize my losses and maximize my gains? --But what are my gains? How can I work this out? Hey, Rex might help. Counseling might slow things down.

Sally already had her calendar out on the dinner table ready to make plans. Lori politely put her hand on the calendar. "Sally, why not do this at my office where you have more room?"

Sally Mae clicked on her ball-point pen. "This table is fine, and the sooner I get some dates set the better. I want to find a time convenient with you, Lori."

"We can do this after your counseling sessions," Lori said. "We're fortunate to have a real professional in our church, Dr. Rex Barkley, doing this for free."

Billy Ray's jaw muscles tensed as he remembered his counseling sessions with Dr. Marshall Evans. "How many sessions are we talking about?"

"That depends on Rex," Lori replied, "but at least six. One good thing is that you won't be charged for a marriage license at City Hall if you do six counseling sessions."

"Money is not an object here," Billy Ray said.

"Well, I do require these sessions because I want you to get off to a good start."

"I think we're off to a good start already," Billy Ray said and then turned to Sally. "Maybe we should get someone else to do the wedding if we want to get married right away."

Like a rabbit sensing an open hole, Lori quickly made her move. "That would work fine with me. I certainly would not object to someone else--"

"Are you crazy, Billy Ray?" Sally interrupted. "Lori is going to do our wedding and that is that! I won't have it any other way. Counseling won't hurt us."

"A lot of wasted time in my opinion," Billy Ray said.

Sally patted Billy Ray on his knee. "Well, you can just keep that opinion to yourself. We'll contact Rex right away and start our counseling. Thank you, Lori, for agreeing to do our wedding."

Lori nodded and dabbed at her salad. Mark never said a word from start to finish.

CHAPTER 17

Lori sat down across from Rex in his office and rubbed her hands together. Maybe I shouldn't have come here. If I tell Rex about my suspicions of Billy Ray, that would put him in an awkward position. So what am I expecting? I can't just tell him to advise against the wedding--that would be unethical. I can't manipulate him. Rex will want his own conclusions. Uh oh, I've sat here too long, and Rex is waiting for me to talk. "I want to thank you for conducting these counseling sessions, Rex. It's a big help. I like your office arrangement. This round counseling table gives it a personal touch."

Rex noticed the hand rubbing and pulled up a chair at the table with Lori. "You didn't come here to talk about my office furniture, Lori. You've got something on your mind."

Nuts! Now what do I say. "Well, I uh, I have reservations about Sally Mae's upcoming marriage. I'm not sure it's a good match."

Rex leaned forward. "You said 'Sally Mae's marriage.' Do you have reservations about Billy Ray?"

Lori rubbed her hands together again. "Well, I--I guess it's a difference in personalities more than anything else. I probably shouldn't have said this much."

"You're not going to bias my opinion. If something's bothering you about this couple, please tell me."

"--Just an uneasy feeling."

"No, it's more than that. If I'm going to do this, we need to meet again after I've reviewed what's going on in my initial counseling sessions. I think you're holding something back."

He's a mind reader. Well, maybe I'm being too careful. I really do need for him to know what's going on with Billy Ray. "I'll give you my opinions after you've made your assessment. I have nothing definite to go on. I'm an amateur. You're the professional. I don't want to interfere with that."

"You won't, but I respect your opinion, and I want your promise to level with me."

"I promise--after you have assessed the situation."

⋏

After two counseling sessions, Rex dropped by Lori's office with some questions.

"I'm not sure what I can accomplish here," Rex said. "Sally does all the talking and Billy Ray seems bored with the whole thing."

"Tell me about Sally," Lori said.

"She's an odd combination," Rex replied. "She comes across as just a cute little southern belle, but I think that's a facade. She uses that to give her an advantage over men, probably copied from her mother. She's actually quite bright and capable of taking care of herself. Billy Ray may be getting more than he bargained for."

"And Billy Ray?"

"Well, he's odd too," Rex thought for a moment. "I can't get a handle on him. I'm not sure that he's capable of the affection that Sally wants."

"Or for that matter with anyone else," Lori said.

"So why are you doing the wedding?" Rex asked.

"I was hoping you would give me a reason not to."

"So you're putting it on me," Rex laughed. "I can't tell whether this marriage is going to work or not. I don't have a crystal ball. The chances are only 50-50 with the general population and I'm sure we both know some very strange people who have made it work."

"I want to know more about Billy Ray," Lori said. "What drives him, what makes him tick? What kind of guy is Sally Mae getting? Is there any way you could help me out on that?"

"Well, I've already suggested that the next counseling sessions be done individually. I'll try to get a better read on Billy Ray."

⚓

Thanks to Sally's persistence, a reluctant Billy Ray came in for counseling and stretched out slovenly in the chair beside Rex.

"I want to make this as painless as possible," Rex said. "I know neither of us wants to be here. Let's just talk about whatever comes to mind."

Billy Ray was caught off guard. Hmm, he wants me to pick my own subject. Is this a way of controlling me? Maybe I better toss it back to him.

"Fine," Billy Ray said, "you choose the subject."

"Well, we can talk about wildflowers or if that's not a good topic, how about what's most important to you in your life?"

"Let's talk about wildflowers," Billy Ray laughed. "No, let's don't. Okay, I can tell you that the most important thing in my life is goal setting."

"Huh, planning out things. Sounds like a business executive."

"That's right. Do you know the history of the Rockefellers?" Hmm, maybe I can take over this interview.

"Yeah, John D. was incredible." Rex said. "Nothing stood in his way."

"Exactly. Focusing on a goal like a tiger moving in on his prey. Anything less is unworthy of a man."

"How about a woman?"

"Nah, I don't think so. A woman doesn't have the balls."

"Literally, huh." Rex said.

"Oh, occasionally some lesbian will make it to the top, but that's not the way God intended it."

Rex crossed his legs in casual posture. "A man's world?"

"Yes sir," Billy Ray replied. "We're the warriors, the hunter-gatherers. We provide for the household."

"What happens when someone gets in the way of your goal?"

"Hah! That's not going to happen if you plan ahead."

"But what if they do?"

"Then it's survival of the fittest, the first law of a free society."

"How far do you think you should go in actual practice?" Rex asked.

"It's not a question of 'should,' but of commitment," Billy Ray paused. "Jesus was absolutely committed to his goal. Nothing stood in his way."

"Except the cross."

"The cross wasn't the end of it," Billy Ray said. "Jesus had a plan with a safety net."

"Do you have a plan?" Rex asked.

"Yes I do! And nothing is going to get in the way of it. Nothing."

"Nothing at all?"

Billy Ray suddenly felt uncomfortable. "Well, let me clarify that. I'm not bothered about bumps in the road--just major obstacles."

Rex paused. "Major obstacles--have you had many of those?"

"A few, but none that I couldn't handle," Billy Ray replied.

"You said you had a plan. Would you like to tell me about that?" Rex asked.

"Not really, it's a work in progress. --Uh well, okay. I think we've talked enough, and I hope you come to the wedding." Billy Ray stood up and abruptly left the room.

Rex was left with one word for his diagnosis. *Weird.*

CHAPTER 18

The next day Rex visited with Lori in her office. Rex tried to find a seat that would accommodate his long legs. "Have you thought about upgrading your furniture?"

Lori laughed. "Maybe I should. Those needle point chairs were donated by Margaret Henshaw. I don't think she had you in mind."

"I had an interesting chat with Billy Ray," Rex said. "Since you're concerned about doing the wedding, I guess it's alright to divulge this info."

"Right, what have you got?"

"I'll tell you one thing. I wouldn't want to get in Billy Ray's way in the upcoming campaign. He's ruthless."

"What makes you think so?" Lori asked.

"I got the image of a tiger stalking his prey," Rex replied. "In fact, those were Billy Ray's words about pursuing his goal."

"Wow, that's intense."

"There's some religious stuff mixed in too," Rex continued. "He mentioned that Jesus wouldn't allow anything to get in *his* way either. So it's all justified. It's not a matter of should or ought, it's a matter of commitment. As Billy Ray put it, major obstacles should be eliminated. Nothing gets in his way, nothing!"

"He sounds like the Blue's Brothers--on a mission from God."

"As long as God doesn't get in the way, yes," Rex continued. "There's one other thing that bothers me. Billy Ray has little or no regard for women; they are the recipients of male benevolence."

"Well, that's sort of a Texas cowboy thing," Lori said. "Women aren't created for decision making, only men."

"I don't think Sally's going to fit into that picture. As a matter of fact, when you search for Sally Lawton on Google, she comes up under Mensa. As I said before, she's not dumb. I think I better talk with Sally and make sure she knows what she's getting into."

⋏

The following week when Lori arrived at her office, Sally Mae was waiting at the door. Sally's southern accent had a sharp edge. "Lori, I need to discuss some things that Rex told me about Billy Ray and I want you to shoot straight on this."

"Fire away."

"I know that Billy Ray has his faults, but I don't think he's crazy," Sally said.

"Did Rex say he was crazy?" Lori asked.

"No, not exactly, but I didn't like the way Rex described him."

"Which was?"

"--As getting his way no matter what. Rex made Billy Ray sound like a woman-hating robot, incapable of affection or compassion."

Lori massaged her hands and thought for a moment. Okay, so Rex gave her the right description of Billy Ray, but I can't just say 'Amen' to it. She'll turn off anything I say. On the other hand, I won't be helping Sally if I act dumb."

Sally pushed for an answer. "I want your opinion, Lori, and I want it in spades. Don't try to spare my feelings."

"It's your decision, Sally," Lori said. "This wedding is yours, not mine. I read the vows, but you have to live with it."

Sally scooted her chair closer to Lori. "C'mon Lori, talk to me. I want to know what you're thinking."

"Alright," Lori got up to get coffee and offered some to Sally. "First off, I need to get some of my facts straight. You moved here from North Carolina when you were in junior high school, right?"

"Yes."

"Billy Ray was a star quarterback in high school. Did you know him well?"

"Not really, I was three years younger," Sally replied. "I admit I was infatuated with him. I loved watching him play and would follow him around in the halls."

"After you graduated from high school, you went to TCU in Fort Worth. Did you see Billy Ray during that time?"

"No--are you going to give me a straight answer or not?" Sally put her coffee aside.

"I'm trying to find out how long you've really known Billy Ray."

"Then just ask me," Sally said. "I graduated from TCU and moved back to Granbury to work with Dad at his farm equipment company. My parents were killed in a car accident shortly after that. I've been dating Billy Ray for six months now, but I got to know him when you started Bible study last year. Is there something wrong with that?"

"Let me ask you this," Lori said, "I know you love Billy Ray, but I want you to look at it objectively. Let's assume he's marrying a friend of yours. What advice would you give your friend for handling some of Billy Ray's less adorable traits? Or is Billy Ray Mr. Perfect?"

"Well," Sally replied, "let me think. I'll admit that not just everyone can get along with Billy Ray. He is headstrong and likes to get his own way. There's no doubt that he's ambitious, sometimes to the max."

"So what advice would you give for getting along with him?"

"Damn it, I don't know. He's like a high spirited Kentucky thoroughbred."

Lori glanced away. Jackass more likely.

"Billy Ray takes patience, forbearance and love without smothering him," Sally continued. "You can't keep a tight rein on him. You have to give him his head and let him find his own way."

"Billy Ray doesn't do well with obstacles in his way. What are the chances your friend would become one of those after the wedding?"

Sally Mae threw her coffee in the sink. "Yeah, well, you have to know when to back off. I see what you're saying."

"I'm not saying it," Lori said. "You are."

"No, you're calling it like you see it. I'm marrying a self contained, self-absorbed man who's not going to be easy to live with. I understand what you're saying, but I'm still marrying him and I want you to do the wedding."

"I'll do what you want, Sally. It's your, uh, wedding."

"You were going to say 'funeral,' right?'" Sally laughed. "I still love you, Lori. You're my pastor and I expect us to be honest with each other. In fact, I'd like to reciprocate with some honest discussion on another subject right now."

"Uh oh, about what?"

"About your Bible study. I know that you want us to have a faith that's really our own. I get that. --But I think you're selling us short."

"How so?"

"You talk about being a fellow traveler, Lori, but you're more than that. You didn't go through three years of seminary just to travel along with us."

"So what am I?" Lori asked.

Sally stood up, then sat on Lori's desk. "I want you to listen carefully because I feel led in saying this."

"By the Spirit? You know, of course, that this puts a silencer on any rational argument I might have."

"Yes, let me finish. I had an experience a few years ago when I went with some friends to look at the civil war memorial grounds in Vicksburg. We started off taking the tour by ourselves but there are over 1000 memorials in the park. We could the see the statues, the incredible pavilions and the markers but we didn't really know what they meant."

"Mark and I went to Vicksburg too," Lori interrupted. "Beautiful rolling hills, tall oak trees, perfectly kept grounds over an expansive area--but too many memorials. We had a hard time putting things together."

"Yes, that's what we found," Sally Mae continued, "so we turned the car around and went back to the administration building to hire a guide. We got some older gentleman who was a retired history professor from Mississippi State. He opened our eyes to a world we would never have discovered on our own. Sometimes we got out of the car and walked over the grounds as our guide talked about the leaders of both sides, the battles and the thousands who died. We had a wonderful tour and an appreciation of what happened there that I will always treasure. Do you understand what I'm saying, Lori? You don't just travel with us. You lead us. You're our guide through the Bible and the history of how people come to faith."

"Wow," Lori said. "That's beautiful. I don't know what to say."

"You can start by acting as a guide for us at our next Bible study. You have a wealth of things to share on our tour."

Lori sat quietly behind her desk after Sally left. So I'm a guide. Maybe Sally Mae really was led by the Spirit. I'm more than a fellow traveler, but I'm not a guru at the top of the mountain. I'm a guide at the bottom going up with the others. So here am I coming to faith again. Thank you, Sally.

CHAPTER 19

Billy Ray sat in his father's old easy chair drinking a Shiner Bock beer. I'm glad I had counseling with Dr. Rex. It put things in focus--bumps in the road and major obstacles. Well said, Billy Ray, well said. Planning is more essential in my life than ever. I've experienced some unfortunate events requiring immediate action. Unanticipated roadblocks create unwelcomed detours. Life can be hard. --But move on, Billy Ray, move on. Detours are no more than just bumps in the road once you find your way.

He downed a second beer. Yes sir, I've had three major detours to overcome. One was my dear departed father, now resting under his favorite oak tree. It was the least I could do. Number two was Hank Casey, my father's close friend, and unfortunately my mother's too as it turned out.

Billy Ray's cat jumped up on his lap. "Hello kitty cat, have you come to hear my story? I think you'll enjoy this one. Hank came to call on me right after my father's memorial service. He didn't even knock at the door--just walked in like he owned the place. I could smell the liquor mixed in with his bad breath."

"What are you doing in my house?" I asked him.

He staggered over to a chair. "Son, I got news for you! You only thought you lost your Daddy."

We talked back and forth. "You're dunk, you stupid old fart."

"That's no way to address family," he said.

"You ain't family."

93

He drooled all over his ignorant chin. "Yes I is. That's what I'm here to tell you. Your mother and I were real close at one time. Yes sir, real close."

"I'm about to kick your butt out of here!"

The stupid bastard wouldn't let it go. "Now hold on, hold on young feller. Hear me out. Your Daddy was no good to your mother. They stopped sleeping together long ago and she came to me for solace. And I sure enjoyed giving it to her. That's how you were conceived!"

"You're leaving now."

"I can prove it! I can prove it! They got a thing called DNA. You compare your blood to mine and see if I'm lying. I'm gonna tell the world the truth, and you're gonna own up to it!"

I grabbed him by his hair and threw him out the door. "Out--now!"

He yelled back. "This is no way to treat your Daddy!"

"You come out here again and I'll skin you alive."

"You need to think through this boy. You need to think it out. You got family! You got responsibilities."

"Well, kitty, after he left I took his suggestion. I thought it through. What if it were true? What if his DNA linked up with mine? He probably forced my mother. There's no way I can have a sot like that running around claiming to be my father! The old fool would probably try to live with me and lay claim to my ranch. So I had to tend to the matter. Two hours later, I took my shovel and knocked on Hank Casey's door. Hank walked out with a beer bottle."

"Well looky here," he said. "The prodigal son! Have you come to make peace boy?"

"In a manner of speaking." I swung the shovel crushing his head. "Now we can both be at peace."

The cat rolled over to get its stomach scratched. "After that, I did some more thinking. Hank's vegetable garden was a half mile from his house, but there was no sense in getting blood in my pickup. I was strong enough to hoist him up on my shoulder and walk the distance. The ground was soft in the garden and it was easy to dig a deep hole. Before I laid him to rest, I found a package of cucumber seeds in his side pocket. Hey, maybe those cucumbers can cover my tracks! I sprinkled the seeds around the grave. Ha! With Hank as fertilizer, they'll probably turn into pickles.

I washed my clothes twice when I got home. There was a metal button missing from the pocket of my western-style shirt--too nice a shirt to loose. I could always buy another button. The killing happened too fast for adequate planning. Could I have missed some detail? No sense in throwing away the shovel--I'm getting good use of it. Oh well, kitty cat, it's time to stop worrying and replaying the scene. It's been six years now, and dead cucumber vines are all that remains. There's nothing there to connect me."

⅄

Billy Ray's thoughts were interrupted when two hands suddenly covered his eyes. "Guess who?" Sally Mae giggled.

The cat jumped from Billy Ray's lap. "How did you get into the house?"

"I found your spare key and had one made for myself. We are getting married, aren't we? It's going to be my house too." Sally Mae looked up at the mantle of the fireplace.

"Why are you staring at my longhorns?" Billy Ray asked.

"I'm sorry, Billy Ray, but that has to go. The stuffed bobcat too."

"Says who!"

"Says your bride-to-be unless you want to get another woman in here," Sally said. "I'm not going to live in this ultra man-cave."

Billy Ray sat up straight. "You need to consult me first."

"No, it's just the other way around, Billy," Sally Mae laughed. "I'm in charge of domestics and homemaking. You take care of the ranch, I'll take care of the house and make a suitable home for us."

"Shouldn't you wait until we're married?"

Sally Mae waved her hands in the air. "Goodness, no! I'm not going to move into a place looking like this. --Say, are you serious about this marriage?"

"Well, uh yes, of course."

"Good. The decorators will be coming tomorrow."

"How much are you spending?" Billy Ray asked.

"It doesn't matter," Sally said. "It's our wedding present from the inheritance my parents left me."

"Our wedding present? Then shouldn't I have a say?"

Sally Mae stamped her foot. "Oh, put a muzzle on it, Billy Ray. You already stand convicted on taste."

"So what should I expect?"

"Well, we need some light and color in this living room."

"It's not a living room. It's a den," Billy said.

Sally circled the room. "Now that I look at it, it's too large to be called a den or a living room. We'll call it the 'great room' and it's going to be elegant--a place where my TCU friends won't be embarrassed when they walk in the door."

"TCU friends?"

"Your bachelor days are over, honey," Sally said. "You're going to wake up to a glorious new day! You just leave it to me. We're going first class."

"Look Sally Mae, I really …"

". . Do you want this marriage or not?"

"Well, I do but …"

". . Then tend to your ranch business and let me take care of the house."

Billy Ray started to argue but Sally stopped him with a look he hadn't seen before. He felt like a student being put in his place by a dominating professor. Never mind, I'll let her have her way and settle with her later.

The next day, the carpenters came. The wooden shutters were taken out and a large window was installed overlooking the ranch. The rustic front door was replaced with a carved oak one with leaded-glass panes. A skylight shone directly over a series of needle point chairs and a sofa substituted for Billy Ray's easy chair. From there the nightmare continued. The painters came and then the decorators.

The den was just the beginning. Every room in the house was luxuriously renovated and furnished. The bathrooms were now replete with new artistic fixtures. A jetted spa-tub and a bidet greeted Billy Ray in the master bedroom. His bed with the leather headboard was replaced with an elegant four poster one with a floral carving. Sally Mae smiled as she surveyed the finished product. It was ready for a party.

✦

Sally Mae invited guests to show off her renovations and included members of the sheriff's department.

As the guests arrived, Sheriff Richards noticed Billy Ray's behavior and took him aside. "Now listen boy, you wipe that scowl off your face. I know things have changed around here, but look how delighted these women are with what they see. Those are votes, my friend. Those are votes! Sally's fixed this place up so that you look like a refined gentleman."

"She even makes me take my boots off on the front porch," Billy Ray complained.

"Well of course," Lyle said. "You don't want to track mud on that beautiful new carpet. You got yourself a fancy gal! Smile, damn it, and greet your guests."

Billy Ray thought about it and to Sally Mae's surprise started greeting their guests with warm handshakes and polite hugs.

Sally Mae hugged him. "Well now, that's more like it!"

Billy Ray had no love for the make-over, but he did understand votes.

Chapter 20

With only six months to go for the election of a new sheriff, the campaign, like the spring weather, heated up. Earl Blanton, Billy Ray's opponent, had good credentials as the assistant police chief of Granbury. He was a quiet man with little experience in public speaking but well respected in the community. The polls between Billy Ray and himself were almost even with a slight edge for Billy Ray.

As Mark Travis entered City Hall, Rob Galloway caught him by the arm. "I have some visitors in my office and we may have a problem. Would you meet me there?"

When Mark came to Rob's office, he was surprised to see Alice Evans and Earl Blanton sitting there. *What now? Why is Earl here?*

Rob poured coffee for the visitors and then spoke to Mark. "Alice shared with Earl the discussion that you had with her."

Not good. What if Earl uses that info in his campaign? "Alice, I thought we agreed to keep this quiet."

"… Mark, I'm sorry if I violated your confidence, but I keep thinking about our conversation. There's only one logical conclusion about who killed my husband and that's 'Billy Ray.'"

"If she's right," Earl Blanton said, "then we need close the barn door before the horses get out."

Mark turned away from Earl. *How am I going to get out of this mess?*

I'm more like a deer caught in the headlights than horses in a barn.

Rob intervened. "Earl, is there something you know that we don't?"

"We know that Dr. Evans' files have been tampered with and Billy Ray's the logical suspect," Earl answered.

"Let's say we brought it to a jury," Mark said, "What's more credible--that someone broke into Dr. Evans' office, found the password to his computer, forged the letter, erased the files, destroyed the notes and left with no signs of a break in--or that Dr. Evans wrote the letter himself?"

"On top of that," Rob joined in, "the investigation itself would be branded as a political attempt to discredit Billy Ray."

"Maybe I should go to the newspaper and tell my story," Alice said.

"The first thing the newspaper will do is contact Billy Ray for his side," Rob countered. "You'll be depicted as a distraught spouse, still grieving over your husband."

"Alice, I grant you it's suspicious," Mark said, "but it's too thin. We need more to go on."

"Maybe I could offer myself as bait," Alice offered. "We could let Billy Ray know what I found out."

"We don't have the resources to protect you around the clock," Rob said. "and even if we did, it's too thin to authorize protection."

Earl Blanton pushed his chair back. "So we elect a mad-dog killer for sheriff?"

"You can't campaign on that," Mark said, "or it'll backfire, and you'll lose for sure."

Alice hung her head in resignation as she left with Earl from Rob's office. "I'm not getting any help here, Earl. I have one other option, a long shot--but I'll have to act quickly."

"Just what option is that?" Earl asked.

"I shouldn't have said anything. You can't be involved, and it's better if you don't know. Let's leave it at that."

"So you're not giving up," Earl said.

"Not at all."

Two days later, Alice arranged a tea-time meeting with Sally Mae at the Iron Horse Inn. The Inn was a large vintage home renovated from the 19th century. After climbing the steps leading to the porch, the foyer opened to a luxurious place for tea not unlike a scene from Gone With the Wind.

Alice waited at a little table covered with lace for Sally Mae's arrival and contemplated her strategy. I need to anticipate Sally's reaction in response to what I say. I can't just out-and-out tell her that she's marrying a murderer, but I need to say enough to create doubt--somehow.

Sally strolled in cheerfully. "Hi there, Alice. What a wonderful place for tea. Has it been opened long?"

"About a month or so," Alice replied. "The tea is authentically British."

"Delightful!" Sally said. "I've been dying to meet you. Billy Ray has told me so many good things about you and Dr. Evans."

Hmm, so Billy Ray knows we're meeting. Good! That should give him something to think about. "I wish you could have met my husband."

Sally unfolded her napkin. "I hope things are going well for you."

"I still have some sad days, but it's been over four years now. I'm adjusting."

"You said over the phone that you had something to tell me."

"Yes. Well, I don't know where to start. It's all so peculiar," Alice replied.

"My goodness, you certainly have my attention."

"Does Billy Ray have any enemies?" Alice asked.

"Uh, no, Billy Ray doesn't have any real enemies--perhaps Earl Blanton, his opponent, but even then ..."

"No, Earl would not be involved in this," Alice said. "He's too much of a gentleman."

"What is it you're trying to tell me?"

"I'm sure Billy Ray told you about my husband, Marshall, who not only was Billy's teacher but his counselor as well."

"No, I didn't know about the counseling part," Sally said.

Alice took a napkin and wiped her mouth. "Oh my, I hope I didn't violate a confidence. Billy Ray had some tough experiences, and Marshall wanted to be helpful."

"What's the problem?" Sally Mae dropped her southern accent.

"Here's my point. Marshall kept very careful records of his clients. Billy Ray's files are missing--except for his letter of evaluation that was sent to the sheriff."

"So?"

Alice casually sipped her tea. "I'm wondering why someone would steal the files?"

"What are you getting at?" Sally asked.

"Well, blackmail. There may be something in Billy's files that could be used against him."

"That's ridiculous," Sally said. "I'm sure there's nothing incriminating or Billy Ray wouldn't be working in the sheriff's department."

"I don't think the evaluation letter was written by my husband," Alice said.

"Why?"

"It's too perfect and it's generic," Alice said. "Marshall always talked about strong points and weak ones--none of which are in the forged letter. The blackmailer could easily prove it as a fraud by producing the stolen files with the real letter."

Sally Mae stared hard at Alice. "None of this makes any sense."

"No, not unless Billy Ray is being blackmailed."

"Alice, this is nuts. I'm not going to mention any of this Billy Ray and I'm asking you to do the same. I know you're trying to be helpful, but it stops here. I don't know where those files have gone and I don't care. Billy Ray is where he should be and I'm not worried about some lunatic with an extortion scheme. Nothing bad is going to happen."

"Maybe you're right," Alice said. "I shouldn't have bothered you with this."

"You did what you felt was right," Sally said, "but let's just let it go at that, okay?"

"Okay, I won't mention it to anyone else. I'm sorry I brought it up."

"No apology is needed."

As Sally left, Alice felt a glimmer of hope. I'm not sure, but maybe I planted a seed--a little dissonance that can take root. I did what I could; I'll let it alone for now.

CHAPTER 21

Later that night, Billy Ray sat down with Sally to eat a grilled steak. Sally seemed quieter than usual.

"How was your day?" Billy Ray asked.

Sally Mae barely touched her steak. "Boring. How was yours?"

"Good. I spoke at a Baptist men's luncheon. I think I got most of their votes."

"How can you tell?"

"They cheered and applauded," Billy Ray replied. "I'm getting good at this speech making business. Lyle Richards is a good teacher."

"Are you still ahead in the polls?"

"Yeah, Earl's not that good in public," Billy Ray said. "How did your meeting go with what's-her-name?"

"Alice Evans? Fine."

"I didn't know you two were friends," Billy Ray said.

"Well, I guess she was lonely. She was one of my Daddy's nurses before he died. We've talked before."

"How is Alice doing with her husband's disappearance?"

"It's been over four years. She's adjusted."

"No one seems to know what happened to him," Billy Ray said.

"No."

"You're awfully quiet, Sally Mae," Billy Ray observed. "Is there anything wrong?"

"Just tired. I'm going to clean up now and go to bed."

"Maybe you're coming down with something. I'll clean up the dishes. You go on to bed."

Sally Mae kissed Billy Ray on the cheek and left to the bedroom. "Thanks for understanding."

Billy Ray loaded the dishwasher and cleaned the grill. Something's up with Sally Mae. What if Alice said something about me? There's nothing she *could* say, no reason. I was in her home for counseling, but we never talked.

Billy Ray left the house and went for a long walk. A conversation with an old friend might clear the air. He's waiting for me now, just over that hill. He was my favorite professor at Tarleton. We had a special bond or so I thought. He never charged me for counseling, and I always felt comfortable in going to him. Our friendship was good for another year after graduation with counseling in his home. Then things took a bad turn. Ah, there he is now under the mesquite trees--right where I left him, number three.

How are you, Dr. Evans, resting well I trust. I'm a little concerned about your wife, Alice. I need to replay our last day together to see if I overlooked some detail your wife may have noticed. You don't mind, do you?

Let me see now. I'd been working in the sheriff's office for a year when I was asked to apply full time for deputy sheriff. I needed a psychological evaluation, so naturally I turned to my good friend, Dr. Marshall Evans. Do you remember your response? You said, "We still have some issues to sort out. I'm not ready to write that letter just yet."

What could I do? I already told the sheriff that you, the great Dr. Evans would send an evaluation letter. The sheriff would wonder why you didn't. --I wondered that myself.

So I parked my truck in a wooded area and waited until you left home. Then I picked your lock, and went into your office. Your computer was on and I found several positive letters of evaluation for others, but nothing on me. Then I went to your cabinet file and discovered your hand written notes describing me as a borderline psychotic with delusions of grandeur.

You old *hypocrite*! What was I going to do now? I needed that letter.

--But then, all of a sudden, the door swung open and there you were watching me going through your files. You were fairly calm about it. "What are you doing in my house, Billy?"

I weighed my options. I might as well tell the truth. "I was wondering why you wouldn't give me a letter of evaluation for deputy sheriff?"

I remember your hurtful words exactly. "I don't think you would be a good fit for the sheriff's office."

"Why?"

"You have some unresolved issues, but at this point I can't help you. I'm not going to report you for breaking in, but our relationship is over. I want you to leave--now."

I walked to the door, then stopped. I couldn't just leave. I tried to reason with you. "Why are you making this so hard? I thought you were my friend."

"I asked you to leave."

"Please don't make me. Can't we discuss this?"

You walked over to me and took my arm. "I'm sorry, the answer is no, now out."

I had no choice. I delivered a quick karate chop to your windpipe. You tried to yell, but no sound came out. The next blow left you unconscious. I bent down and clamped my hands over your nose and mouth. That was it. There was no blood or evidence of a struggle.

I backed my truck to your back driveway, loaded your body, and started to go to my ranch. Then I thought of something. The letter--maybe there's a way of handling it. I covered your body with a tarp and walked back into the house. I looked through your things--letterhead stationary in your desk drawer, and what's this? A signature stamp, but did you use it? Yes! I found copies of other letters with the stamped signature. That made it simple--no forgery required.

The rest was easy. I used the computer to cut and paste from those positive evaluations I discovered earlier. Then I straightened things up, took a trip to my ranch, and here you are. --Hey, I'm glad we had this little talk. I remember everything now and I left no stone unturned. No problems.

✦

Billy Ray returned to the ranch house and found Sally Mae in the rocking chair on the front porch. His thoughts turned again to Alice Evans. *Why am I worried? There's not a shred of evidence, especially after all the care I took. Even so ...*

Sally stood up to greet him. "I couldn't sleep. I need you to scratch my back. You look deep in thought."

"I was thinking about our wedding date," Billy Ray said. "It's coming up in two months. Are you still okay with it?"

Sally laughed. "What? --getting married to you? Yeah, I'm cool. How about you?"

"As long as you're happy, I'm happy." Billy Ray sat down, pulled Sally onto his lap and kissed the back of her neck. *There's really nothing to worry about. Sally Mae's fine and Alice is not a concern. I don't have a problem.*

CHAPTER 22

Later that week Billy Ray was called into the sheriff's office. Lyle Richards greeted him with his usual big smile, and the two men sat across from each other at the conference table.

"It's time to take it up another notch," Sheriff Richards said. "We can't let the campaign sag in the middle from lack of attention."

Billy Ray shuffled his feet. "What more can I do? It's one speech after another, group after group. I'm worn out."

"You need to be seen as an active member of the community."

"I go to church."

"Which limits you to Presbyterians--not enough to get you in the public eye."

Billy Ray shrugged. "What do you suggest?"

"Do things to be seen. Buy a season ticket to the Opera House on the square and go to all their plays. Sally Mae will love it and people will respect you for supporting our theater."

"I'm not much on plays."

"Grin and bear it. Show a little class. Get out where people can see you. Do you play golf?"

"Golf is for sissies."

"I play golf," Lyle said.

"Well--some sissies."

"I know you played football, but is there any sport that you can play where people in the community might watch you--tennis maybe."

"I played racquetball in college."

"That's good! It makes you look like you're concerned about fitness. So join the YMCA and get season tickets at the Opera House. You'll have visibility in the community."

"Alright, if I have to."

⬧

Sally Mae was delighted that Billy Ray bought season tickets to the Granbury Opera House. She loved plays and enjoyed dressing up and going out. After the second play they attended, people recognized Billy Ray and some shook his hand and wished him well.

At the Y, Billy Ray chose a Monday before noon to warm up and recoup some of the skills he learned in college. He practiced by himself for about fifteen minutes when he heard a familiar voice.

"Hello Billy Ray," Celesta opened the door while he was practicing. "We have the court at noon but you're welcome to play with us."

"Who's *us*?"

Lori walked in. "I'm *us*. Didn't know you played."

"Not very well. I hope you don't mind hitting a few balls with me."

"Ever play cutthroat?" Celesta asked.

"Yes," Billy Ray replied.

"Then warm up and let's play." Celesta said.

Lori slowly opened her equipment bag. Is Billy Ray going to be a regular? Is this what I have to look forward to? Noon is the only time I can play. --Well, there's no choice for now. I'm stuck.

Lori won the first game with Celesta barely losing from a poorly returned ball by Billy Ray. The match was closer during the third game when Billy Ray developed his kill shots. He was strong and hit the ball hard, but with not much finesse. During one point with Lori serving, Billy Ray returned the ball by slamming it into the small of Lori's back. She bent over in pain. "Give me a second."

"I'm sorry, Lori," Billy Ray said. "I was concentrating on hitting the ball."

Lori shook it off. "That's alright."

After a few more points with Billy Ray serving, Lori hit a hard backhand with the ball smashing into his ear.

"Damn!" Billy Ray yelled. "Damn, that hurts!"

"I'm sorry, Billy Ray," Lori said, "I was focusing on the ball."

"Maybe it would be best if we called 'hinder' or tried not to hit each other," Celesta said. "I don't want to be next."

Both Billy Ray and Lori nodded in agreement, and the game preceded without incident.

Celesta invited Billy Ray back next time and Lori winced. There's no getting away from this maniac and now I'm literally hemmed in!

▼

The next day, Sheriff Lyle Richards called Billy Ray back into his office. Lyle clapped his hands together. "I've got the perfect event for you. We could not ask for a better break. You may not like it, but you've got to do it if you want to win the election."

"What now? Is there no end to this?"

Lyle joined Billy Ray at the conference table. "I've already signed you up so let me explain. People need an opportunity to view you from several different angles. You are a supporter of the arts, you believe in physical fitness, you are capable of protecting the public--but you also are a man of compassion. In particular, you care deeply about women and children. That's the next step."

"So what have I got to do? Kiss babies?"

Lyle leaned across the table. "Billy Ray, I want you to take this seriously and listen to me. There is a wonderful charity supported by the prominent people in Granbury. It's called Elsie's Place, and it's for free dental care to poorer women and children."

"I'll write a check," Billy Ray said.

"Spoken like a Presbyterian," Lyle responded. "No, you'll do much more than that. You'll participate in their big fund-raising gala that they host each year."

"How?"

"Well, the fund-raiser revolves around a contest called "The Handsome Hunks of Hood County.""

"I've heard of that and I'm not doing it!" Billy Ray protested.

"Shut up and listen," Lyle said. "I'm the campaign manager and you'll do what I say or you can get somebody else."

"Alright, alright," Billy Ray said. "What do I have to do?"

"There will be twelve contestants. First of all, you'll get your picture taken for the calendar. I've signed you up for Mr. September. You'll be on every woman's wall two months before the election."

"I don't want to pose for a calendar!"

"Again, shut up." Lyle said. "There's more. On the night of the gala event, the contestants will stroll down a run way and make their pitch."

"Hell no!"

"Billy Ray, this is an opportunity you cannot afford to miss," Lyle said. "You'll be performing before the elite, several hundred of the wealthiest in the community. Women will be yelling and screaming and giving their money. These are not just votes, they're influential votes. Do you want to be sheriff or not?"

"What happens on this 'gang plank?'"

"You'll go out twice, once in formal attire and once in costume with a sense of humor."

"I don't have that."

"What, a sense of humor or a costume? No problem," Lyle laughed. "I've got just the outfit for you. You'll dress as a fisherman with lures pinned all over you. You'll have a casting rod with a soft purse on the end as a lure. You cast it out in the audience. When women put money in the purse, you reel it in and put the money inside your shirt."

"Why not my pocket?"

"There's nothing sexy about a pocket. You're a hunk, remember? You put the money inside your shirt to encourage fantasies--and votes."

"Then what?"

"You go back stage and come back for the voting results. The vote depends on how much money you collected. So don't expect to win. There are two doctors competing in the group so they'll probably collect the most money. They have lots of practice in doing that."

"If I can't win, then why …"

"Nobody cares whether you win or lose. The important thing is caring about Elsie's Place. That's how you'll be remembered at the polls."

"I'll be glad when this whole thing is over."

"It's never over," Lyle said. "If you win the election this time, then you start thinking about the next one. You have to keep up your public persona. How are you coming with the theater and the Y?"

"I actually enjoyed one of the plays--about a fiddler and an old Jewish guy who had to marry off his daughters," Billy Ray said, "but not so good with racquetball at the Y. There's only one court with two times when I can play--noon with the B league, and evening with the A team. I'm not good enough for the A league, and Lori Travis plays at lunch time. I played with her and another lady. Lori didn't seem happy with it."

"If things are strained between you and Lori, then back off." Lyle said. "Don't force her to be with you. That creates resentment and you don't need that. Go play with the A team."

"I'm not good enough."

"Hell, you're an athlete. Practice, practice, practice--do it right before the A team plays. Sooner or later, they'll invite you to join them."

"I guess I could play doubles if I had a good partner."

"It'll help with your macho image. Combined with your sensitive love of the theater, you'll be the most interesting man in Granbury."

Billy Ray left Lyle's office with his head down. I didn't sign up for all this stuff, but I guess I'll have to tough it out--speaking engagements, racquetball, live theater, and now a clown at a charity. What's next?

CHAPTER 23

After dinner, Lori assisted Mark in loading the dishwasher. Mark noticed the frown she wore.

"Something's bothering you," Mark said. "Want to talk about it?"

"Yesterday, Billy Ray showed up for racquetball," Lori replied. "I don't know what to do if he wants to play again."

"Hey, maybe I should go with you," Mark said. "Billy Ray and I will challenge you and Celesta. I can hardly wait."

"Yeah, right," Lori said. "I'm sure we'll all have a wonderful time."

"I wonder why Billy Ray wants to play you gals?" Mark asked.

"I don't know. You can tell he's played before. Once he gets back into shape, he could be tough."

"So he's out to beat you?"

"Maybe. I don't really care--just so he stays away."

A few minutes later a phone call came from Celesta. Lori was laughing when she hung up. "Good news from Celesta! Billy Ray is now playing with the A team! Celesta said that he has big red welts all over his body to prove it. That little rubber ball may not look like much but a kill shot from those big guys will leave a red blister."

Mark lifted his water glass. "Here's to Billy Ray. May his welts increase!"

Lori folded her arms and sat back in her chair. "Just tell me one thing. Do you honestly think he killed those men? I mean *really*. I still have a hard time believing that."

"Maybe not one hundred percent," Mark said, "but if he forged that letter from Dr. Evans …"

"Then he would have to kill Dr. Evans to make it work," Lori said. "The problem is logic--or what people perceive as logic. A jury is not going to buy into the forgery argument. It's simpler to think that Dr. Evans wrote the letter himself."

"That's what I told Alice."

Just then there was a ruckus out on the back yard. BR was yowling and something else was screaming. Mark ran out on the patio. "No, that's not possible! Our cat is facing down a red tailed hawk. "

Lori and Mark stood spellbound watching the battle. BR charged the hawk time and time again until the hawk flapped its wings and furiously took off. Several feathers were left on the ground.

"That hawk must have swooped down and missed. BR, you're one lucky cat. That big old bird could have carried you off!" Mark exclaimed.

"My money was on BR." Lori picked up her cat and examined it for scratches. "He looks okay, ready to go another round."

"That fight's not BR's style," Mark said. "BR likes to sneak around bushes and jump out on an unsuspecting prey. He's a stealth killer, not an open combat guy."

"I wonder how Billy Ray does it," Lori said, "--if he is a killer. Maybe the answer is as simple as BR, stealthily approaching his goal, overcoming obstacles along the way."

"Part of it may be in fooling the public with a favorable picture of himself." Mark pulled up a chair for Lori on the patio. "--So Billy Ray joins the Y, goes to the Opera House, and charms groups with speaking events. He has a crafty old campaign manager in Lyle Richards who probably is acting like a GPS for Billy Ray. I wonder where he's headed next?"

"Billy Ray or Lyle Richards?"

"Both. Billy Ray is learning from a master politician," Mark said.

"I don't think I can stay in the same town with a 'Sheriff Billy Ray,'" Lori said.

"We'll manage," Mark said. "Let's stay out on the patio for a while. The weather's nice and we can enjoy the sunset."

"How about some wine to go with that?" Lori retrieved a bottle of Merlot and two glasses from the kitchen. For a while they sat quietly enjoying the fresh air.

"I have something to ask," Mark broke the silence. "Do you know about Elsie's Place?"

"I do," Lori said. "It's a wonderful charity and they have a fantastic extravaganza with handsome young men vying for the title of hottest hunk."

"Yeah, well, it's coming up in two months and there's a calendar with it. It's called 'Hunks of Hood County.' Each contestant poses for a particular month."

"Let me guess," Lori smiled. "My husband has been asked to be a hunk!"

"Uh huh. I've been asked to be Mr. August because I'm so hot. It's for a good cause and other guys are involved too. I think I might do it. Do I have your approval?"

Lori paused and looked at the reddening sunset, "I'll have to give that some thought--other women staring at my husband with lust in their hearts."

Mark grinned. "What's wrong with that?"

"Have you no shame?"

"I have to keep my options open," Mark said. "You may not love me forever."

Lori shook her head with her long red hair blowing in the wind. "No sir! I'm not going to let you do it. You are closed for business."

"Final answer? My one chance for getting on a calendar?"

"Well, I can't deny you that," Lori laughed. "So let's think about what you're going to do on the run way. Do you understand what you're getting into?"

"What do you mean?" Mark asked.

"It's done for laughs. You have to dress up in something comical--not superman. There were two of them last year--much to their embarrassment."

"How about the Lone Ranger?"

"Too obvious. Someone probably has that idea already," Lori said. "Unfortunately, you won't know who's doing what until the night of rehearsal."

"How do you know all this?"

"Our next door neighbor, Andy, did it last year. He was one of the hunks that showed up as superman," Lori said. "Some don't decide on what to wear until the last minute. That's how they ended up with two supermen. We need to think of something unique that no one else would think of. Let me work on that. It'll be fun. "

"I wonder who the contestants are?" Mark said.

"That's not disclosed until later because some chicken out."

"I may be one of those."

"No you won't," Lori said. "It's a worthy cause, and last year they raised $75,000. You'll enjoy it. It's a blast!"

"Okay, you can be my manager."

"Nothing new in that," Lori nibbled his earlobe and they went back inside.

The Hunks' contest also had the attention of Buster Conley and Sammy Alfred, two mechanics who owned a dilapidated auto shop six miles north of Granbury. They had made enough money robbing jewelry stores in Dallas to buy the shop but were now faced with a cash flow problem.

"I don't think this idea is doable," Buster said. "There are too many people in one room."

Sammy wiped grease from his face. "Yeah, but it's like Mardi Gras. They're yelling and screaming and no one is paying attention to the money. They're drinking like crazy and focused on the hunks."

Buster emptied the oil from the car they were working on. "I still don't get it."

"Look, I told you," Sammy said. "I saw the whole thing when I was working as a janitor last year. Each hunk has a crew collecting money in cans with their hunk's picture on it. Then the money is dumped in the head lady's bag at the front table. She's sitting right next to the runway as one of the judges. She's yapping her mouth off and won't be looking."

"So you just walk up, take the bag and she's going to let you do that?" Buster waved his hand dismissively.

"Well, I'll need you to create a distraction," Sammy replied.

Buster tossed his socket wrench on the table. "How am I going to do that?"

"Use your imagination. Think about what would happen in a restaurant to really get their attention? Something loud and surprising that makes people stop and look."

"Maybe if a naked lady walked by," Buster laughed.

"I keep hoping you're not as stupid as you look. How about if you just threw up all over the place?"

"Let's think of something else," Buster replied.

"We have time to work out the details."

"Do we pack some artillery?" Buster asked.

"Absolutely not. That's the beauty of this plan. There's no need for guns. We'll be dressed up all clean and shaven with sports coats and ties. No one will notice us because we'll look like everyone else."

Buster was still not convinced. "Won't people spot you carrying the bag?"

"No, I've got this whole thing planned out. I'll bring a large briefcase with little bottles of free wine samples for everyone at my table. I'll tell them I'm working with a distributor. That way they won't be suspicious of the briefcase. Once the briefcase is empty, I'll quietly go up, swipe the Hunk's money sack and slip it inside the briefcase."

"--But uh, but they'll see you walk up," Buster said.

"I won't walk straight up to the table. I'll get up like I'm going to the restroom. You'll be seated at a table on the other side of the room. When you see my signal, that's when you create the distraction. Then I'll turn and get the money," Sammy said. "This is not rocket science. Nothing will go wrong if you do your part."

"Hmm, how much do you think we'll make?" Buster asked.

"Last year they collected $75,000. These people are rich. A lot of the collection will be in cash."

"Wahl uh, sounds too good to be true," Buster said.

Sammy pulled the lever on the grease rack. "Do you have a better idea?"

"No."

"So what's it going to be?"

"Boy howdy." Buster shook his head. "Shucks, I guess I'm in."

"Good."

CHAPTER 24

The big night came for the Hunk's contest at the convention center. Over three hundred people sat at their tables with cocktails and wine waiting for the first hunk to appear on the runway. Back stage out of sight from the crowd, the twelve hunks assembled waiting for their turn. When Mark walked in dressed as the Flash, Billy Ray at first didn't recognize him. "Oh hello, Mark. So you're the Flash. Out chasing bad guys?"

"Hi there, Billy Ray. My, my! That's a well pressed fisherman's suit you're wearing. Fishing for votes?"

Billy Ray peaked around the corner at the crowd. "Sure, I thought I might find one or two out there."

"I'm certain you're here for the best of reasons."

"Of course," Billy Ray replied. "We're like Robin Hood--taking from the rich to give to the poor. It's for a good cause."

Mark turned to see Rob Galloway dressed in green tights and a feathered cap. "Speaking of Robin Hood …"

"Where's your bow and arrow?" Billy Ray asked Rob.

Rob raised his eyebrows and smiled mysteriously. "It's a surprise. Wait and see."

A few minutes later Rob was the first to go down the runway. He carried a lighted bow and soft plastic arrows with paper clips tied to a string. He carefully launched them into audience.

"Ladies, I mean you no harm and bid you a pleasant evening. Please return my arrows with expressions of your love and caring." The response was generous with twenties and hundred dollar bills attached to the arrows and returned to Robin Hood.

Not to be out done, Mark sprinted out onto the runway enthusiastically. "If you want to know why I am called the Flash, hold up your money," Mark shouted.

There were several unfortunate remarks as to why he might be called the Flash. One woman sipping a large margarita yelled, "Hey Flash, that was quick! Was it good for you?" The crowd laughed and applauded.

"You will not distract me from my mission!" Mark said. "If you love me, ladies--hold up your money!"

Mark took a deep breath. Here comes that broad jump I did in college. I hope I still have my stuff. Mark took a running start and flew off the runway startling the nearby judges. The audience applauded. He ran from table to table quickly gathering up money and jumped back onto the runway. "The Flash thanks you for your generosity, ladies!" Mark tried not to show he was out of breath as he made his exit.

"How much did you get?" Rob asked as Mark made his way backstage.

"Let's see--one hundred, two, three, four--wow, over a thousand dollars," Mark replied. "This crowd is really into this! What do we do with it now?"

"Find one of your crew members and put it in the can," Rob said. "Each dollar counts as a vote for you."

The other hunks, dressed anywhere from a caveman to a comic book character, competed just as vigorously with thousands of dollars collected. Their crew members continued going out to the tables all through the event soliciting more dollars for votes.

The hunks came out a second time dressed in formal attire presenting the judges with bribes, such as candy, champagne and costume jewelry. Then each contestant went out into the audience again pleading for more support. The cash came flowing in.

∧

Sammy and Buster sat at their tables watching as the last hunk returned backstage. Then they waited for the official announcement of the winners. During that time, the chair woman separated the checks and stacked the bills in a banking bag. As Sammy predicted, her attention shifted to the runway as the final announcement came. Sammy rose from the table with his briefcase and walked toward the restrooms. As the audience began to applaud for the runner-up, Sammy signaled Buster for the distraction. Buster released two remote operated furry rats which he sent scurrying under the tables. He yelled at the top of his voice, "It's a rat!"

People screamed and scrambled from their tables. Sammy made his move and reached for the bag. However, Lori was seated close by and saw what was going on. Without thinking and in one quick move, she folded her metal chair and with her highly practiced backhand clobbered Sammy with a rabbit punch just behind the back of his neck. Sammy dropped to the floor like a stone. All during this time, several videos were taken of the runway, some of which captured Lori's feat with the chair.

The hunks heard the crowd shouting "He's stealing the money! Stop him! Stop him!" Even though he didn't have the money, Buster panicked and ran for the exit. The chase was on. Billy Ray, hoping for a photo op, led the hunks hurdling over chairs and tables--but there was no need. Earl Blanton, seated at a table next to the exit, sent Buster flying with a clothes-line punch.

Afterwards everyone was talking. "Best Hunks' Contest ever! Did you see what Lori did? That gal's got spunk! More spunk than the hunks!" The videos showing Lori's knockout delivery were shown over and again on every surrounding media with interviews of both Lori and Earl. For weeks to come, Mark was proudly referred to as Lori's spouse. Mark was especially comforted by one thought. Maybe now they'll forget about the Flash.

⅄

Lori received a letter from the Hood Country Jail and gave it to Mark at dinner. "Here, check this out."

"Mm, the handwriting is worse than mine," Mark read the letter aloud.

"Dear Lori,

My mother was a Prezbitarian and I think I'm one too. Buster and I would like Communyun. The sheriff said that he would make arrangements for next Friday at 4 pm. Would you do it?

Love,

Sammy and Buster

Mark was laughing so hard that he had to stop eating. "Well, are you going to serve Communyun to those Prezbitarians?"

"Yes, want to come?"

"Uh, no."

"That's alright--I'm taking Junie. She can protect me."

"You talked to the sheriff?"

"Yep--Lyle said he would make the arrangements."

Sheriff Richards indeed made the arrangements. When Lori and Junie arrived at the jail, Billy Ray greeted them at the door.

"Come this way," Billy Ray said locking and unlocking the metal doors with a clank. He motioned to a small room with a six foot table and folding chairs. "Have a seat here and I'll go get the prisoners."

A few minutes later Sammy and Buster arrived dragging their ankle chains. "Hi Lori, thank you for coming!" Sammy moved to hug her, but caught himself as he tripped over his bracelets.

"This means a lot for us," Buster said.

"I was worried that you might refuse to come after what we did," Sammy hung his head. "I guess forgiveness for sumptin like this is hard. I'm glad my brother is taking over the shop. Do you think God will forgive us?"

"Yes, I do." --Probably not Hood County.

"Can the deputy take Communyun with us too?" Buster asked.

"If he wants," Lori looked at Billy Ray who nodded 'yes' and sat down at the table.

Junie shifted nervously in her chair. "Can we get started?"

They passed out the elements of The Lord's Supper and Lori repeated the words of the Institution. "This is my body … this is my blood."

Everyone very reverently participated. Then after the benediction, the door opened and the Hood County photographer for the newspaper made her entrance.

"This is wonderful," the photographer set up her camera. "May we take a picture."

Lori could hardly refuse. *Now I know what Lyle meant by 'making arrangements'--publicity arrangements, complete with Billy Ray taking Communion.*

The newspaper and photo came out the following week with the title "Places in the Heart" with the subtitle "the deputy, the prisoners and the pastor taking Communion together." Billy Ray was quoted as saying "This is what the church is all about." The paper went on to comment that "Pastor Lori Travis adds a special touch to her ministry--serving Communion to one of the robbers she knocked out during the Hunks' Contest."

Mark choked with laughter as he read it. Lori snatched the paper away from him and said, "You go in the other room and you stay there until you stop laughing." Mark came out once but lost it and had to go back in again. Lori continued to serve Communyun to Sammy and Buster until they were transferred to the state prison.

CHAPTER 25

Two weeks after the attempted Hunks' robbery, Earl Blanton was invited to dinner by Alice Evans. He had mixed feelings as he drove into her driveway. Why did she choose me as a guest? With her looks, she could certainly do better than some craggy looking ape like me. --It's probably about her missing husband but what can I do?

Alice greeted Earl at the door. "Thank you for coming, Earl. I hope you like pot roast. It's ready to be dished out."

Earl presented a bottle of red wine. "It smells great. If I wasn't hungry before, I am now."

"Sit down and I'll bring you a plate."

Alice tried to engage Earl in some preliminary small talk, but Earl wasn't good at it. His sentences were short without commentary. After some awkward pauses, Alice finally showed her hand.

"Earl, I don't want to be seen as taking advantage of you," Alice began, "but you're in a unique position and I know you want to help. Neither one of us wants to see Billy Ray become sheriff. There's got to be a way to stop him. There's got to be. I thought I could let it go after talking to Sally Mae but I just can't."

"You talked to Sally Mae?"

Alice went over her conversation with Sally Mae. As she finished, Earl put down his fork. "Let me see if I understand this. You told Sally Mae that someone was trying to frame Billy Ray by forging his psychological evalua-tion? That makes no sense. What were you trying to accomplish?"

"I wanted Sally to confront Billy Ray about it," Alice said. "And maybe Sally would think twice about marrying him."

"You're not thinking straight. If Billy Ray is what you think he is then you're putting your life in danger."

"I know that," Alice said, "and I'm giving you a letter that should be opened only if something happens to me."

"What!?" Earl moved his chair closer to Alice. "I'm not stupid, Alice. You're naming Billy Ray as your killer in case he succeeds. That won't work. People will think that you're just sick with grief. That's not the first time something like this has been tried. I've seen it before. I'm telling you it won't work! You won't be around to argue your case, but Billy Ray will."

A deep sadness came over Alice. "Then you do something. You're his opponent so you have a right to stop him."

"I wish I could think of something."

"What do you need?" Alice asked. "I have Marshall's appointment book. The last of his clients to see him alive was Billy Ray. The appointment is right here in his book. Look, I can show you!" Alice got up from the table to re-trieve the appointment book.

"Was the appointment on the day Dr. Evans disappeared?"

"No, Marshall was missing a week later on Tuesday."

Earl finished his pot roast. "Then I don't understand the importance of the appointment. I don't see how it connects."

Alice slumped down in her chair and began to cry. Earl reached over to comfort her but she moved away.

Alice struggled to regain her composure. "I guess it's just no use. Billy Ray is going to become sheriff and there's nothing we can do. You're not even going to fight him, are you?"

"Wrong, I'm going to do everything I can to stop him."

Alice spoke in a hoarse whisper. "You can at least mention that Billy Ray is unstable. He's deeply disturbed and dangerous, not someone people would want as sheriff. You can do that much, can't you? Don't let him become sheriff--please."

"I'll try. I really will try." Alice hugged him and held onto his arm as they walked to the door.

⚓

Earl started to get into his car when he noticed Alice's next door neighbor watering her flower bed. It was a warm summer's evening and the sun was slowly going down. The woman waved to him, and he went over to talk. Why am I doing this? It's been over four years. The sheriff probably already interviewed her. --Nothing to gain, but nothing to lose either.

The woman put down her watering hose as Earl approached. "Hi, I'm Earl Blanton and..."

"Oh, I know who you are. You're running for sheriff against that good looking Billy Ray. Lots of luck."

"Do you know Billy Ray?"

"I've seen him over the Evans' house a time or two. My name's Emma, by the way, Emma Bedford," Emma took off her garden glove and shook Earl's hand.

"Good to meet you Emma and I'm glad you're keeping up with politics."

"Well, you seem like a nice enough fellow," Emma said, "but I think Billy Ray is going to win."

Earl played dumb. "I guess Billy Ray was a friend of the Evans. Do you remember the day Dr. Evans disappeared?"

"Yes, it was on the day I was packing up to go help my sister in Atlanta. She had hip-replacement surgery and no one was there to take care of her."

"How long did you stay with her?" Earl asked.

"A good two months. My sister's older than me, and it took a while to get her stable."

"The day you were packing--when was that?"

"Tuesday."

"How do you know the day? That was over four years ago."

"I always water my flowers on Tuesday. I remember coming out onto the porch. And I remember seeing Billy Ray going into the house--just did get a glimpse of him."

"Really! Did he see you?"

"No, his back was to me as he went into the house."

"Did you see his face?

"No, but I would know that good looking youngster anywhere--back, front, sideways. It wouldn't matter. It was Billy Ray alright."

"Did you see his car or truck?"

"No, come to think about it. I guess he was parked under a tree somewhere trying to find shade."

"Did you see him leave?"

"No, I was busy packing to see my sister," Emma said. "Say, you sure are asking a lot of questions. What are you getting at?"

"I'm just trying to piece things together for Alice. She's still distraught."

"Poor thing. It's so awful," Emma said. "I don't know how my answers are going to help her."

"I suppose you already had lots of questions from the sheriff?" Earl said.

"No, as I said, I was gone for two months. I found the sheriff's note in my door when I returned but I never called back. I really don't know anything."

"Thank you for your time," Earl said.

"I'm glad you're helping out with Alice--such a sweet lady," Emma said. "and I would vote for you as sheriff, but Billy Ray is just too cute."

"I didn't know it was a beauty contest," Earl muttered as he went back to his car.

⅄

One week later, Earl was called into The Hood County News for an interview. The interviewer was Samantha Doyle, an ace reporter especially adept at ferreting out her subjects on controversial issues.

"The race has been a quiet one so far," Samantha said. "You're behind in the polls. Is there anything you would like to say that might make a difference."

"I think people should take a very close look at both candidates," Earl replied.

Samantha eyed him keenly. "What would they find if they looked up close and personal at Billy Ray?"

"Well, for one thing he's young and inexperienced--better looking than me of course."

"Do you think looks will make a difference?"

"I hope not, but Billy Ray does have some advantages. He has some important friends and supporters like Sheriff Richards, the Rev. Lori Travis and uh, hmm …" Earl paused.

"You were going to mention someone else?" Samantha asked.

"Well, I was going to say Alice Evans, but Billy Ray was closer to Dr. Evans."

"Dr. Evans, the psychologist?"

"Yes, in fact Billy Ray was one of the last ones to see Dr. Evans before he disappeared."

Samantha wrote that down on her notes. "How do you know that? Did Alice Evans tell you?"

"No, I heard it from a neighbor next door to Alice."

"That must have been Emma Bedford--an interesting neighbor, she's been around Granbury a long time."

"Yes, I think that was her name," Earl said. "Listen, I don't see the importance of this. Billy Ray's a good friend of the Evans."

"Of Alice?"

"Well, as I said--not so much of Alice as Dr. Evans who helped out Billy Ray with some counseling."

"That's why it's important," Samantha said. "Billy Ray might know something that would help solve the case."

"I hadn't thought of that," Earl said. "--but I hope you don't bother Emma. She's such a sweet lady."

Samantha laughed. "Everybody knows Emma. She would love to be in the paper. I'll talk to Billy Ray and to Alice too and get their take on it. Of course, I'm also going to dig around and get a more complete background picture of you both. That's my job."

"I'm not making any accusations," Earl said.

"I didn't think you were."

"Good, because I'm not."

⋏

After the interview, Earl drove over to the DA's office to give a report on his experience with Emma. Earl found a receptive audience with Mark and Rob.

"This is hilarious," Rob said. "Even if Samantha doesn't print it--which she will--Emma is all that's needed for this to go county-wide."

"I hope I haven't put Emma at risk," Earl said."

"No, it's too public," Mark said, "and Billy Ray's not that stupid--if he's the killer."

"Well, it's beginning to look like he's involved," Earl said.

Rob exchanged glances with Mark. "Let's see how it plays out. It's a good day's work, Earl, but don't get too cozy with our office. You need to keep your distance and play it cool. We don't want this to look like a campaign conspiracy."

"Yeah, with Samantha on the hunt, we need to be careful," Mark added, "so please keep us informed, Earl, but don't come to visit."

After Earl left, Rob grinned and turned to Mark, "It's getting interesting. I can't wait to hear what Billy Ray says."

"The newspaper comes out Friday," Mark replied. "We'll see."

⋏

Mark and Lori eagerly awaited the delivery of The Hood Country News. When it came, Lori retrieved the paper from their front yard in her bathrobe and ran back to the house clutching it in her hands. "It made the front page!"

"Let me see!" Mark and Lori huddled together taking turns reading the paper.

Lori read the headline: "Candidates Have Close Ties With Missing Person"

Mark continued: "Apparently, both candidates for sheriff have close connections with Alice Evans and her husband Marshall Evans who has been missing for the past five years. In talking with Alice Evans, this reporter learned that Earl Blanton has been of help and support to her during this time. She denies any romantic connection."

"That should start the tongues wagging," Lori said. "Let's see--The article goes on for a while about Earl's interview and then gets into Billy Ray's background, etc., etc. Ah, here's the good part:

"But perhaps of even more significance is the link between Billy Ray Larson and Dr. Marshall Evans. Candidate Billy Ray had been in counseling with Dr. Evans for almost three years leading up to the psychologist's disappearance. The following Qs and As were recorded by this reporter with permission from Billy Ray Larson:

Question: "Billy Ray, were you a friend of Dr. Marshall Evans?"

Answer: "I would hope so. At least, I thought of myself as his friend."

Q: "Isn't it also true that you were in therapy with Dr. Evans as a patient?"

A: "I don't think Dr. Evans would characterize our relationship that way. When I took his class at Tarleton, he generously offered free counseling to his students.

I was one of the students who went to him and our relationship continued after college."

Q: "Your counseling relationship?"

A: "Yes, Dr. Evans helped me in resolving some issues in the deaths of my parents."

Q: "You may not know this, but you were seen by a next-door neighbor going into the Evans' home the day of his disappearance. The neighbor reported that she saw you, but not the vehicle you were driving."

A: "Well, let me think about that. It was four or five years ago. As to the vehicle I was driving, it was probably my diesel truck. It's very noisy. I usually parked away from the Evans' house in case someone was taking a nap. Uh, I'm trying to remember the details of the visit. It was a while back..."

Q: "Do you need some time to think and come back?"

A: "No, I have nothing to hide."

Q: "I wasn't implying that, but if you saw him on the day he disappeared then anything you might recall could help in the investigation."

A: I honestly don't remember the exact day. The last time I visited Dr. Evans--let me think--yes, it could have been on that day or the one right before he disappeared. I went to see him about his letter of recommendation. I wanted to thank him."

Q: "Recommendation for what?"

A: "Actually, it was a letter of psychological evaluation about my suitability as deputy sheriff."

Q: So your saw Dr. Evans?

A: Yes.

Q: "Do you have his letter?"

A: "Sheriff Richards has it. It says that I am suitable and well qualified for the job."

Q: "Can you shed any light on the disappearance of Dr. Evans?"

A: "I wish I could. The public should know that any information relating to Dr. Evans' disappearance would be appreciated."

Lori put down the paper and turned to Mark, "So what do you think?"

"It's good," Mark replied.

"His reply?"

"No, the interview. He was forced to admit that he was with Dr. Evans the day he disappeared. And the explanation about the parking of his truck was thin."

"Yes, but the general public is not going to give that a second thought," Lori said. "I bet most people will buy his explanation without batting an eye."

"Well, the general public is not doing the investigation. We have him at the scene and that's an important step."

"Are you going to bring him in for questioning?"

"No. We still have some more spade work to do."

"I guess Rob Galloway will approve your digging."

"With a witness seeing him at the scene, you bet!"

"Maybe it's enough for Sally Mae to rethink the wedding," Lori said as they dressed for work. "All I can say is thank God for Ms. Emma."

Chapter 26

Billy Ray finished his third beer, and paced up and down on his front porch. How could that Emma woman possibly have seen me? I was careful, looked around twice when I picked the lock. No one in sight. I opened the door and looked again. No one there. So how...?

Billy Ray stopped pacing. Wait! The door mat, that damned door mat! I tripped over it as I went into the house. Yeah, that must have been the moment when Emma saw me. Well, that's not good. It set me up with that newspaper reporter so she could zero in on me. Damn it, it may cost me the election. At least I played it cool and made no denials. Take a breath, Billy Ray, have another beer and mellow out.

Sally Mae drove up and Billy Ray staggered out to greet her.

Sally Mae clenched her teeth. "Billy Ray, you're drunk."

"Well, uh, wouldn't you be? The newspaper is against me and I'm--I'm going to lose the election."

"You will if you don't stop hitting the sauce."

"I'm not usually this way, uh honest." Billy Ray collapsed into his rocking chair and held up a bottle to Sally Mae. "Would you like something to drink?"

"No, I would not. We need to talk."

"I thought that's what we were doing."

Sally Mae kicked the empty bottles away from her feet. "You've been keeping things from me. I had to learn about your counseling sessions from Alic--uh, the newspaper. What else are you hiding?"

"Nothing! What are you talking about?"

"I want to know what happened the day Emma saw you. Did you just go into the house unannounced?"

Billy Ray fought his way through the beer fog. *I've got to be careful. Sally Mae's smarter than I thought. This marriage thing may not be a good idea, but it's too late for that now. The truth, I've got to stick to the truth--at least part of it. The truth can be just as deceptive as a lie.*

Billy Ray leaned back and spoke softly. "You're right, Sally Me. I went in unannounced. I always do that at their house. I called around for Dr. Evans but he wasn't there."

"The newspaper said you saw him."

"I did. He came in a little later, just as I was about to leave."

"I don't think you're being straight with me, Billy Ray. You told the newspaper that you hid your diesel truck because you didn't want to wake anyone up. But now you tell me that you went into the house yelling for Dr. Evans."

"I wasn't hiding my truck," Billy Ray suddenly realized his contradiction. "Okay, maybe I was. Would you want people to know that you were going in for counseling? Hell, I don't know. It was four years ago. No one's going to believe me, no matter what I say."

"I want to believe you. At least I don't think you had anything to do with Dr. Evans' disappearance."

"Well, thank you for that."

"One thing more, now that we're being honest," Sally Mae said.

A headache followed Bill Ray's fourth beer. "There's something else!"
"Something Alice told me. She thinks that you're being framed."

"How?"

"She thinks your letter from Dr. Evans was forged and someone stole the original to blackmail you."

"That's ridiculous," Billy Ray pulled himself up from his chair and leaned on the porch rail. "I don't know what to say. It's absurd."

"That's what I thought too," Sally said, "Maybe I shouldn't have bothered you with it. You have enough worries."

"Look, Sheriff Richards has my letter with Dr. Evans' signature. I have a copy, uh, somewhere or other, but I can't remember what it said."

"It must be okay or Lyle Richards wouldn't be your campaign manager."

Billy Ray tried to shake the fog. I can't let her badger me with more questions. "Sally Mae, right now I need to be alone and get over this hangover. I'm sorry you had to see me this way."

"I hope it doesn't happen too often."

"Aw, you know me better than that," Billy Ray said. "Of course it doesn't."

"Well, pull yourself together. You have a campaign to focus on," Sally walked back to her car.

"Thanks again for coming over." Billy Ray gathered up his beer bottles and went back into the house. He wondered what else Alice had told Sally Mae but he knew better than to ask. He had enough talk for now.

CHAPTER 27

"Oh no, no!" Lori hung up the phone and sat down.

Mark put down his newspaper. "Someone die?"

"No, but something almost as bad. Help me straighten up the house. Margaret is coming over, and bringing Judy and Virginia."

Mark put the dishes in the dishwasher. "Ah, the three amigas. Isn't it past their bedtime? It's almost eight."

"I liked it better when they weren't so fond of us," Lori said. "I have you to blame for that. They became your trusty sidekicks when you interviewed them."

"They were helpful."

" My detective hunk, the little old lady magnet."

Lori was putting up the vacuum cleaner when the doorbell rang. The three amigas walked in the door with big smiles.

"I love your house," Margaret said, "even if it is one of the new ones."

"And right across from the library and Shanley Park," Judy joined in. "It's so pretty at Christmas time."

"It's pretty right now in the summer time," Virginia added.

Margaret motioned the others to sit down." I guess you're wondering why we're here. We want to share with you something we're very proud of."

"Tell us," Mark said.

"Some of us in the church have gone together and rented out the Convention Center," Judy said. "We're organizing a debate, along with dinner, for Billy Ray and Earl."

"How nice," Lori said. "When's it going to be?"

"Four weeks from now on Saturday, September 28," Judy said. "And we're buying your tickets."

"Oh my," Lori shifted uncomfortably in her chair. "Uh, Saturday is not a good night for me. I need that time for finishing up my sermon."

"Judy, did you say Saturday?" Virginia asked. "It's not Saturday, but Friday."

"That's right," Margaret said. "It's on a Friday--so there's no problem. You'll be at our table to cheer Billy Ray on."

Mark held out his hand like a traffic cop. "Stop just a minute. Is it wise for ministers to get involved in politics?"

"Well, you can bet Earl's minister will be there!" Virginia said. "I can't imagine Lori not supporting one of our members on something this important."

"Can I think about it?" Lori asked.

"No ma'am, you certainly may not!" Margaret said. "You're going and that's that. If anyone objects, they'll have to deal with me!"

Lori rubbed her hands and took a deep breath. "Okay, I guess we'll be there."

"Maybe not both of us," Mark protested. "I have to look at my schedule."

Judy shook her finger at Mark. "Mark, we would be very disappointed if you're not there with Lori. Billy Ray needs all our support."

"I'll have to check."

Margaret squeezed Mark's knee. "Well, you better have a good reason. That's all I've got to say."

After they finished their tea, the three amigas left with the satisfaction of a mission accomplished. Lori collapsed onto the sofa like she had been run over by a truck.

"Maybe you should go back into the law business," Mark joked. "I hope you have a good time cheering on Billy Ray."

Lori looked hard at Mark. "You are going to that debate whether you want to or not."

"No I'm not."

"Yes you are. You're not leaving me alone on this one."

"It's going to take a lot of loving for this to happen," Mark said.

"You already get that."

"You have no idea how much more ..."

Just then the cat-door clattered and BR came in holding a little dove in his mouth.

"Oh no, BR--you, you bird murderer!" Lori yelled.

Mark took the dove from BR. "He's just doing what cats do. It's still alive. Let's go outside and put it on a branch or something."

"Fine, and let's sit out on the patio and make sure BR doesn't go after it again." Lori took two wine glasses from the cabinet. "I need to shake off our visit with the three amigas. "

Lori and Mark sat quietly, drinking their wine and looking at the full moon. BR jumped up on Lori's lap as Mark's eyes slowly began to shut.

Lori held up the cat and eyeballed him, then put him back on her lap and petted him. What am I going to do with you, BR? You're an awful killer and here you are wanting love. Alright, you're my cat and I'm not going to stop caring about you.

The horrible thing is that I care about Billy Ray too. I'm his pastor. I wish I weren't but I am--even if he's done terrible things. I don't know how to help him. He needs to be stopped if he's done what we think. I worry about Sally Mae. What do I do, Lord? Help me out here.

After a while, Lori noticed Mark nodding off to sleep. She took his arm, guided him off to bed and hoped that BR would not bring in another present.

CHAPTER 28

One week after the newspaper interview, Billy Ray was still obsessing over the article. Sleep and his appetite for food eluded him. Sheriff Lyle Richards observed Billy Ray's change of mood and called him into his office. Lyle pulled up a chair next to him at his conference table. "Listen to me boy, you need to get a grip. You're looking like something the cat drug in. Are you worried about that newspaper interview?"

"Yeah."

"It seemed to me you handled it well," Lyle said. "The only issue is your counseling. There was no reason for you to hide that. In fact, most people will respect your doing it. Nowadays, it's like going to a doctor."

"Okay, but there's something else. That Emma woman saw me at the house the day Evans disappeared."

Lyle put his hand on Billy Ray's shoulder. "Is that what's bothering you? So what? You didn't kill him, did you?"

"No."

"And no one is going to believe that you did," Lyle said. "Dr. Evans gave you a clean bill of health. He was in your corner all the way."

"Yeah, but that reporter, Samantha what's-her-name, made it look like I was hiding something," Billy Ray said.

"I didn't read it that way," Lyle responded. "You explained why you parked the truck away from the house. It was a matter of courtesy. That diesel would wake up anybody."

"I don't know what to think."

"Well, I do, and I think you're acting paranoid. I liked the newspaper article. We can use it to our advantage."

"How?"

Lyle leaned closer to Billy Ray. "It give us publicity for the forum coming up at the Conference Center. You couldn't ask for a better situation to have a debate. First off, your church friends are paying for the cost. That fact alone gives you credibility--you're respected by your church. I'm surprised that your opponent agreed to it, but he did."

"I'm not comfortable speaking to a large group of people."

"You will be after we've rehearsed it," Lyle said. "There are two things you need to remember. First, you'll be among friends. You can laugh with them and have a good time. I'll show you how. Second, you won't have to talk long at all. They'll be eating dinner and will prefer a short positive speech."

"A positive speech? What do I say about Earl Blanton?"

"You compliment him but don't say too much. You respect what he's done for the community. You tell the audience that it's a privilege to run against a person of his experience and character--but stop there. Then you say "Here's what I want you to remember about me, blah, blah, blah. I'll fill in the blahs for you."

"Why do I mention Earl's experience and character?"

"Because it heads off Earl at the tracks. You can bet Earl's going to mention the same thing. If you do it first, then Earl will struggle to find something else to say. Also, the audience will be less likely to listen to something they've already heard. Of course, you don't want to paint too rosy a picture of Earl--just enough to inoculate the audience against his own self portrait."

"Huh, I would never have thought of that."

"I majored in public speaking, and I have the experience," Lyle said. "You have the best coach available. Aren't you lucky?"

"Yeah!"

"You have to promise me one thing if I get you elected."

"What?"

"I don't want my deputies fired because of you. If you become sheriff and still want my help for your second election, then keep my deputies. They're good people-- well trained--and you'll need them."

"Okay, I see no problem with that."

"Well, there is one deputy that may be a little let down," Lyle admitted. "That's my chief deputy, José Moreno. He expected me to put him up for sheriff."

"Uh, that might be a problem," Billy Ray said.

"It's not. I've talked to José; he's actively campaigning for you--putting up signs and everything. He realizes that he's more likely to stay employed if you are elected. You can count on his loyalty."

"So I need to keep José as my chief deputy."

"Absolutely, and he's bi-lingual. You'll need him when you go out into the field."

"Right, I'll do that."

"Now back to the campaign," Lyle continued. "There's a couple of things you might want to consider. I hear by the grapevine that Earl and Alice Evans are dating."

Billy Ray shrugged. "What's that got to do with anything?"

"Well, maybe nothing, but Earl's easily embarrassed," Lyle answered. "You don't want to appear mean about it, but you might mention it as an aside--something to preoccupy Earl."

"I don't know how to do that, and I'm not comfortable with it."

"Fine, but there is one thing you must do. You need to visit Ms. Emma."

"Why?"

"Ms. Emma and I go way back. I've heard that she likes you and plans to vote for you. She knows a lot of people, and you need to cement your relationship with her."

"What do I say?"

"Oh, come on. Use your charm and common sense. Make your visit look routine like you're going door to door soliciting votes. When you come to her house, look delighted to see her. She'll probably insist you come in. She thinks you're cute."

"I guess I can do that."

Sheriff Richards discussed Billy Ray's presentation for the debate and set up times for rehearsals. Billy Ray left his office with a confident stride. *Lyle makes good sense. He's right, I don't need to worry as long as I don't act that way. I'm sorry I had to promise to keep his deputies, especially that José Moreno who would like my job. I hope he doesn't become a major obstacle, but I can deal with it if he does.*

⚔

Billy Ray canvassed Emma Bedford's neighborhood as Lyle suggested. When he arrived at Emma's, she eagerly took his arm and guided him into her living room.

"What a wonderful surprise," Emma said. "Billy Ray in my home! Sit down and have some tea."

"Well, I can't stay too long," Billy Ray said. "I'm out beating the bushes trying to get enough votes to become your sheriff."

"You've got mine, Billy Ray," Emma beamed. "You certainly have mine!"

"You don't know how good it is to hear that," Billy Ray said. "Everybody in town knows you and respects your opinion. If people know you're backing me, I'm sure to have their votes too!"

"Oh, you're exaggerating."

"No ma'am, I'm not. In this town, you carry a lot of ..." Billy Ray started to say 'weight,' but noticed Emma's rotund figure, "uh, influence. People really like you, a lot."

"That's sweet, Billy Ray. And I will support you anyway I can."

"Hmm, that's a pretty generous offer. Do you mean it?"

"Just try me," Emma replied.

"Okay, just for starters, are you going to the debate July 12th?"

"Honey, I've already got tickets for myself and three of my friends."

"Wow! You are serious," Billy Ray took a sip of tea. "I wonder if--no, no, that's too much to ask."

"Tell me."

"Well, right after I'm introduced at the debate, I'm going to thank people and point out some folks I enjoy seeing."

"I hope you point to me!" Emma said.

"I sure will, and I'm wondering if you will do a little something extra just to show your support."

"Name it."

"I hesitate to ask this. I don't want to embarrass you."

"You're not going to embarrass me. Just tell me what you want me to do."

"I'm going to point to you and say "Now there's someone we all know and love just for being herself. Ms. Emma, stand up and take a bow!"

"Oh my! You're going to say all that?"

"Something like that. I'll work on it, but I would love it if you stood up and said, 'Billy Ray, you've got my vote!"

"I can do that!" Emma laughed. "Then what are you going to say?"

"Uh, I'll be modest and say 'Thank you, Ms. Emma, but Earl's a good candidate too."

Emma slapped the table and laughed. "Billy Ray, you are as clever as you are pretty. I can't wait for the occasion! You will knock them dead."

"I hope not. Only live people can vote!"

"If you win, would you let me throw you a victory dinner?" Emma asked.

Billy Ray rose and took a bow as he started back to the door. "I would be most honored. With you in my corner, victory is at hand."

Emma gave Billy Ray a hug that took his breath. He gave her a kiss on the cheek to round things off. I'm getting pretty good at this; Lyle would be proud.

Chapter 29

Holding a debate for county sheriff in the Granbury Conference Center made it a special occasion. The new Center, with its Dallas Cowboy Stadium appearance on the outside, was expensive to rent. Mark and Lori were attending the center for the second time after Mark's previous appearance in the Hunk contest.

Mark noticed the fashionable attire around them as they walked in. "Hmm, my 'Jacque Pen-Nay's' suit doesn't quite fit in."

Lori whispered in his ear. "You look fine. At least you don't have a gut. Here's our table in the Billy Ray section and, oh my, look at those embossed name cards."

"Fancy! The card even shows what we're eating." Mark helped Lori to her seat.

"Right, I ordered you the filet and chose the salmon with crab sauce for myself," Lori said.

"Thanks. I wonder where the three amigas are?"

Lori nodded to Margaret, Virginia, and Judy who were standing over at the bar. "Be nice. They're probably ordering wine for us."

"Okay, but I'd be more comfortable sitting at one of Earl's tables," Mark said.

"Keep your voice down. Here they come."

Judy held up a bottle of wine as they came to their table. "Oh my, look at our good looking minister! What a beautiful suit--tailored perfectly."

"Lori would look good in anything," Margaret said.

"Just some old duds that I used to wear in court," Lori replied.

"We'll be the *judge* of that," Virginia laughed at her own joke.

"And Mark, you look good too--really good," Judy ogled him.

Virginia shook her head at Judy. "Shameless hussy."

Mark outwardly smiled with an inward groan. It's going to be a long evening.

After the wine was poured for the second round, the three amigas talked nonstop. They freely interrupted each other without actually listening to what the other was saying. Mark looked around for a way out and saw Rob Galloway's table next to the one with Earl and Alice.

"Excuse me," Mark said as he walked over to Rob Galloway.

"Have a seat," Rob said. "My wife had to go see her sister at the last minute, so I have an empty chair."

"I'll take it," Mark said. "I can't get a word in edgewise at my table even if I wanted to. My ears are tuckered out."

Earl walked over from his table, his hulking figure fitting tightly into his tux. "Hey Mark, it's good to see you here."

"Are you ready for the great debate?" Mark asked.

Earl sighed. "Actually, no. I wish I were someplace else."

"Me too," Mark said. "How's this debate supposed to work?"

"There's not much to it," Earl answered. "Billy Ray won the toss so he's going first. We each have five minutes with a three minute rebuttal. After that the audience writes out their questions and the MC reads them out. I already know the one I want to answer."

"What's that?" Rob asked.

"The one that asks 'When are we going home?'"

"That'll get my vote," Mark said. "The sooner, the better."

Just then a waiter came to the table. "We're sorry, there's a delay because the salmon that was supposed to come in fresh from Alaska failed to get here. We just now discovered it. You can choose either chicken cordon bleu or steak."

Earl's expression turned hopeful. "Huh! With dinner postponed, maybe people won't stay around to hear us."

The dinner arrived forty five minutes later much to the exasperation of the attendees. Earl was right. People were already planning to leave. The MC, however, sensed the problem and went to the mike while everyone was still eating.

"Well, these things happen," the MC said, "so let's get started right now. Keep eating but enjoy the debate. Billy Ray, we will begin with you!"

Billy Ray laughed as he walked to the podium. "I can't compete with good food. I'm going to keep it short and simple. First of all, I see some special people in the audience. There's my worthy opponent, Earl Blanton, seated next to Alice Evans. What a charming couple!"

Earl was caught off guard and choked on his steak with a hacking sound. Billy Ray took a step toward Earl.

"Hey Earl, I'm sorry. Was it something I said? Are you alright?"

"Fine, fine," Earl took a drink of water to recover.

"You know, Earl is one of the finest law officers we have," Billy Ray continued. It's just a shame that he has to be running against me. Otherwise, I would sure vote for him!"

Billy Ray waited until the audience stopped laughing. Then he turned toward Emma Bedford. "I don't have time to acknowledge everybody, but I want to mention a favorite of mine, someone widely acknowledged as a much loved matriarch in Granbury. Ms. Emma, stand up and take a bow!"

Emma started to say her line but was dumbfounded to see people standing and applauding. Her voice was soft as she spoke through her tears. "Billy Ray, you, you're going to make a wonderful sheriff."

The audience laughed and Billy Ray applauded her. It worked out better than he expected.

"Win or lose, Ms. Emma," Billy Ray said. "You have made my day."

Billy Ray's speech was short and to the point, highlighting his training and appreciation for Sheriff Richards. He told the story, with some embellishments, of the drug raid with Mark Travis. He praised Mark and Rob Galloway, and expressed his hope to work with them. Then he turned toward Sally Mae who had been sitting next to him at their table.

"I want to say one last thing. There is one vote that counts above all others, even if the election goes the other way. Sally Mae, as long as I have your vote, that's what really matters. And everyone, everyone here, all of you are invited to our wedding on November 12th. Our pastor, Lori Travis, will preside at the ceremony. Well, there she is now, seated right over here in my section. Lori, we love you! Thank you, everyone. Please finish your dinner. I yield my remaining minute to Earl Blanton!"

Earl tried valiantly but Billy Ray had captured the audience, and almost everyone turned back to their dinner. Finally, Earl made a summary statement and ended with, "I uh, I'd appreciate your vote." Neither candidate offered a rebuttal and no questions at all were handed to the MC. The dinner delay and the coaching of Lyle Richards had won the day for Billy Ray.

Chapter 30

One week after the debate, Sheriff Richards sat across from Billy Ray at the Lone Star Restaurant waiting for their lunch to arrive. Lyle motioned the waiter to come over.

"Do me a favor, would you?" Lyle asked the waiter. "See that lady sitting by herself in the back corner?"

The waiter looked over in that direction. "The older lady?"

"Put her ticket on my tab."

"What if she wants to know who's picking up her ticket?" the waiter asked.

"Tell her 'the sheriff.'"

Billy Ray looked blankly at Lyle. "Why are you doing this?"

Lyle sat back in his chair, studying Billy Ray as if he were seeing him for the first time. Huh! He questions a small action of compassion. He's missing something. Why couldn't I have seen this before? He lacks caring and he's not going to understand my saying so. How can I teach him the importance of it? Maybe if I approached it as a strategy. "Listen to me boy, and listen well. I'll tell you a secret of how I kept my job as sheriff all these years. Without it, you'll become a one term sheriff."

"What does that got to do with paying for that lady's lunch?" Billy Ray asked.

Lyle took out his billfold. "Well, everything. It's what's known as LARK."

"Lark?"

"Yes, LARK. It stands for 'Little Acts of Random Kindness.' It's a movement that started some years ago. I got into the habit of it when I first ran for sheriff. If you want to stay in office, it makes all the difference."

"Explain."

"It's not enough to be a good law officer. People have to feel that you are a good person, kind hearted and generous. So you look for opportunities to do little acts of kindness. If you do one a day, the word gets around. People will say "That's our sheriff. He knows how to treat people. He's the right man for the job."

"So I pick up people's tickets at restaurants. Sounds like a good way of going broke."

Lyle put his hand on the table. "Shucks, Billy Ray! You've got enough money to do that for someone every day. --But I'm not talking about just restaurants. Use your imagination. A family's trying to get to the hospital. You turn on your siren and get them there. A child falls down on the playground and has a skinned knee. You grab your first aid kit and help her out. Someone calls about a missing dog..."

"I'm not going to waste my time on a dog!"

"That's not the right attitude. You take down the description of the animal and promise to be on the lookout for it. Then you post the description on the board. Are you going to be a good guy or not?"

"That's not the way I do things."

"No it's not, but when you get into the habit of doing these things, you'll enjoy what people say about you. And you'll like it even more when they vote for you!"

Billy Ray scowled. "Are you sure this LARK thing will work?"

"Well, not when you frown like that. Smile when you do a good deed and people will smile back at you. I can tell you that it's worked for me. You want to be the people's choice for sheriff, don't you?"

"Yes, I do."

"Then put LARK on your calendar--once a day. It's not that hard."

"It just doesn't sound like me," Billy Ray said.

"It's not what it sounds like, it's what you *do* that counts."

Billy Ray shuffled his feet. "LARK--well, maybe. What have I got to lose?"

"Only the sheriff's office," Lyle said, "but with LARK you're going to make it for the long haul."

As Billy Ray left the restaurant, Lyle heard him muttering, "Huh, little acts of kindness--so where do I go from here?"

⋏

Two weeks later, Lori came home from the Seekers' Bible study and joined Mark on the patio. She laughed, shook her head and sighed.

"Was Bible study that strange?" Mark asked.

"Billy Ray showed up."

Mark tilted back his chair. "Rats, you said he had stopped coming. What changed his mind?"

"I don't know, but you should've been there. You wouldn't believe it."

"Believe what?"

"The new Billy Ray," Lori replied. "He spoke of kindness and compassion."

"What? You're joking."

"No, I'm not," Lori continued, "and he was very convincing. We were studying Matthew 25--you know, the passage about doing good deeds unto the least of these."

"Uh, that's the one about giving a cup of water to the thirsty and visiting those who are sick and in prison?"

Lori stood up from the table. "Yes, now listen to what Billy Ray said. It was something like 'I have come to a new realization. God may call us for different lines of work, but we are all called for doing acts of kindness. This passage is a call for all of us, not just to sit around here and talk, but to do the things it says for the needy. We shouldn't wait for these people to come to us. We should go to them.'"

Mark put down his glass. "Huh! That sounds like one of your sermons, very close to what you preached a few Sundays ago. What's going on with this guy? Do you think it's genuine?"

"I don't know," Lori said. "Those dark blue eyes of his are hard to read. It certainly sounded sincere. He even volunteered to serve on our Outreach and Mission Committee."

Mark tossed his napkin onto the table. "No, no, I'm not buying this. The leopard doesn't change his spots--at least not this quickly."

"Sally Mae said that she's noticed a change in Billy Ray. Maybe it's a walk-in."

"A walk what?"

Lori laughed. "A 'walk-in,' where an outside spirit takes over a body. Don't worry, I'm not serious, but that's the way it seemed."

"It has to be a ploy--something to bolster his bid for sheriff."

Lori sat back down. "That occurred to me, but you should have been there. He seemed so--so committed."

"Yeah, well, maybe committed for a lock-up."

"I hate to be naive, Mark, but I don't want to give up hope entirely. Maybe Billy Ray can change."

"I really, really doubt that."

"I guess time will tell," Lori said.

"Oh c'mon," Mark picked up his empty glass. "You're not getting sucked into this. It'll all stop after the election."

Lori took Mark's arm as they went back inside. "You may be right." "Which is another way of saying I may be wrong," Mark replied.

Lori's hair brushed against Mark's face. "I'm still Billy Ray's pastor. A pastor has to look for the good in everyone."

"Good luck with that." Mark hugged Lori from behind as they headed off to bed.

CHAPTER 31

Billy Ray was in his patrol car driving six miles north of Granbury when he noticed an old Pontiac pulled over on the other side of the highway. He crossed the grass median and pulled up behind it. A middle aged man and a woman were in the front seat. The woman was crying.

Billy Ray walked to the passenger's side. "Ma'am, is there a problem here?"

"Yes, oh yes. I'm Elsa Greenlee and this is my husband, Jerry. The car's dead and Jerry can't make his interview at the plant. We think it's the battery."

"I know it is," Jerry rested his head on the steering wheel, "and we don't have the money to replace it."

"How do you know it's the battery?" Billy Ray asked.

"I know because I'm an engineer--or I was until I was dismissed from my job a month ago. I have an interview at the nuclear plant in twenty minutes, but there's no way I can make that now."

"My husband Jerry's a good man, officer," Elsa said. "He worked for the City of Ft. Worth for the last twenty years. --But three years ago, this new horrible boss, Brad Patrick took over and my husband argued with him. Patrick wanted to fix things in a way that would cause a hazard. Jerry wouldn't do it."

Billy Ray propped his elbow on the car window. Could this be a LARK moment? "Who's doing your interview at the plant?"

"Randolph Akins. He's the VP in maintenance."

"Randy? I know that guy--done a little fishing with him. Why don't you call him?" Billy Ray asked.

"No cell phone."

Billy Ray paused. What would Sheriff Richards do? "We need to act fast. Pop your hood and let's unscrew that battery."

Ten minutes later, sirens blaring, Billy Ray was on his way back with a new battery. He contacted Randy Akins through dispatch.

"I hope this is about fishing," Randy said.

Billy Ray turned off his sirens. "Here's the deal. I'm helping out this guy, Jerry Greenlee, who needs a new car battery."

"Uh huh!" Randy replied. "He's supposed to be here in five minutes and I'm closing out the interviews at five. Too bad, his resume looks good."

"I'll tell you I what know," Billy Ray said. "He had this boss, Brad Patrick, who fired him and . . ."

"Patrick?! Yeah, I know the guy," Randy interrupted. "A real arrogant asshole. Tell me what happened."

"Jerry got canned because he argued with Patrick--something about causing a possible hazard," Billy Ray said.

"And Jerry stood up to Patrick. Well, well, how about that!" Randy chuckled. "I want to meet this Jerry Greenlee. How soon can you get him here?"

Billy Ray turned the sirens back on. "Less than an hour."

"I'll wait for him. Call back with his license number and make of car so I can get him through security."

Billy Ray knew that Randy collected cars. "The car's over thirty years old, a Pontiac Firebird Esprit in pretty good shape."

"Really! Hell, that's a classic. I want to see the car too," Randy said.

Billy Ray did the battery installation himself so that Jerry would stay fresh for his interview.

Jerry started his car and revved up the engine. "I'll pay you back."

"No you won't. This one's on me. Now follow me and we'll get to the plant ASAP." Maybe this isn't such a good idea. This couple won't be eligible to vote for me until the next election! I hope this LARK business pays off some time soon.

Otherwise, I'll end up with dirty hands and a waste of time.

⚹

On the following Sunday, attendance was back up from summer vacations and the beginning of the school year. The presiding elder rose from his chair behind the pulpit and called for announcements from the congregation. Joe Michaels immediately and enthusiastically strolled up to the podium and took the mike.

"I have a wonderful story and a blessing to report," Joe said. "I want you to picture this. Think about a couple who had given up hope and were stuck out on 377 coming from Cresson. There they are--sitting with a dead battery, no money, and no way for the husband to make it to an important interview at my plant."

"Joe, don't go longer than my sermon," Lori said in an audible whisper, getting a laugh from the congregation.

"I'm on a roll. Let me finish," Joe replied. "Then comes an angel in the form of one of our church members. He's wearing a badge and stops every-thing he's doing. Out of his own pocket, he buys and installs a battery, calls the plant, makes it right for the interview, and guides the couple to the plant."

The congregation strained their necks looking around for the hero of Joe's story. Their attention focused on Billy Ray sitting on the back pew.

"The interview was a success, but all the man could talk about was the good Samaritan who rescued him," Joe continued. "He said that 'If people in Granbury are anything like this deputy who came to his aid, then this must be God's country!' Everyone at my plant is talking about it. They are talking about our own Billy Ray Larson!"

The congregation broke into a loud applause and tried to get Billy Ray to stand up. Billy Ray nodded appreciatively, but remained seated with Sally Mae kissing him on his cheek and wrapping her arms around him.

Lori preached a good sermon, but at the end of the service, the hand-shakes went to Billy Ray. Sally Mae stood hugging him the whole time.

After the congregation filed out the door, Mark escorted Lori to their car. He was laughing.

"What on earth are you laughing about?" Lori asked Mark.

"It's either laugh or cry. --Billy Ray as a do-gooder! I have to give him credit. It's a good strategy."

Lori cocked her head to one side. "Suppose he keeps on doing good and gets into the habit of it? Would he eventually change and become a good person?"

"Do you really believe that's possible?" Mark said.

"Maybe. There's a story I came across about an enchanted mask. Do you mind if I tell it?"

"Sure, if it's one of your good ones."

"It's the story about Bemas, an evil man who fell in love with a woman who was both kind and beautiful--but he knew she couldn't love him the way he was. So he found an enchanted mask of a saint and started wearing it. People looked at his new saintly face and started coming to him for help. Eventually the woman agreed to become his bride. Bemas married the lady and continued to wear the mask, but after several years, he could no longer stand his hypocrisy and took off the mask. He looked in the mirror and there to his surprise was the face of the saint looking back at him!"

"Good story," Mark said. "Let me guess the moral. If we behave a certain way long enough, with community backing and a loving spouse, change is possible."

"Yes, and as Billy Ray's pastor, that's what I'm hoping," Lori concluded.

"And like Bemas, Billy Ray will have the wonderful love of his new wife," Mark added. "That puts a lot on Sally Mae--you're also her pastor, right?"

Lori sighed and was silent. Mark continued, "Billy Ray has to be willing to change and I don't think he has the heart for it. Just answer me one question. Do you feel good about this upcoming marriage?"

"I'm not sure."

"Lori, I trust your intuition. Do you feel good about this marriage or not?"

"I'd like to feel good about it. I really want to."

"--But you're conflicted."

"I'm just hoping, Mark. I'm just hoping and praying."

⚐

Later that night, Lori got out of bed and walked outside to the patio. She rubbed her hands together and started pacing. *God, I'm looking to you for an answer because I don't have one. Sally Mae and the congregation really want this marriage. If I refuse, I might as well look for another pastorate. They won't understand it and they won't forgive me. --But if I do the ceremony, I'm not sure I could forgive myself. It's tearing me apart!*

Mark joined Lori on the patio. "What's going on out here? Are you beating yourself up over Sally Mae's wedding?"

"Well, you said it yourself," Lori replied. "I'm Sally Mae's pastor just like I'm Billy Ray's and between the two of them …"

Mark put his arm around Lori. "Alright, so you're in a double bind and I'm not helping. You need to talk to someone else. Call Rex Barkley. Maybe he can put things in a different perspective. In the meantime, come back to bed. You're not helping anyone by losing sleep."

Mark gently led Lori back to bed, then rubbed her back until she was quietly breathing.

⚐

The next Wednesday Lori sat impatiently in her office waiting for her psychologist friend, Rex. She held the wedding book in her hands, with only two weeks left before the nuptials of Billy Ray and Sally Mae. Finally Rex arrived ducking slightly to get through the door.

Rex noted the troubled look on Lori's face. "You sounded urgent over the phone."

Lori flipped thought the pages of the wedding service. "It's this thing. Now that it's really happening, I'm wondering if I'm right."

"It's their choice," Rex said. "You've expressed your reservations to Sally."

"I haven't told you everything," Lori said.

"Okay, do you want to tell me now?"

Lori pulled up a chair next to Rex. "Shut the door and have a seat. What I'm about to say stays in this office. Okay?"

"Fine."

"It all started when Mark talked to three of our women."

"Members?"

"Yes, gossips really--but I don't want to name them," Lori said.

Rex laughed. "I probably know who they are."

"Never mind that. Mark talked to them about three missing persons. Billy Ray has connections to all three."

"Closely?"

"Yes--well, two of them for sure--Billy Ray's father and Dr. Evans. The other missing person is Hank Casey, a close friend of Billy Ray's father."

"I remember a Dr. Marshall Evans who spoke at a mental health conference when I was in graduate school," Rex said.

"Yes, that's the one. He's been missing for four or five years now. Alice Evans is convinced that Billy Ray was involved."

Rex shifted his long legs for a more comfortable position. "Maybe you better fill me in on the details. I'm not sure where all this is going."

Lori discussed Mark's interviews with Alice and Earl, and his experience with Billy Ray on the field.

As Lori was concluding, Mark stood up. "Wait! Does Mark believe that Billy Ray murdered those people? I know he's an egomaniac, but from what I've read about him on those shoot-outs, he seems to be something of a hero. What does Mark...? "

"Mark says he's nuts. He thinks Billy Ray kills without thinking and without remorse."

"That is disturbing," Rex said. "So where are you on this?"

"I don't know. If you had asked me that question three months ago, I would have agreed with Mark," Lori replied. "--But Billy Ray has changed. You should hear him in Bible study! He's not only in favor of giving that cup of cold water, he follows through with what he says. I've heard from more than one person how Billy Ray is helping out in the community. He's building houses for Habitat and even delivers food for Meals on Wheels."

"Yes, but think for a minute," Rex said. "How many politicians seem to be doing all sorts of good things, only to discover later their feet of clay?"

"On the other hand," Lori replied, "if he gets into the habit of doing good …"

Rex walked over to the coffee pot. "Yeah, I know. We're shaped by our good habits, but not entirely. We're also shaped by our ambitions and goals. Billy Ray seems to be more in that category. The end may justify the means. If he can get what he wants by taking on the role of a do-gooder, then maybe murder isn't needed for a while."

Lori stood up and leaned against her desk. "Oh my Lord, do you think that's it? His murders are just on hold?"

Rex filled his coffee cup and sat down. "Let me back up. It's really hypothetical. You don't know for sure that Billy Ray did those murders. In fact, if I were on a jury, given your evidence, I would probably abstain or vote 'not guilty.'"

"Then I don't know what you're saying."

"I'm not sure either," Rex laughed. "I'm trying to look at it from both sides. I'm not saying that Billy Ray is or is not a murderer, but let's assume that Mark's suspicions are correct. Here's the way I would profile it. From what I know about Billy Ray, the question is *not* how he treats people when things are going well, but how he treats them when they create problems for him. What does he do to them then?"

"And right now, things are going very well for Billy Ray," Lori said. "Nothing is in his way."

"Well, even if things get in his way, they would have to be major hindrances," Rex paused. "We've been over this before, remember? Billy Ray doesn't worry about bumps, just roadblocks."

"So he wouldn't kill just for the sake of killing?" Lori asked.

"No, if he's a killer--and that's a big *if,* he may not even enjoy it," Rex replied.

"--But he wouldn't feel bad about it," Lori surmised.

"It would sort of be like taking out the garbage," Rex said.

"That's chilling. There's no remorse to it."

"That's right, but let me say this again--it's all hypothetical," Rex said. "So what are you going to do?"

"About the wedding? What would you do?" Lori offered Rex another cup of coffee. "I really need some guidance."

"Lori, a good counselor leaves decisions up to their clients."

Lori held Rex's hand. "I don't need a counselor and I don't want to lose any more sleep on this. I need someone I respect to help me put this thing in perspective--and that's you!"

"Okay, help me review the situation," Rex said reluctantly. "We've both talked to Sally Mae, and she's still Billy Ray's biggest cheerleader--a true believer."

"Right, and she's thrilled with the new Billy Ray."

"So what's the problem? You've done everything you can."

"Well, I don't have to do the ceremony. I can tell her no."

"With the enthusiasm of the congregation for Billy Ray, you'll lose members if you do that."

"--But I'll keep my integrity."

"And lose your effectiveness as a pastor--so it's Catch-22."

"You're not helping," Lori said.

Rex leaned back in his chair. "Alright, I could lose my license for this, but I'll play the guru. Here it is. Do you want to take notes?"

"Just tell me."

"Lori, you can't lose your congregation over this. You have to do the ceremony, but you need to keep your integrity too. So here's how you get off the hook."

"I'm listening."

"You go ahead and risk your friendship with Sally Mae. You really have no basis for saying that he's a killer. As I've said before, I know some power-crazed execs just as driven. What you *can* do is to tell her that you have a very bad feeling about what she's getting into. Don't sugar coat it. Tell her directly and bluntly."

"She'll insist that I do the wedding anyway."

"Probably," Rex agreed, "but guess what? You're off the hook because you've absolutely done everything you can. It's Sally Mae's decision. You can't ruin your ministry over this. You just can't! So do the ceremony and go on with your life."

Lori sighed. "I wish I knew for sure how all this will turn out."

"Time will tell."

"I wish you hadn't said that," Lori said.

CHAPTER 32

Billy Ray was finishing his third bottle of Shiner Bock when Sally Mae came dancing out to join him. "I'm so proud of you I could just bust! You are the best thing that ever happened in Granbury. I hope everybody in the whole county comes to our ranch after the wedding."

Billy Ray reached down into the cooler for another bottle. "I can't believe you're offering steaks for everyone. Are you sure we'll have enough."

"More than enough. I've had three of our Angus cows dressed out."

"Why don't you just slaughter the whole herd--uh, might as well with the drought going on."

Sally Mae counted the bottles under his chair. "Billy Ray, how many beers have you had?"

"This is my last one," Billy Ray replied. "I'm not uh, I'm not drunk."

"Better not be, because I need your full attention. I've got a great idea we need to discuss."

"Lay it on me, and uh, thanks for including me in on it."

"You've been doing a lot of charitable work, Billy Ray, and I love you for it."

"Thanks again."

"--But your time is going to be limited after you're elected sheriff," Sally Mae continued.

Billy Ray waited for Sally Mae's conclusion. "So?"

"So here's what I've been thinking…"

Billy Ray leaned forward and waved his hand. "Here it comes. Drum roll!"

"Are you sure you're not drunk?" Sally Mae asked.

Billy Ray lifted his bottle high in the air. "Just mellow, and eager to hear your point if you've got one."

"Two things. When you're elected, you need to continue your charitable work, but you're not going to have much time as sheriff."

"Hmm."

"I want to take some of your money and some of mine from my inheritance to form a Billy Ray Foundation."

"A what?"

"A Billy Ray Foundation and I've got a great idea for its purpose."

Billy Ray put down his bottle. "Wait a minute, what kind of money are we talking about?"

"A half-million each," Sally Mae replied, "and don't tell me you can't afford it. I've seen that pile of hundreds in your safe. I've already talked with an attorney about our tax advantages. You'll be pleased to hear what he said."

"I'm not pleased to hear about any of this. You're talking about a lot of money!"

"Wait until you've heard what I have planned for it," Sally Mae said. "I've already talked to the Friends of the Library."

"Friends of what?"

"I'm on the library committee, and we desperately need to expand our program for poorer children who have reading problems. We plan to provide several adventure rooms designed to attract kids, with challenging games to take them from one level to the next. One room has a swamp with alligators they have to get through. Another has a virtual space trip for advanced levels. There will be computers generating holographic images with action figures to help them along. No kid can resist it. I'm very excited about what our money will do, but it won't be just us. The foundation will encourage other donors. I've already applied for the 501C3 non-profit status."

"Sally Mae, you've jumped the gun on me."

"It's still your choice. You don't have to do it, but I've already told the committee that I plan to contribute" Sally Mae answered.

"Be quiet for a minute and let me think." Billy Ray slumped back into his chair. Hmm, maybe I shouldn't object. It might get me out of this LARK business, especially if I turn the foundation over to Sally Mae. I can talk about my limited time as sheriff. I won't have to build houses and deliver meals. With what I've got stashed away from the oil leases, a half-million is chump change.

"I'll do it on one condition," Billy Ray announced.

"What?"

"You take over the phone calls of people wanting help, and you manage the foundation," Billy Ray said. "You can use that TCU business degree of yours to make the whole thing work! When I become sheriff, I want to be left alone."

"Billy Ray, I am the luckiest girl in the whole world!" Sally Mae said. "You are a sweet, wonderful man, and I promise not to let you down!"

Billy Ray accepted Sally Mae's hug and strolled out by himself for a walk in the pasture. Hey, it's not all that bad. With Sally Mae taking over, I can be generous without having to work at it. If Sally Mae only knew the money I really have. I could build that library twice over and still have enough for whatever I want. I'll make sure they put up a large Billy Ray plaque so that they won't forget my generosity.

⚓

The day of the wedding came and Sally Mae sat alone in the brides' room. As she was fastening her wedding dress, the door swung open. Alice Evans stood in the half- lighted doorway, moving forward like Fruma Sarah, the ghostly wife from Fiddler on the Roof. She spoke in a raspy voice. "I've had no sleep and I prayed about this all night long. You must not go through with this!"

"Alice, are you alright?" Sally Mae asked.

Alice took hold of Sally Mae's hands. "I know what this looks like, but you've got to listen. You remember that letter I told you about--the one I said was forged?"

"Yes, but what are you doing here, Alice?"

Alice held on to Sally Mae. "I need you to understand what really happened. It wasn't someone else. It was Billy Ray who forged that letter. He did it after he killed my husband."

Sally Mae broke loose and moved back. "You're not wanted here, Alice."

"I know this sounds crazy, but you must listen. You are marrying a murderer!"

"Alice, I want you to leave."

"You are making a horrible mistake. You're in danger and you don't know it. O Lord, what can I do to make you see …"

"Alice, get out now!" Sally Mae took a step toward Alice. "Leave!"

"I can't, not until you …"

Sally Mae grabbed Alice by the wrists and dragged her to the door. "You've had your say and now you're going."

Alice was surprised by the strength of Sally Mae. The door slammed in Alice's face, and the lock clicked on afterwards. Alice pounded on the door. "I can't let you do this!"

"Alice, you're having a breakdown. I'm calling the police."

"No, I'll go. I warned you as best I could." Alice left sobbing.

What in the world! The woman is plainly nuts. Maybe I should call someone or talk to Lori. No, not Lori--she weighed in on me last week. There's probably not much that can be done anyway. Should I tell Billy Ray? --Maybe later. I don't want anything upsetting this wedding.

Sally Mae took her place at the back of the sanctuary waiting to be cued in by the traditional wedding march. Lori stood at the front ready to receive the wedding party. The wedding march played, and Sally Mae was escorted down the aisle with her uncle, Drew Lawton. She held back the tears, remembering the car accident that took her parents four years ago.

At the front, she joined hands with Billy Ray. Sally Mae's well proportioned figure was highlighted in a tailored white dress that departed from the traditional wedding gown. Billy Ray looked like Prince Charming immaculately groomed in a perfectly fitted black tux. The two together were everyone's pick for homecoming king and queen.

Lori administered the wedding vows, but hesitated before giving Sally Mae hers.

"Do you, Sally Mae Lawton," Lori swallowed hard and then repeated, "Do you, Sally Mae Lawton, take this man, Billy Ray Larson, to be your wedded husband?"

"I do." Sally Mae knew that her initials, SML, would not change, but began to wonder about other changes. It wasn't just Alice; Lori had expressed her reservations too. Sally Mae shook it off. *This is just nuts. I'm marrying a wonderful guy. Well, too late now. It'll be good.*

At the conclusion of the ceremony, both the organ and piano played loudly as the couple walked out quickly to their limousine. The reception followed with a long line of cars going out to the ranch. With the whole county invited, many other cars were waiting at the gates. After the toasts were made, Sally Mae took the microphone.

"I am married to the most generous man in Hood County. I am very pleased to announce a gift to our entire community--the creation of the Billy Ray Foundation that will provide an adventure wonderland, a learning center for our children. Billy Ray, would you like to say something?"

"The credit goes to my lovely bride," Billy Ray said. "However, I have looked at her construction plans, and it's going to need more money than we originally thought. Therefore, I am putting up an additional million dollars for matching funds. When you see Sally Mae's plans, I'm sure this will be the most exciting project for children this county has ever witnessed. I hope you will give generously."

"Oh Billy Ray, Billy Ray!" Sally threw her arms around her husband and wept for joy. The crowd applauded loudly and the newspaper photographer took one picture after another.

Billy Ray wiped the barbeque sauce from his chin. That should do it. I'll be seen as a champion of children, and Sally Mae has a large enough foundation to keep her out of my hair. Now I can tend to my mission and fulfill my destiny.

Chapter 33

During breakfast on the morning of the election, Sally Mae brought in The Hood County News. "Here's the final tally. You won by two hundred votes."

"What!" Billy Ray grabbed the paper. "I could have lost! After all the people I helped, this is the way they repay me! I wish I knew who voted against me. Those stupid ingrates!"

Billy Ray threw his breakfast into the trash and then drove up to the sheriff's department. I can't walk in angry like this, and in the long run, what does it matter how close it was? I have plans for the future. Getting elected sheriff is just a starting point. I'm still God's chosen. The others around me are merely stepping stones."

Lyle Richards was waiting for Billy Ray inside the hallway with bottles of champagne for the staff. "Congratulations to the newly elected Sheriff! Of course, you won't be installed until March. --But you have established yourself as a true champion of the people. I'm proud of you."

"Thanks Lyle," Billy Ray watched as Lyle poured a glass for him. "You didn't have to do all this."

"Yes I did, especially since I have some final advice for you. Let's go to our office and talk." Lyle wrapped an arm around Billy Ray's shoulders and marched him to the office.

"I just want to remind you of some of the things we agreed to," Lyle Richards said. "First of all, there's your deputies. I don't want any one of them dismissed. They all need to know that their job is secure."

"Don't worry. I'm not going to fire anybody," Billy Ray said.

"It's especially important that you work closely with José Moreno," Lyle continued. "He's your chief deputy--a good man who's been in this department for fifteen years. As I told you before, he's bilingual. He's saved me a lot of grief not only in watching my back, but also in helping me get along with the Mexican population. Do you speak Spanish?"

"A little."

"Well, we have a growing population of Mexicans and you'll need José for interpretation as well as his expertise as an officer."

"I'll welcome his help," Billy Ray paused. "I wonder why you didn't support José as sheriff? I remember your saying he wanted it."

"There was no way that José could beat Earl Blanton," Lyle said. "I think José understands that. This town is still 90% white with lots of gray hair. They like José, but…"

"They'd like him better trimming their lawns."

Earl frowned. "I wouldn't go that far. They respect José as a deputy, but I doubt he could beat Earl Blanton for sheriff."

"I see."

"I know you'll treat José with respect and I'm sure he'll treat you the same way."

When Lyle left, Billy Ray shut the door, sat behind the sheriff's desk and buried his face in his hands. If I were José, I would be pissed, really pissed. Fifteen years is a long time to wait. I don't want him watching *my* back. He might be looking for a convenient accident. That's what I would do. Of course, accidents can happen either way."

When March came and Billy Ray was installed, Sally Mae stood at their ranch door and welcomed his staff as they came to her special get-acquainted dinner. Everyone was dressed in western attire. Billy Ray wore Sally Mae's favorite shirt for him on which she sewed a replacement for a missing brass button.

José was the first to notice Billy Ray's shirt. "That's a handsome shirt. Nice buttons with a Texas star, except for this one on the top. Is that a lightning bolt?"

"Yeah, but Sally Mae said no one would notice the difference," Billy Ray said.

"Uh, well, really it's not that noticeable," Jose took a step back. "It's a great looking shirt--red and blue Texas colors. It looks tailored."

"It is."

Sally Mae joined the conversation. "What are you boys talking about?"

"I was complimenting his shirt," José replied.

"He noticed your new button," Billy Ray said.

"I'm surprised he did," Sally Mae said, "but if you like I can sew on all new ones and make them the same."

Billy Ray flicked his nose. "I'm going to give this shirt to the Salvation Army."

"You'll do no such thing," Sally Mae said. "I love that shirt."

"Think I'll get another beer," Billy Ray walked away.

Sally Mae laughed. "He's so sensitive."

José laughed too. "Well, there's nothing wrong with a sensitive sheriff with a lovely wife."

Sally Mae tried to untangle her gold necklace. "Nuts! José, would you mind unlatching this thing? It's all twisted up."

"Sure." A minute or two went by before José finally figured out the latch. "Got it! I don't know how you put this thing on by yourself."

Billy Ray watched the interplay between José and Sally Mae. Something's going on there. If José thinks he can mess around with my wife, he's got another thing coming. I may have to straighten out Sally Mae too. The next thing you know she'll be inviting him over to dinner.

Two of the deputies, Allison and Tiffany, came over to see Sally Mae. "You have a beautiful home," Tiffany said. "How about a tour?"

"Thought you'd never ask!" Sally Mae led the way going from room to room. A crimson red sunset brought them outside. In a burst of enthusiasm Sally Mae went to the garage and rolled out her electric golf cart with its heavy duty tires, and motioned Tiffany and Allison to get in. The women chatted and laughed as the cart bumped along over rocks and hills covered with a wildflower array of bluebonnets, red paint brushes and yellow coreopsis.

Billy Ray stayed at the house looking at his Rolex and drinking a beer with Walt, a taciturn deputy with little to say. Finally, the women returned home and the last of the guests left.

⚓

Later that evening, Sally Mae wanted to celebrate the success of her party with Billy Ray. She sat down beside him and took his hand. "I'm so glad we did this. I really enjoyed getting to know your staff and they all seemed to have a great time. We'll do this again. I think it helps in building trust and a sense of friendship."

Billy Ray removed his hand from Sally Mae's. "I'm more interested in getting their respect than friendship. I'd like to fire one or two of them but I can't do it because I promised Lyle to keep them on."

"Why would you want to fire anyone? They impressed me as competent and good to work with. That's especially true of José. He seems like the kind of deputy who would work well with the public."

Billy Ray bit his bottom lip. "José wanted to be sheriff. I'm not sure I can trust him."

"He was certainly friendly with me."

"Yeah and I didn't like it," Billy Ray said.

Sally Mae squeezed his hand. "José is charming, but I married someone I like even better."

"Just stay away from him."

Sally Mae removed her hand. "Billy Ray, I'm sorry--but I'm not putting up with jealousy. I'm not going to live that way. I want everyone on your staff to feel welcome in our home."

"Right, never mind what I want."

"On some things, yes, but jealousy is not one of them. It's nuts and I don't do nuts."

"You need to remember your marriage vows," Billy Ray retorted.

Sally Mae stood up with her hands on her hips. "And you need to stop acting like a child. This discussion is over and I don't want to hear it again!"

"Fine!" Billy Ray picked up a beer and went outside slamming the screen door after him. Sally Mae reopened the door and followed him.

"If you get drunk, you can just go someplace else. You're ruining a wonderful evening. I worked very hard in making your staff feel welcomed and appreciated. You get your act together and you do it now!" Sally Mae went back into the house slamming the screen door behind her.

Billy Ray sat sulking with his beer on the front porch. If she really knew me, she wouldn't act this way. I'm David and she's Bathsheba. I'm the warrior here. She doesn't get to choose who is welcome at my ranch. She can learn that the easy way or the hard way, but she'll learn.

CHAPTER 34

One week after Sally Mae's party, Sheriff Billy Ray received an alert from the Huntsville State Prison. Three prisoners, two of them serving life sentences for murder, had escaped. They were last seen headed north in the general direction of Cleburne and Granbury. Later that afternoon, Billy Ray's dispatcher ran into the main office. "Sheriff! Those murderers--they're here in Hood County! I just heard from Allison and José."

"Calm down and give me the details," Billy Ray said.

"They're holed up outside of Thorp Springs. José and Allison have them sighted in an old farmhouse."

"It's always an old farmhouse." Billy Ray strapped on his Colt 44. "I need two more deputies, whoever's closest to the scene. I'm on my way. Tell José not to do anything until I arrive."

As Billy Ray drove out to the farmhouse, the story of Uriah came to mind. It's so simple, now that I think of it. The best of plans are. Put Uriah out front. Then draw back and allow the enemy to kill him. Huh! It worked once for King David.

When Billy Ray drove up to meet his deputies, the four of them were hunkered down seventy yards away from the farmhouse. José whispered to Billy Ray. "I don't think they've seen us yet. What do you want us to do?"

"Let's see if we can take them alive."

"That might be difficult considering who they are," Allison said.

"Well, maybe it won't be as hard as you think," Billy Ray replied.

"Here's how I want to handle it. First of all, José, I want you to take this bullhorn and go armed with a launcher and a tear-gas propellant."

"And do what?"

"Do you see those three trees at two o'clock?"

"Those hackberry trees fifty yards from here? They're only about eight inches across--not much cover."

"Those trees are close together and you'll have plenty of cover when we start shooting," Billy Ray said.

Tiffany grabbed Billy Ray's arm. "Sheriff, this is not a good plan. Hackberry trees are trash trees--unsubstantial. An assault rifle would rip them apart."

Billy Ray glared at Tiffany. "Look, I'll go myself if you want. José can stay here and take charge of the operation."

"No, no, I'll do it," José said. "What exactly do you want me to do?"

"Well, don't try to make a straight line run from here. Go through the woods behind us and make your run at twelve o'clock. We'll start shooting as soon as we see you make your turn."

"Uh, maybe it would be better to start shooting before I make my turn, not during. I'll signal you."

"Good idea. After you get to the trees, use the bullhorn and tell them to surrender."

Allison spoke up in a hoarse whisper. "No! They'll hear the bullhorn and know where to shoot!"

"Allison, I know what I'm doing. Let me be the sheriff," Billy Ray said. "If they start shooting, we'll fire back and keep them busy. José, when you see that happening use the launcher and fire the tear-gas through their window."

"Maybe I better take some extra propellants," José said.

"Right. I'm going to take Allison and flank them from the left," Billy Ray turned to Walt and Tiffany. "You two stay here and use your assault rifles to give José plenty of cover fire. Allison and I will do the same."

Three minutes later, with everyone in position, José gave the signal and the deputies started firing. The convicts fired back and José barely made it to the trees with bullets flying all around him. Then there was a pause as both sides stopped shooting.

José used the bullhorn. "You're surrounded, come out with your hands on top of your heads."

The convicts immediately opened fire in the direction of the bullhorn. One of the hackberry trees went down and even though José was wearing a vest, the tree bark cut into his face and unprotected areas. Bullets ricocheted all around. José wiped the blood from his face, grabbed the launcher and fired a tear-gas grenade at the window. *Missed!* He reloaded and fired a second one that succeeded, exploding in the farmhouse. In the quiet that followed, the convicts came out gasping for air.

Billy Ray raised his rifle to shoot, but Allison put out a restraining hand. "They've dropped their guns. No need to shoot." The deputies took the convicts into custody and called an ambulance for José.

Later that day, Billy Ray held a press conference. "Our deputies all performed with precision and valor. We're particularly proud of Chief Deputy, José Moreno, who suffered severe lacerations as he courageously took the point position and launched the tear gas. I'm glad to report that although his wounds required over a hundred stitches, Deputy Moreno is on his way to recovery at the Granbury Hospital."

Pretty boy José is not so pretty now. Maybe I'll call him Deputy Scarface.

Billy Ray took questions from the media and introduced his deputies. He stopped when he noticed Sally Mae with a gift basket.

"What's the basket for?" Billy Ray asked.

"I'm going to visit José at the hospital. Want to come?" Sally Mae replied.

Billy Ray knew it would be expected. "Uh, well, okay."

On their way to the hospital, Sally Mae turned to face Billy Ray. "I talked to Allison about what happened. I was curious about how José was all cut up and none of the rest of you had a scratch."

"José was just doing his job, that's all."

"Not quite all. You sent him on that mission," Sally Mae said.

"I told him I would go if he didn't want to. Somebody had to do it."

"Right, but it was your plan, huh Billy Ray."

"It worked and José got credit for a job well done," Billy Ray said as they arrived at the hospital.

⅄

They took the elevator to José's room and found him watching TV.

"I thought you would look a lot worse than this," Billy Ray grinned.

"Disappointed?" José said.

"He looks pretty bad to me," Sally Mae said. "--stitches all over his face. What happened?"

"Bark from hackberry trees--not very good cover," José replied.

"Hackberry trees! You're lucky to be alive if that's what you were hiding behind." Sally Mae gave José her basket. "Here's some things to cheer you up."

"A care basket--first one I've gotten! Are these cookies home made?" José asked.

"Yes they are. I worked all day over a hot stove just for you," Sally Mae laughed.

"Sheriff, you've got a great wife, but next time I'm going to take you up on your offer, and let you use the launcher."

"What did I tell you?" Billy Ray said to Sally Mae, "I told you I offered to take his place."

"Yes he did," José conceded, "and the sheriff gave me lots of credit. I'm not complaining. I'm a hero."

Sally Mae took hold of José's hand. "Nearly a dead one."

"Let's don't wear him out," Billy Ray said. "It's time to go. He needs to get well and come back to work."

Sally Mae bent down over José and nuzzled his face with a kiss. "That's for being brave and stupid."

"Come back any time!" José laughed, then groaned.

Billy Ray was deadly silent as they left the hospital. He had a dream the night before of José making love to Sally Mae. He swallowed his anger and put it away for later at a better time.

Chapter 35

Three weeks later Billy Ray was greeted with the familiar sounds of joking and laughter coming from José's office. *That damned José starts every morning by making coffee for the deputies. This morning's going to be different. They'll be drinking coffee in my office, thanks to the special coffeemaker I just purchased--no mess, no fuss, and no more coffee with José.*

Billy Ray walked outside his door. "Hey everyone. Coffee's ready in my office if you're interested."

"What you got, sheriff?" Allison walked into his office with Tiffany.

"Hmm, an individual cup maker." Tiffany moved back to the door.

"Not bad," Allison said, "but you need to try José's--grown in Mexico and roasted in San Antonio. José has a special way of brewing it. It starts out the morning just right."

"Come join us," Tiffany said as they went on their way to José's office.

Billy Ray closed the door. *Damn it! I'll let them have their coffee and then I'll cut it short by having a staff meeting. Maybe that'll stop their hob-nobbing and get them on the job.*

After twenty minutes, the sounds of laughter penetrated Billy Ray's office. As he swung open José's door to announce the staff meeting the laughter abruptly stopped. "Staff meeting in ten minutes."

Billy Ray went back to his office. I bet they were talking about me. José's the ringleader. It's not enough that he's charmed my wife. Get rid of him and it'll all stop. My first try didn't work too well, but I'm not done yet.

✦

The next several weeks passed without incidence or violence; there were no calls requiring major police action. Billy Ray grew more sullen with the office situation, and he sat on his porch in the evenings with his empty beer bottles. The screen door swung open as Sally Mae came out. "I can't live with these dark moods of yours, Billy Ray. We need to do some serious talking."

"Huh, so now what? You want a divorce?"

"I want you to talk to me," Sally Mae replied. "What's going on with you?"

"Nothing that you and José couldn't fix."

"José?" Sally Mae pulled up a chair and sat next to Billy Ray. "Have you gone crazy? José is not the problem. It's you."

"Have you been seeing him?"

"No."

Billy Ray slumped in his chair. "Everybody wants to see José. Everybody! He's a real charmer that one--a lover and a charmer."

"Well, he's not mine."

"You don't find him charming?" Billy Ray wiped the beer from his chin.

"Well, of course. José is just what you need to keep people happy at the office."

"He's taking over the office. Whenever there's a question, do they come to me? No! They go to José." Billy Ray threw his beer bottle from the porch, crashing it on the rocks.

Sally Mae stood up and put her hands on her hips. "So that's what this is all about! You've gone nuts and you're going to make everybody else nuts. You need to get a grip! You were the one who got elected sheriff, right? What else do you want? Those deputies are your deputies, not José's."

"My deputies--hah!" Billy Ray said. "I might as well not be there. And getting elected? --Barely, just barely. If I hadn't spent all that money on charity, I wouldn't be in that office."

Sally Mae's eyes narrowed. "I thought you enjoyed helping people."

Billy Ray threw another beer bottle. "You and that damned foundation. A lot of good that did me."

Sally Mae moved back to the door. "You need help, Billy Ray. I can't stand it anymore. I didn't sign up for this."

"I'm sure you and José will be very happy together." Yeah, maybe I can arrange a double funeral.

"I don't want you sleeping in my bed tonight," Sally Mae said.

"I'll sleep where I damned well want too," Billy Ray said. "This is my ranch. Do you hear me? Mine!"

"Then I'm sleeping in town. Let me know when you're sober."

Billy Ray grabbed Sally Mae's arm. "You'll do no such thing! You're my wife and …"

Sally Mae slapped Billy Ray across his face and wrestled her arm free of his grasp. "I don't know who you think you are, but that rough stuff is out!"

Billy Ray covered his face with his hands in supplication. I better make this right. I can't have her going into town and badmouthing me. I've got to come up with some sweet talk fast. "Wait, please. I'm wrong. I know I am. You've been nothing but kind and patient. My drinking is getting out of hand. Please don't leave me. I love you and I need your understanding. It's just seems like José is taking over the office. I don't know what to do."

Sally Mae put her hands on Billy Ray's shoulders. "Well, I do. You need to show that you're a good boss and have their concern at heart. You're having a birthday next week and we'll have the staff over for dinner."

Damn! I can't stand the idea of José in my house again. Well, for now I'll just pretend to go along with it. "What a wonderful idea. We can invite Lyle Richards and his wife too."

"Don't forget Mark and Lori Travis," Sally Mae added.

"Invite them all. It'll be a great birthday." I'm not done yet. I'll act sick the night before and we'll have to cancel the whole thing.

Sally Mae simply rescheduled the event. Not to be outdone, Billy Ray came up with another excuse for delaying. Finally, Sally Mae gave up on the party and decided to talk with Lyle Richards.

Billy Ray was busy with paperwork when a loud knock came at his office door. Lyle walked in immediately afterwards. "What on earth is going on with you, boy! I just had a talk with your wife."

"Is there a problem?"

"The problem is you," Lyle replied, "and it's not just Sally Mae that has a problem. The people on your staff aren't happy either. They say you're cutting them short. Don't give me any denials about it. Tell me what's going on."

Billy Ray's eyes turned down to the floor. "Alright, let me be honest with you. The people on my staff don't come to me with problems. They go to José. Every morning starts the same--coffee with José. I don't have a staff. José does."

Lyle stood up and started pacing. "You are such an idiot! Of course everyone goes to José. I went to him myself. He's a great sounding board. You should be delighted to have him on your staff. He keeps everybody working together! That's a big plus in an office."

"Sally Mae sure likes him."

Lyle sat back down and laughed. "There would be something wrong with her if she didn't! Are you worried that José will run off with Sally Mae?"

"I don't know."

"Well, the way you're acting who could blame her? You stay on your front porch drinking beers and ignore her when she tries to talk you. Then you make up some phony excuses for not having her party. If I had a son-in-law like that, I'd shoot him!"

Not if I shoot you first you meddling old goat.

"I'll tell you what I'm going to do about this," Lyle pointed his finger at Billy Ray. "I'll be dropping in on you from time to time. I'm responsible for your election and by dangies, you're going to stop all this sourpuss stuff and make a good sheriff and a good husband. Sallie Mae and everybody here deserves a lot better than you've been giving."

"I'll make changes," Billy Ray said.

"So what are you going to do?" Lyle leaned forward.

"I'll start by having coffee with José and the rest of them."

"Fine. Then what are you going to do for Sally Mae?" Lyle asked.

Billy Ray smiled to offset his reluctant tone. "I'll help her plan my birthday party."

Lyle patted Billy Ray on his back. "I'll be there and I'll be watching."

Billy Ray stared at the door as Lyle left. *I should never have married Sally Mae. She's a lot smarter than I thought. She's got me right by the short hairs--for now.*

⅄

Two weeks later Sally Mae's party was in full swing with an expanded guest list. This time, Billy Ray was actively greeting and hugging his guests. He made a point of putting his arm around José's shoulders, and loudly laughing and talking with those around them.

Sally Mae stood in front of the fireplace and made an announcement. "This a very special time for us. Today, because of three very generous donors, the Billy Ray foundation has doubled! We now have four million dollars, and construction will begin after we receive another million which we anticipate soon!" The crowd broke into applause.

Billy Ray joined Sally Mae and raised his margarita glass. "I want to propose a toast to those wonderful donors, and to the hardworking staff of the sheriff's department whom we are honoring tonight--with special mention of José Moreno who every morning makes the best coffee in all of Texas."

"Here, here!" Allison clinked her glass with Tiffany and Walt. Others followed suit laughing and cheering.

Mark whispered in Lori's ear, "Do you think Billy Ray is bi-polar?"

"Shh, save it," Lori said.

⅄

Later driving home, Mark repeated his question, "I'm serious. Is he bi-polar?"

"Maybe he's learning to be a happy sheriff like Lyle, his mentor," Lori yawned. "Of course, it might have been the margaritas. I still have a buzz from it."

"I think he's playing a role," Mark said. "It's like he was in a horse opera, starring Billy Ray as the happy rancher."

"At least it's not the righteous warrior."

Mark eased up on the accelerator. "Do you want my opinion?"

Lori kissed his cheek. "Why not? You're going to give it to me anyway."

"Billy Ray takes the path of least resistance. If a party makes things easier for him, fine. If not, then he'll make people disappear."

"Sally Mae is still there and seems happy. Right now, that's good enough for me," Lori yawned again. "You know, we've been down this road before. Aren't you tired of investigating Billy Ray? I'm ready to move on to something else."

"Well, I'm not. I think I'll call the FBI--maybe talk to Max," Mark said.

"What? Max Sanford?"

"Yeah, he owes me big time."

Lori snuggled up to Mark. "Yes he does--especially after you solved a case for him, and let him have all the credit."

" Got him a promotion too," Mark said.

"I know Max pretty well," Lori said. "I worked with him when I was an Assistant DA. He's had some success, but basically he's like a Hollywood depiction of an arrogant Fed--tall and smooth, speaking in a deep bass. He wants big cases easily solved with his name at the top of the headlines. He's certainly not interested in cold cases that are local."

"Max appreciates my detective work. I can guide him along."

"Look," Lori said, "you need to wait until it's something really momentous, and then you can cash in on the Max card. Of course, you'll have to make it sound like it's his idea. Save it until you really need it. "

"I suppose you're right."

"I know I am."

"Well, maybe."

"You always have to have the last word, don't you?" Lori said.

"Do not."

"Do too.

"I'll let it go," Mark said, pleased to have the last word.

Lori curled up and slept on Mark's shoulder the rest of the trip home.

Chapter 36

Right before dawn, Billy Ray woke up with Sally Mae lightly snoring beside him. He walked into the darkness of the great room and poured some more tequila into his already loaded margarita pitcher. After two glasses of it, he fell asleep on the sofa. He jerked up straight when he heard the ghostly voice of his father. "Ha! So you're the great warrior, vanquishing all who stand in your way. And now you can't even control your own house. That little wisp of a girl has you hogtied. She's made a fool out of you. You are nothing but a party clown. Your own deputies laugh at you. Fool!"

"Shut up old man!" Billy Ray staggered to his feet. "No one makes a fool of me. You just watch."

Billy Ray bumped open the door of his bedroom. "Get up little girl! You have work to do!"

Sally Mae tried to shake the cobwebs from her sleep. "What on earth! What are you doing?"

Billy Ray grabbed Sally Mae and slung her over his shoulder. "I'm taking over as lord of this manor. You're going to earn your keep as an--uh, uh, a ranch hand!"

Sally Mae tried to break free but Billy Ray stumbled through the great room finally making it through the front door.

Sally Mae beat on Billy Ray's muscled back. "You're going to fall down and hurt us both you idiot! Put me down! It's cold out here you fool! I'm in my pajamas!"

Billy Ray opened the barn with his free hand. "You're going to learn, uh …Let me see, what are you going to learn? Hmm, Ha! I know. You're going to be a heavy equipment operator. Let's go over to this front loader. You're already uh--well, quite a little operator, aren't you? So up you go into the cab, and I'll turn on the switch. Good! Now let's see you do your job. Move those rocks out into the pasture."

"Alright, move out of the way, stupid!" Sally Mae in one quick motion shifted gears and shot out of the barn.

Sally Mae lifted the big rocks and moved them to the pasture as Billy Ray watched in astonishment. "Hey, what--where in the hell did you learn that!"

"You have a short memory, dummy. My daddy sold these things and I demonstrated them to his customers." Sally Mae jumped out of the cab and ran into the house. Billy Ray stumbled to the front porch and collapsed into the wooden rocking chair.

Moments later, Sally Mae walked out of the house with her bags packed. Billy Ray watched her get into the car. "Where are you going?"

"None of your business, jerk!" Sally Mae pulled out of the driveway with the dust flying.

Sally Mae slowed her car when she got to the highway. If I divorce him, then what would happen to the foundation? I'm not going to disappoint the parents and children of our community. So what are my options? I don't want Billy Ray coming after me, so...

Sally Mae called Lyle from her car speaker and gave him the details.

Lyle listened intently. "Did he hurt you?"

"No--maybe a bruise or two. I still believe there's good in him, but this drinking has got to stop."

"If you think drinking is the problem, maybe I can fix that--unless he's an alcoholic. I'll pay him a visit and try a little tough love. "

Sally Mae rubbed the bruise on her arm. "He's a mean drunk."

"Yeah, well I'm meaner. You stay away for a while, and leave Billy Ray to me." .

Once again, Lyle sat across from Billy Ray in his office. "Just sit there and shut up," Lyle's face turned red. "Don't you say a word! I'm not interested in what you've got to say. I'm here to tell you what's going to happen to you, if you don't shape up and shape up right now!"

"Well, what …"

"Did you hear me? I said shut up and listen. You'd better listen boy!"

"Please calm down." Billy Ray said.

Lyle hovered over Billy Ray. "Damn you. Shut your mouth! I'm going to say this just once. I am on the verge of publicly withdrawing my support of you and expressing my regrets in the Hood Country News. That's going to happen if I ever hear of you mistreating or speaking disrespectfully to Sally Mae. And if I ever catch you drinking again, you'll be washed up for sure--if I have anything to say about it--which I certainly do!"

Billy Ray averted his eyes. "I uh, I didn't mean to uh …"

"I don't want to hear your lying excuses. You've been warned." Lyle stormed out of the office.

Billy Ray swallowed his rage. That old bastard doesn't know who he's dealing with. I'll let some time go by and then take care of it once and for all.

⚓

The next few weeks when Billy Ray came home, he silently sat on his front porch drinking root beers. He limited his conversation with Sally Mae to blank stares, short phrases and a complete absence of affection. Sally Mae knew what was going on and had her own way of countering. When the Hood Country News came out on Friday, Billy Ray read the headlines: "Billy Ray Foundation a Success: Construction to Start Soon."

"We reached our goal last month," Sally Mae said in an interview. "That happened when my wonderful, generous husband went beyond what he has done thus far, with an additional million dollars."

Billy Ray cornered Sally Mae in the kitchen. "I did what!"

"You can always deny it," Sally Mae laughed. "You wouldn't talk to me about it so I made the pledge for you. I know you want the foundation to succeed."

"How do you know I've got that kind of money?" Billy Ray asked.

"Don't be ridiculous," Sally Mae said. "I pay the bills. I know every penny you've got."

Billy Ray walked out onto the porch and stared across the pasture. Ha! So she thinks she knows what I've got? I have tons of money stashed in places she'll never find. Well, why not play along--the good hearted, generous Billy Ray. I'll even make a speech when Sally Mae hosts the big event. She'll get no credit. I'll put up a Billy Ray plaque without her name on it. In the meantime, I'll play it cool. I don't want another visit from Lyle.

Chapter 37

Two months later, Mark Travis was interrupted from his work by two visitors. Mark stared at one of them in disbelief. Except for the yellowed teeth, he bore a startling resemblance to Billy Ray.

"We understand you've been working our daddy's case," the Billy Ray look-alike said.

"I'm sorry. Have we met?" Mark said.

In one motion, the other man took off his baseball cap and swatted his brother. "Where are your manners, Wynn! I'm Hiram Casey and this one here is my brother, Wynn. For the past twenty three years--after the divorce--we've been living with our momma's folks in the Cumberland mountains. Wynn was just a baby."

"So you're Hank Casey's boys," Mark looked at the Ruger Blackhawk strapped on Hiram's waist. "That's a big gun. Got a permit?"

Hiram showed his badge. "Don't need one. I'm a deputy."

"We want to know what happened to our daddy," Wynn said.

Mark turned on his overhead fan. "I can tell you that there are three missing men in this town and I'm working all three cases. I haven't made much headway."

Hiram patted his Blackhawk. "What do you suspect? Are the other two linked with our daddy somehow?"

"Well, your daddy was a very good friend of ..."

"Yeah, Eddie Larson," Hiram interrupted. "Tell us something we don't know."

Mark looked closer at his scruffy visitors. The room began to absorb their odor. "You might check with Eddie's son, Billy Ray. He's the new sheriff in town and was acquainted with Hank. I'm sure he'll be glad to see you."

Hiram rolled his eyes. "Yeah, yeah, we know that too. Come on, Wynn, we're wasting our time here. Let's go see the sheriff."

As they walked away, Mark continued to stare at Wynn. Except for the beard, he had the same walk, same blue eyes, about the same height and weight of Billy Ray. It's weird--almost a dead ringer.

⚓

When Hiram and Wynn Casey walked past the offices of the sheriff's deputies, José and Tiffany trailed behind to see Billy Ray's reaction. They were not disappointed. Both Wynn and Billy Ray stood staring at each other in silent amazement.

"We're Hank Casey's sons," Hiram said. "I'm Hiram and this here is my brother, Wynn--and uh, hey! You know what? Wynn looks a whole lot like you!"

Billy Ray sat back down behind his desk. "Yeah? What can I do for you?"

Hiram scratched the stubble on his chin. "We're inquiring about our daddy, Hank Casey. You were a friend of his?"

"My father was," Billy Ray replied. "They went fishing and hunting together."

"Then maybe you can tell us more than that dumb Mark Travis," Hiram said.

Billy Ray's nose began to twitch, but he wanted to learn more about their plans. "Uh, how long are you going to be in town?"

"I've got to get back to Tennessee, but Wynn will be around looking for a lawyer to settle up things on the ranch," Hiram said. "It's been six years now. If you can't find our daddy, then maybe he can be declared legally dead. Anyway you look at it, he's better off that way--not much use to anyone alive."

Allison, listening in the open doorway, whispered to Tiffany, "What a nightmare, living with *that* son!"

"Dad wasn't much, but I still hope we can find out what happened," Wynn looked steadily at Billy Ray. "Do you think we look alike?"

Billy Ray broke eye contact. "Maybe somewhat."

"We could be brothers," Wynn said.

"We're not. Stuff like this happens."

"So what can you do for us?" Hiram asked. "Can you do a final search, enough for a good faith effort to declare him dead?"

Billy Ray had a sudden inspiration. "I'm going to assign my top deputy to you." He walked past them down the hallway. "José, would you come to my office please?"

Billy Ray put his arm around José. "I want you to meet my chief deputy, José Moreno. José knows this town inside and out. He's yours to work the case for as long as you're here."

"That's fine with me," Wynn said. "A good Mexican knows how to smell out trouble."

José took a step back. There's got to be some tactful way to tell this guy to take a bath.

"I'll tell you what--and I'm delighted to do this," Billy Ray smiled. "I'm going to ask José to stay with you on your ranch for a while. José is a good investigator. Maybe between the two of you, you'll come up with something."

⚓

José opened the windows as he drove Wynn out to his Hank's ranch. He knew that he could not stay in the same house with him for very long. He thought of an approach that he hoped and prayed would work.

"Tell me something, Wynn. How are you with the ladies?" José asked.

"I don't know. I took a year at the Cumberland Community College, but it didn't seem to help with the gals. So, José--how are *you* in that department?" Wynn replied.

"Well, to be honest, I have a great love life," José said.

"Really!"

"Yes indeed. Want to know my secret?" José smiled.

"Well--yeah, sure," Wynn said.

José paused. "Maybe I shouldn't say anything. You wouldn't believe it if I told you."

"Try me."

"Something I sort of discovered by accident. It's a little like cat fishing. Are you into fishing?" José asked.

"I'm good at cat fishing."

"I can believe that--uh, I mean a man of your caliber would know stuff like that," José said. "Well, let me get to my point."

"Please do."

"Catfish are attracted by the right scent and it takes a good fisherman to come up with the right formula."

"Are you saying ladies are the same way?" Wynn asked.

"Yep--and I can prove it to you. I know exactly what to use."

"Maybe I should try it," Wynn said.

"When is your birthday, Wynn?"

"Next month."

José pulled over into a Walgreen's parking lot. "I'm going to give you a birthday present that will put you in my debt forever."

"What?"

"You'll see." A moment later José returned with a bag. "Now before I give you this, let me say that you're going to have to use this every day. In fact, when I see a lady I want to ask out, I use it twice a day before I ask."

Wynn reached for the bag. "What is it?"

"It's something simple--been around for a long time."

"Let me see!" Wynn tore open the bag and pulled out the contents. "Hey, are you kidding me?"

"Yes, it's Old Spice, but look at what it says on the label."

"Hmm, it say 'especially formulated.'"

"They've been working on this stuff for years and believe me, Wynn, they finally got it right," José said. "It's like a magnet, but the soap alone won't do it. You have to use the shampoo and the deodorant too."

"What's this toothpaste doing in here?" Wynn asked.

"It's a special whitener. Women like white teeth too."

"Why are you doing all this for me?" Wynn asked.

José put a hand on Wynn's shoulder. "Someone once did the same for me. I'm passing it on. I can't wait to see the results for you. The gals will come running."

Wynn studied the label. "You're a good guy. I'm going to start using this stuff tonight."

Thank God. Got to get rid of those clothes too. That scent's not going to go away in a washing machine.

"Why are you frowning?" Wynn asked.

"How long have you had those overalls?"

Wynn tugged at his suspenders. "A long time. They're my work clothes. I'm a carpenter back home. People living in our mountains know that I'm good with my hands. I build just about anything. I make good money."

"Those overalls are awfully beat up."

"No reason to buy another one."

José tightened his grip on the steering wheel. How can I find a polite way to tell him about the smell? "Let me put it this way. Do you have a favorite fishing lure?"

"So we're back to fishing?"

"Bear with me. A good lure will not only attract a fish; it'll trigger them."

"Yeah, I know that. Some fish will be attracted to a lure and swim around it, but it won't trigger them. They won't bite. So what's this stuff you just bought me?"

"That Old Spice is a wonderful trigger, but we need to work on the attract part. Those old smelly overalls have got to go. You need new ones and some city stuff as well."

"I didn't realize my overalls smelled!"

"Do you sleep in them?" José asked.

"Sometimes."

"Well, no wonder! Hey, there's a Wal-Mart not far from here. We might as well do this thing right and go first class," José said. "Later on, when you're in a party mood, we'll go to the Haggar outlet and get a fancy suit."

"What's wrong with right now?"

"Let's get you cleaned up first with that incredible Old Spice stuff. You might run into a good looking gal."

After Wynn cleaned up, José took him shopping. Wynn rarely went to a big city and the stores in Granbury delighted him. At Wal-Mart, he came out from the dressing room in new overalls and asked the clerk to get rid of the old ones. The clerk made a hasty departure to the outside dumpster. After that, Wynn went from store to store until he had found a new sport's coat and no longer looked like a hillbilly.

"My friend, you are now ready for a social life," José said. "It's Friday night and I know of a nice bar. Let's get a beer and see what happens."

Sure enough, Wynn met a nice lady and forgot all about José. José watched their interplay with satisfaction. Huh, Wynn has toned down his hillbilly accent; he's not all that dumb, really. Well, mission accomplished. Even if Wynn doesn't find his father, he's going to be one happy dude. Who knows? He may even settle down here.

CHAPTER 38

That next Monday, Mark was greeted by Rob in his office. "I'm curious," Rob said. "I know Hank's sons paid you a visit. I'm wondering why they left so quickly?"

"Wynn and Hiram? I saw no reason for them to stay."

"Didn't you want to interrogate them?"

Mark waved his hand in the air. "Fumigate, maybe."

"So that was it. You just wanted them to get out of your office."

"Yeah, well--okay. Maybe I should have at least questioned them. Let me think about it. I do know that Hiram left town, and Wynn is staying at his father's ranch."

After Rob left, Mark clicked on his computer and typed out some possible questions for Wynn. I just hope I can stand the smell. Maybe I can get Wynn to come out on the porch. Mark found the phone number and called Wynn who invited him over.

☙

When Mark drove over to the ranch, he was greeted by a well groomed man that he first thought was Billy Ray. "I'm looking for Wynn," Mark said.

José laughed. "You're looking at him!"

The slight aroma of Old Spice had taken the place of what was there before.

"I didn't recognize you without the beard and uh …"

"What can I do for you, officer?" Wynn asked.

Mark sat down beside Wynn. "Well, I have a few questions about Hank. Some of them might not make any sense but ..."

"I'll be glad to cooperate anyway that I can." Wynn listened attentively.

"First, can you remember the last time you heard from your Dad?"

"That would been six years ago, right around the time he disappeared. I remember it was the year when Billy Ray had his father's funeral, although the body had not been found," Wynn replied.

"So did you hear from him before or after the funeral?"

"As I remember, it was the same week as the funeral."

"Talk to me about Hank. What sort of man was he? I know he liked fishing with Billy Ray's father. Were there other things he enjoyed? Do you remember anything out of the ordinary?"

"He liked poker and he drank a lot of beer." Wynn said. "He also liked gardening. Come to think about it, there was one thing that was kind of odd. Three months after he was missing, Hiram and I went out to his garden. It was overgrown with cucumbers. He liked cucumbers, but not that much. The vines had swallowed up everything. --But that's probably not important."

"What about friends. You mentioned poker. Did he have a fishing or poker buddy that he might have confided in?"

"Well, there's Melvin McCrary. He owns a bar, built like a log cabin, a few miles down Tin Top Road. They were poker buddies."

Mark took out his pad and pen. "One thing I might ask Melvin is about the ladies who knew Hank."

"Melvin would know more about that than I would. Dad always did have an eye for the ladies."

"Must run in the family," José laughed.

"When Dad was younger, he was very handsome," Wynn said. "The alcohol did him in later on."

"If you think of anything else that might help, please give me a call," Mark handed Wynn his card."

"I appreciate your interest." Wynn shook Mark's hand and walked him to the door.

Mark drove over to Tin Top Road and found Melvin McCrary's bar nestled in a grove of trees. Melvin was there laughing loudly with his red-necked customers.

"Good afternoon, Melvin," Mark began "I'm …"

"I know who you are, officer. I've seen your picture in the papers," Melvin extended his hand. "Can I get you a beer?"

"No, I just need to ask you a question or two about Hank Casey."

"Hank? What has it been now--five years?"

"More like six," Mark replied. "I had the opportunity of talking with Hank's sons recently and your name came up as a good friend."

"Hank and I were buddies," Melvin said. "I miss him. What do you want to know?"

"I understand he was quite a ladies' man," Mark paused for an answer.

"Yeah--hey, come on back to my office. We don't need to be talking about that out here," Melvin motioned Mark to follow. The office, reflecting Melvin's demeanor, was decorated with the heads of animals including an armadillo, a skunk and a jackrabbit.

"Hank was active with several women," Melvin said. "It's not a subject I would want to discuss in public, but if it will help with your investigation …"

"It might," Mark said. "Did he have a favorite? Were any of these women married?"

Melvin shuffled his feet. "Yes to both questions. Can I answer off the record? I wouldn't want this to get out."

"It won't. I'm just trying to put things together."

"Well, the woman was Eddie Larson's wife, Barbara. She died giving birth to Billy Ray. I think old Hank really loved her. Eddie probably knew about it and didn't care. Their marriage was pretty much over anyway."

"Do you remember anything in particular that Hank told you about Barbara?"

"If this gets out …"

"It won't."

"When Billy Ray was born, Hank was sure that it was his baby. He talked off and on for twenty years about telling Billy Ray that he was his daddy," Melvin said.

"Was Hank really planning on doing that? When did he last talk about it?"

Melvin popped open a beer. "Well, I think the last time he mentioned it was right before the funeral. Yeah, I remember it now. Hank sat there right at my bar and told me he was going to tell Billy Ray--tell him he was his daddy. I told him he was drunk, and to let some more time go by, but he said enough time had already gone by. He was determined to do it right then and there."

"You think Hank went to see Billy Ray during the memorial service?"

"Uh huh, that's when it was. Thought it was a bad idea." Melvin emptied his unfinished beer in a flower pot.

Mark asked a few more questions and then wrapped up the interview. "Thanks very much, Melvin. You've been helpful, and I'll keep this confidential."

"Just don't talk about Hank's connection with Billy Ray," Melvin said.

"I won't." Mark drove away, reviewing the situation. Wow, the pieces are beginning to fit together. Yes indeed--Billy Ray had a motive.

CHAPTER 39

Mark Travis sat by the table of their back patio looking out onto Lori's landscaped yard. The lantana was just beginning to bud and the desert willow was displaying its large pink flowers. His mind was focused, elsewhere. *So what have I really got? Maybe not as much as I thought, not enough to convince Rob.*

Lori came out to join him. "Iced tea?"

"Huh? Oh yeah. Thanks," Mark stood up and pulled a chair over for Lori.

"You look like you're trying to figure something out," Lori said.

"Clues," Mark replied.

"So that's it. Your mind is in the clues' closet," Lori laughed at her own pun.

"Let me guess. You're pondering the mysteries of Billy Ray."

"You think I'm obsessed," Mark said."

"True, but if you've got something new I want to hear it," Lori replied.

Mark recounted his visits with Wynn and Melvin. "Here's what it amounts to. The last time Wynn heard from Hank was six years ago, right before the memorial service for Billy Ray's father. Then Melvin mentioned Hank's affair with Billy Ray's mother, Barbara, something I already knew from Margaret Henshaw and the other two amigas."

"Hank was having an affair with Billy Ray's mother?"

"Yes, and we need to keep that under wraps. Apparently, Hank was sure that Billy Ray was his biological son. Hank told Melvin that he was going to announce that to Billy Ray. "

"That Billy Ray was his son."

"Right, and he was going to do that at the time of the memorial service for Eddie Larson," Mark continued.

Lori listened with interest. "It sounds like bad timing on Hank's part, but something you would expect from a drunk. So Hank was going to walk up to Billy Ray and say 'Billy Ray, I am your father!'"

"I doubt Billy Ray was thrilled to hear that. Hank had wealth as an oil rancher, but he was a drunken sot--not someone Billy Ray would want as a relative," Mark said.

Lori shook the hair from her eyes. "You think Billy Ray killed Hank because of that disclosure? I don't think a jury would buy it."

Mark moved his chair at an angle to face Lori. "Okay, so what is your take on it? I can tell you that Hank's son, Wynn, is a dead ringer for Billy Ray."

"Well, you've been doing your homework; I'll give you that," Lori replied. "I may share some of your suspicions, but I'm still not convinced. Maybe I don't want to be."

"Why?"

"Look at all the good things Billy Ray has been doing. His foundation has brought in a lot of money, and it's going to make a big difference to children. I thought--I hoped that Billy Ray was coming to faith--maybe leaving the warrior-king image behind and becoming a real disciple."

"I think Billy Ray is more than a warrior-king. He's locked into this own darkness," Mark said. "He's a psychotic killer."

Lori reached out for Mark's hand. "Oh my! If you really believe that, you've got to prove it, for Sally Mae's sake if no one else's."

"I'm trying."

Lori picked up her gardening tools and went over to her flower bed. Just then BR came down from a tree after unsuccessfully stalking a squirrel. BR jumped up on Mark's lap with a peculiar Siamese yowl that sounds like the beginning of a conversation.

Mark rubbed the cat's head. "Hey there, BR, maybe you can tell me. You're a stealthy animal, watching and waiting. How would you make a kill and not leave a trace that would be questioned? You wouldn't want to leave blood evidence on your own property, right? So how about doing it at the victim's place? Blood traces from the victim wouldn't be suspicious there, would it, especially on a ranch?"

Mark became aware of Lori struggling with a weed. "I guess a gentleman would volunteer to help you."

Lori laughed. "It's something I enjoy and you don't, but you can keep me company."

"What are those vines you're working with?" Mark asked. "They're all over the ground."

"Asian Jasmine. You described it correctly. They're ground cover."

Mark stood up. "So now, you're covering up the grass I put in."

"I'm just covering up the portion around our bushes. Asian Jasmine stays pretty throughout the year."

"Ground cover--wait a minute," Mark began to pace around the Jasmine, "That's it! That's it! Cucumbers, cucumbers! I think I know …"

"Know what?"

"Where Hank is."

Mark pulled out his cell phone. "José, it's Mark. Is Wynn there with you?"

"No," José replied. "He's out on a picnic with his new girlfriend. I don't expect him back until late."

"Good. I don't want him around--not for this. You and I have some digging to do. Can you find someone else to help?"

"There's a yard worker here whom Wynn and Hiram hired to keep up the place. I guess I can enlist him," José said. "Where are we going to dig?"

"Ask the yard worker if he remembers the spot where those cucumbers started coming up six years ago. That's where we're digging."

"What are we digging for?"

"Maybe nothing. Maybe a body."

One hour later, the three men were busy with their shovels in Hank's garden.

The yard worker remembered the cucumbers, but was less sure of their exact location. The vines had long since dried up. The garden was in an area similar to the foundation of a small house. Mark hoped that they could finish their digging before Wynn came back.

José brought his shovel up. "I think I'm on to something. The ground is somewhat raised here."

Mark went over to dig with José. "Yeah, it looks promising."

"How deep do you think we should dig?" José asked.

"I don't think the killer would have time to go six feet." Mark breathed heavily as he increased his speed, and José matched his effort.

Four feet down José touched something with his shovel. "Whoa!" José backed off from his dig. "I think we need to go slow."

"Find something?"

"Maybe," José carefully spread out the dirt from the spot. "Take a look."

"You found it!" Mark began pulling the dirt away with his hands. Together, they uncovered the white bones of a skeleton clad in overalls. "I'll call the coroner's office. We need to keep the body intact."

"What about the sheriff's office?" José asked.

"Hmm--let's do that later. I don't want too many people here. This investigation started with my office, and I want to follow through."

José leaned on his shovel. "I better not wait too long. Billy Ray's going to be angry if I don't inform him. I'll call Billy Ray when the coroner brings out the body. That way, you'll have a chance for a first look."

After the coroner came, the skeletal remains were carefully lifted up. José called the sheriff's office, and Billy Ray immediately started out for the ranch. Mark, however, instructed the coroner to drive to the lab and followed him there.

José was left looking at the empty grave. Now what? How am I going to explain this to Billy Ray? All that's left is an empty hole. There's nothing here to see. I better call Billy Ray back and...

Something in the dirt of the grave caught the sunlight. José crawled down into the hole to retrieve it. He picked up the small object and stared at it. A brass button with a Texas star! Could this be the sheriff's button? What's it doing in the grave? There has to be some reasonable explanation. I need to hang on to it and think about how to handle this. There's no way that Billy Ray could be involved with the murder.

José placed the button in a small plastic bag and put it in his pocket. Then he took out his cell phone and redirected Billy Ray to the coroner's lab. When he finished his call, he looked up and there was Wynn staring at the open grave. Wynn was now a handsome young man, well dressed and clean--with white teeth thanks to a dentist.

Wynn started to cry. "You found my father, didn't you?"

José put his arm around Wynn. "Yes, Mark Travis thought this might be the place."

"Do we know who did it?"

"Not yet, but it brings us closer," José said.

"I dread calling my brother. Hiram never forgave our father after the divorce when we moved back to mom's home in the Cumberland's. Dad couldn't leave women alone. Mom knew about it, and Dad didn't seem to care. Hiram had a hard time with that. I don't know about the funeral arrangements. Can we bury Dad on the ranch?"

"I'm not sure," José replied.

"What about paying respects, maybe a viewing?"

"There's nothing left after six years," José said.

"Maybe cremation would be better. That way, we can sprinkle his ashes over the garden he loved so much."

"I think that would be a good idea," José held on to Wynn's arm, comforting him.

Wynn started back to the house with José. "You've been a good friend. I'm glad you're here. Well--I guess now I'd better call Hiram. I wouldn't want him to find out from someone else."

Chapter 40

Two days later, José sat in his office staring at the button. *I've got to tell some-body. I can't ignore what I found. Maybe I should tell Mark. He'll know what to do.*

José left his office and drove to Mark's. The secretary greeted him.

"Mark isn't in yet," she said, "but he's on his way. Would you like to wait in his office?"

"Yes, thank you," José replied.

As José waited, he began to have second thoughts. *Once I show him the button, there's no going back. What if Mark goes after Billy Ray? That might be very wrong and I'd be responsible. I should go now and give this some more thought.*

Mark walked in his office just as José started to leave. "Hey José, sorry to keep you waiting. Now that I've got you here, please sit down and have a cup of coffee. I want to talk to you."

"Did you find out anything at the coroner's office?" José asked.

"Yes, Hank's sons were able to identify a small metal plate on Hank's right leg from a tractor accident," Mark said. "As far as the murder weapon was concerned, his skull was fractured from a heavy blow to the head."

"That doesn't sound like a careful plan," José observed.

"No it doesn't. The skull was smashed in from the front, so he was facing the killer."

José closed his eyes and opened them again. "Maybe someone he knew."

"Yeah, and someone very strong. Hank was a big man, not easy to kill. And putting him in that grave took some muscle," Mark noted.

"Where do you think Hank was killed?"

"Probably murdered on the ranch, don't you think? Why else would he be buried in the garden?"

"It's hard to say. It was six years ago," José muttered.

Mark offered José a refill on his coffee. "Was there something you wanted to tell me?"

"Uh, not really--just wanted your thoughts on the investigation."

José got up from his chair and Mark walked to the door with him. "I've spent some time working on this case, José. Maybe we can keep each other informed."

"That would be good," José said as he left.

⅄

A call came in to Billy Ray's office about a drug robbery from the hospital pharmacy. An anonymous tip followed as to a possible location of the suspects, and the deputies went out to investigate. Billy Ray stayed in his office, brooding. The discovery of Hank's remains was too close to home. After a while, he picked up the phone and called the newspaper. When the reporter arrived, Billy Ray gave an official report.

"Obviously, the killer surprised Hank and perhaps used a convenient object, such as a stone or a hammer. My guess is that it was a robber who may have been familiar with the ranch, but thought that Hank was away. It was a horrible act of violence; the killer may have been someone in the vicinity, perhaps someone he knew. However, it all happened a long time ago, and we don't want to alarm our residents."

"Could this have been an act of passion?" the reporter asked.

"Yes, it could," Billy Ray replied. "My thinking is that the person who committed the act did so without planning."

"You say the killer might still be in the vicinity?" the reporter asked.

"I didn't say that," Billy Ray paused. "I said the killer may have been living in the vicinity at the time it happened--someone who knew the ranch."

"Then the killer may still be here," the reporter surmised.

An idea came to Billy Ray. "Well, it's possible, but let's hope not. I'm not ruling anything out."

When the reporter left, Billy Ray looked through his files. Was there someone who might be a logical suspect? I'm glad I kept the shovel. Now it might come in handy. It'll fit the impression of the skull fracture, of course, after I pick the right suspect. The connection has to be a strong one, someone close to him with a motive. Hold it--hold it just a minute! Of course, of course! He was right here in my office.

Billy Ray's thoughts were interrupted with the deputies celebrating in the hallway. They burst into Billy Ray's office with the news.

"We got them! We got them! --evidence and everything!" Allison dumped the hospital drugs marked in plastic bags on Billy Ray's desk. "Look at this haul. There's enough *morphine* to kill fifty people! There's Oxycodone, Hydro-codeine, Percocet and all sorts of good stuff."

"Good job!" Billy Ray said. "I'll lock this stuff up in my office safe. We'll catalog it later for the D.A." Billy Ray held up the vials of morphine with syringes in the same package.

"My aunt was accidentally given an overdose of morphine," Tiffany said. "The doctors thought her respiratory system had shut down--nearly declared her dead."

"How much did she get?" Walt asked.

"About ten milligrams. The nurses got their charts wrong and she got two shots within an hour," Tiffany replied.

"I know morphine is a strong drug, but I didn't know it was that strong," Walt said.

"Well, that's what my aunt told me, and her blood pressure dropped way down.--That stuff can kill you."

Billy Ray listened with interest and then changed the subject. "Who were the robbers who took the drugs?"

Walt laughed. "A husband-and-wife team. Not too smart. He left his bill-fold at the scene. Allison and José are processing the two of them, now."

Billy Ray waited until they left his office, then concealed five vials of morphine and examined one of the empty syringes. *This syringe looks big enough to do the job. It won't do for my Hank Casey situation, but there are others I need to consider. Can morphine be traced in the body? No matter. This stuff will leave no blood evidence, and that's good enough for a burial with my new excavator at the ranch.*

⚘

The memorial service for Hank was held in the chapel of First Baptist. The deputies were in attendance along with Billy Ray. Wynn said a few words of remembrance, but Hiram remained seated in his church pew.

When the service ended, José invited the brothers out to lunch. Wynn accepted, but Hiram declined. "I'm going back to the ranch to get a few items. You two go ahead."

Billy Ray overheard Hiram's remarks and rushed to pick up the shovel at his barn. Then, he drove to Hiram's ranch and walked out into the pasture. When Hiram came out of the house, he waved him to come over.

"I want you to see something," Billy Ray said. "I think I found what might be the murder weapon."

Hiram followed Billy Ray who was carrying a hoe out into the pasture.

"How can that be after six years?"

Billy Ray pointed with his hoe to a shovel in the dirt. "Pick it up and see what you think."

Hiram took the shovel and examined it. "What am I supposed to see? I don't understand…"

Billy Ray pulled out his Colt 44. "Look out! There's a rattlesnake!"

Hiram drew his Ruger Blackhawk. "Where?"

"Coming toward me!" Billy Ray trained his gun as Hiram turned his head.

"I don't…"

Billy Ray fired. Hiram slumped lifelessly to the ground, his pistol falling from his hand. Blood oozed out from his head. Billy Ray wiped the hoe clean, and wrapped Hiram's hands around it to get his fingerprints. Then he put Hiram's pistol in his lifeless hand and squeezed off a shot into the air.

"You missed me, Hiram." Billy Ray laughed, and called Allison on her cell phone.

Allison arrived twenty minutes later with Walt and Tiffany. They stared in disbelief at Hiram's dead body.

"What happened?" Tiffany asked.

Billy Ray paced around the scene like a tiger. "I know it's incredible. I came out here after the funeral to look around for a possible weapon. I had a feeling that the weapon might be something in the barn--something heavy and blunt. When I drove up I saw Hiram out in the pasture digging with a hoe. I don't think he saw me. He seemed startled when I came up on him. I saw the shovel on the ground and was going to ask about it, when he drew his pistol and fired. He missed, and I didn't. It happened very fast."

"Did you call José?" Allison asked.

"No, I thought he was with you," Billy Ray replied.

"He's having lunch with Wynn," Tiffany said.

"Oh no," Billy Ray said sadly. "How am I going to break the news to Wynn?"

"Leave that to us," Walt replied. "It's better not coming from you."

"We'll see if the shovel matches up with the skull impression," Allison said. "You've been through enough. Go home and rest. We'll take it from here."

"I can't believe this," Tiffany said. "First Wynn's father and now his brother. The only real friend Wynn has is José."

Allison roped off the scene with yellow tape. "This murder makes sense when you think about it. We all heard Hiram say that the old man would be better off dead. Maybe it was Hiram's plan that we find Hank's grave. That way half the ranch would be his, free and clear."

"It seems odd after all this time," Walt said. "In another year, Hank could be declared legally dead. Why not wait until then?"

"Who knows?" Tiffany shrugged. "Poor Wynn. I'm glad José is with him."

Billy Ray looked over the scene as he got into his car. No loose ends. Case closed.

CHAPTER 41

The next evening, Mark and Lori read the headlines of The Hood County News: "Sheriff Guns Down Killer" with the sub-text, "Billy Ray Larson solves six-year-old mystery."

Mark held up the newspaper and shook it. "How can anyone be stupid enough to believe this story! After six years, Billy Ray has a sudden inspiration to look for a long lost murder weapon and wouldn't you know it, he found it and shot the killer!"

"Everybody I've talked to thinks it's just wonderful," Lori said. "Billy Ray is the talk of the town. Finally--a good man has come along to save us."

Mark settled into his easy chair. "So--have you finally seen the light about this psycho?"

"Don't worry. Any doubts I had about Billy Ray are gone," Lori said. "I wish I could talk some sense into Sally Mae. She needs to get out of there."

"Sally Mae's going to stand by her man. There's nothing you can do."

"Well, maybe I can…"

The doorbell rang. Mark went to the door and was surprised to see Wynn standing there.

"I--I have to talk to someone," Wynn said. "I started to talk to José, but he's too close to the situation. May I come in?"

Lori peered around Mark and said, "Yes, of course, come in and have a seat. May I get you something to drink?"

"No ma'am, do you mind if we talk?"

"I'll leave you two guys alone."

Lori made a hasty retreat to the bedroom, but Mark followed and blocked her egress. "I need you to come back in."

Lori whispered in his ear. "I'm sure you can handle it."

"I don't know what to say."

"I don't either."

"If you come back in, I'll owe you big time," Mark said.

"It's not a pastoral problem," Lori said.

"Yes it is," Mark said. "This young man needs comfort and so do I."

"Nuts! --Oh, alright, but you take the lead." Lori walked back into the living room with Mark.

"What can we do for you?" Mark asked Wynn.

"None of what the sheriff said made sense to me," Wynn said. "I keep going over and over it. I want to know what you think about it."

"You obviously have some questions," Mark said.

"I know my brother and Dad didn't get along," Wynn said, "but Hiram wouldn't kill him. He's no killer."

"Getting the ranch might be a motive," Mark said.

"Why would Hiram wait six years? --And there's one other thing that's bothering me, Mark. How did *you* know to look in the garden?"

Mark hesitated.

Lori spoke up. "I think it was the cucumbers."

Mark nodded his head in affirmation. "Yes, I got suspicious when I learned about the cucumbers. It sounded like somebody was trying to lay a ground cover."

"Cucumbers? Hey, that's right. I was the one who told you about it," Wynn said. "That makes sense. Thanks for putting it together."

"What do you want me to do?" Mark asked.

"I'm asking you to find out what really happened," Wynn said.

Mark paused for longer than comfortable, so Lori spoke up again. "Are you asking Mark to investigate the sheriff?"

"Well, I don't know. The sheriff's story doesn't make sense to me. What do you think?" Wynn asked Lori.

"I think Mark would have to be careful about an official investigation. You don't want people to know that they're under surveillance." Lori said. "Evidence could be destroyed."

"Hmm. It seems to me that you're something more than a minister, ma'am. You make more sense than most preachers I know."

Mark leaned over closer to Wynn. "So let's do it on an unofficial basis. We would have to keep quiet about it. Can you do that?"

"Yes sir."

"One thing for sure--we can't include José on this," Lori said. "He's not in a position to investigate his own office."

"I'd like to know what he thinks," Wynn replied. "José is a good friend."

"Please leave José completely out of it," Mark said. "I'm not going to do this unless you promise that."

Wynn frowned. "Would I be putting José in danger?"

"I don't know. Just don't discuss the case with him," Mark said. "Agreed?"

"Okay, I promise."

Mark observed Wynn closely as he walked to the door. Huh! It's like watching twins, the good one and the evil one.

When they were alone again, Lori had a question for Mark. "Tell me something detective, just where and how are you going to investigate?"

"What do you mean?"

"It seems to me you've turned over every stone and knocked on every door possible. There's nothing left to investigate," Lori surmised. "Am I wrong?"

Mark scratched his head. "No, I'm afraid you're right. I don't want to give Wynn false hope. Maybe I can work it from another angle. I'll let out little pieces of information I already have and create some dissonance for Billy Ray."

"Just what information are you going to put out," Lori asked, "that Billy Ray could be Wynn's brother and that his brother murdered his father?"

"No that would be stupid. Wynn would confront Billy Ray for sure."

Lori stood up like a trial lawyer. "Well, then let's think about this. What other bits of info can you release? How about Alice Evans believing that Billy Ray killed Dr. Evans?"

"You know very well I can't do that either. Let me think about this."

"I thought that's what we're doing," Lori responded.

"You're painting me into a corner. All my options look stupid."

"Exactly," Lori sat down, resting her case.

Mark spoke directly into Lori's ear. "So what are your thoughts, smarty?"

Lori thought of racquetball. "Just do something that keeps the ball in play. Don't go for a kill shot right away. Get set up for it."

"As soon as I figure out what that means, I'll do it," Mark backed off and changed the analogy. "Okay, so it's *not* time to lay down my cards. One play at a time, right?"

Lori stretched and yawned. "Something like that. It's been an interesting evening, but it's time for bed. Good night, detective."

"Good night, pastor."

CHAPTER 42

José knew that Wynn would expect him to have first-hand information about his brother. Before lunch time, José took off early and went to see the coroner. The coroner, Frank Garner, was surprised to see José. "I just completed a detailed report on Hiram Casey and sent it to the sheriff. I have nothing more to show you."

"Tell me about the gun," José asked. "Was it loose in his hand?"

"Not exactly. His hand was closed around it, but it wasn't a death grip."

"Could you tell if he fired a shot?"

"There was gun powder residue on his hand," Frank said. "Why are you asking this? You can get my full report from the sheriff."

"You've told me what I wanted to know," José said and left to drive back to his office.

The coroner watched as José pulled out of the driveway. After a few minutes, he dialed Billy Ray and described his conversation with José.

"You say he asked about the gun," Billy Ray flexed his fist, "about the dead man holding it?"

"Yes," the coroner replied. "He seemed interested in whether the hand was open or closed. I told him the gun was loosely held."

"Good," Billy Ray said. "I'm glad you told him exactly what happened."

"Maybe I shouldn't have bothered you with this. It just seemed odd," the coroner said. "I hope I didn't get José in trouble."

"No, not at all. I want my deputies to feel free to ask questions. I appreciate your call," Billy Ray hung up the phone down and sat back at his desk. I've got to be careful on this one. I don't want José to feel skittish. I want him relaxed like a steer prepared for market. I'll pretend to be like Lyle Richards, friendly and available with nothing to hide.

That afternoon, Billy Ray asked José to come to his office. José came in holding two cups of coffee.

"I'm glad you like my coffee," José said.

Billy Ray smiled. "You do great work. Close the door. I have some personal stuff I need to talk about. I've lost a lot of sleep these past few days."

"You're thinking about the gun fight with Hiram Casey?" José asked.

"I can't get it out of my mind. I keep going over and over it, wondering if I could have done something differently. It's wearing me down."

"I know exactly how you feel," José said. "Five years ago I had to kill a woman in a gun fight. It was horrible. I couldn't stop thinking about it."

"How did you get over it?"

"I finally got a prescription from my family doctor. It helped me feel less anxious," José said.

"I hate to ask, but do you have any of that stuff left? I know I could go to a doctor and ask for it."

"I guess there's no harm in giving you the ones I have left," José answered. "That way if it helps, you can call your doctor for more."

"I would really be grateful," Billy Ray said. "Is there anything I can do for you?"

"Well, I don't know. I'm worried about Wynn, Hiram's brother," José said. "Wynn and I have become very good friends. I know he's hurting. He's going to ask for details about the shooting."

Billy Ray pulled out a file from his desk drawer. "I have the report right here. You can show him this if you like."

"No, I went by the coroner's office today and got some information that I think will make things easier for Wynn," José said. "For one thing, it was obvious that Hiram fired it."

"I'm glad you're good friends with Wynn," Billy Ray said. "Please keep me advised on how things are going with him. If there are any other details I can provide let me know."

Billy Ray watched as José left. Well, that changes things. I don't have to kill him, at least not right away. And I can use that prescription thing he's giving me as a turning point in my life. I'll pretend to take the pills, and start going back to church and Bible study to emphasize it. That way any lingering suspicions about the Hiram shooting will go away. Of course, I need to stay away from Wynn. I don't want to be pressed for details.

⸺

For the next several weeks Billy Ray settled into his more subdued way of life. Lyle was glad to hear about the prescription therapy and the church-going Billy Ray. Sally Mae was less sure, but grateful for any sign of positive change. Billy Ray poured on the charm, shook hands constantly at church, and wore a smile as big as the Joker's.

Mark, however, saw this charm campaign as a possible opportunity for turning the tables on Billy Ray. A few days later, he had lunch with Wynn, who was impatient for information. Halfway through their meal, Wynn put down his fork. "I'm hoping you have something helpful to tell me."

Hmm, maybe I should have run this by Lori, but it works, it will keep the ball in play. "Wynn, what I'm about to say may seem absurd, but it could be a game changer."

"I don't have anyone else to turn to," Wynn said. "You're it."

Mark consumed the last bite of his hamburger. "Here's the deal. It may be risky, but I think you need to rattle Billy Ray's cage. Billy Ray has started going back to church and Bible study. That's where you need to be."

"Are you kidding?"

"Not at all," Mark replied. "Think about it. How would you feel if you were Billy Ray? There you are suddenly faced with Hiram's brother twice a week?"

"Are you thinking that Billy Ray murdered Hiram?"

"Well, if he didn't, then there's no harm done with your going to church."

Wynn stopped eating his lunch. "What if he did?"

"That's an hypothesis I want to test, if you're willing to help. I believe that Billy Ray has set a course for himself. He wants to be seen as a nice guy, with nothing to hide. His plan calls for going to church twice a week. If he's guilty, then you're the last person he wants to see. Just your being there can put the screws to him. Sit behind him at church. Sit right across from him at Bible study and make eye contact."

"It's going to feel weird going to church by myself," Wynn said.

"Take a girlfriend. She'll love our church."

"Do I have to join?"

"No."

"Okay, it sounds crazy to me," Wynn said, "but I don't have a better idea. When should I start?"

"Next Sunday. Bible study is on Wednesday."

"Huh. That's a lot of religion."

"Stick to it and always smile when you talk to Billy Ray. That's *his* strategy and it's time someone used it on him."

Mark picked up the check. "You know, maybe I'll go to Bible study too--give Billy Ray a double whammy."

That night, Lori was caught off guard when Mark told her about his plan. "You told Wynn what!"

"Yeah, I know. I should have discussed it with you before," Mark said. "But, if it's going to work, then it needs to be done soon."

"Well, that's just great. It's hard enough preaching every Sunday without some plot going on right in front of me."

Mark hung down his head. "I'm sorry."

"No, you're not--but don't feel bad. I have a little surprise for you too."

"What?"

"I bought season tickets to the ballet at TCU. Guess who's going with me?"

"Me? This is cruel and unusual punishment!"

"Your sentence will be carried out immediately, beginning next Saturday night."

"Well, at least I won't feel so bad about what I've set up at church."

"Getting back to Wynn, your plan worries me. What if it puts Wynn in jeopardy?" Lori asked.

"I thought about that," Mark said. "I told Wynn that it's risky, but Billy Ray is crazy, not stupid. There would be too many coincidences with Hank, Hiram and then Wynn killed too."

"You need to go to Bible study and keep an eye on it," Lori said.

"Wow, first the ballet and then Bible study!"

"Well?"

"Yeah, I'll go to both." Ha! She doesn't know that I'm already planning on Bible study.

Lori patted him on the chest. "Good boy."

Chapter 43

The next Sunday morning, Billy Ray and Sally Mae came in early to take their seats in the middle pew of the semi-circle auditorium. Sally Mae turned to see the unfamiliar couple who had moved in directly behind them.

"My goodness," Sally Mae addressed the woman of the new couple. "You must be visitors. I know that because I certainly would have remembered your husband. He bears a striking resemblance to mine."

"So I've been told," Wynn responded. "I'm Wynn Casey and my lady friend is Crystal Brighton."

"It's a pleasure having you here. We hope you like our church. I'm Sally Mae Larson, and this is my husband, Billy Ray."

Billy Ray turned around, slowly. "We've met, but I don't think Sally Mae has. I'm sorry if this is awkward."

"Not at all," Wynn responded. "Crystal is a Presbyterian so we're just shopping for a church."

"How nice," Sally Mae said. "Crystal, how long have you been a Presbyterian?"

"Ever since I was a little girl," Crystal said. "I moved here from Chicago a few months ago. I'm an RN at Lake Granbury Medical Center."

Sally Mae turned to Wynn. "What was your name again?"

"It's Wynn, Wynn Casey."

"Any relationship to ... oh, oh my," Sally Mae turned helplessly to Billy Ray.

"I'm Hiram's brother. It's okay. I'm slowly getting over it. Terrible things happen, and we have to go on," Wynn said.

"I'm so proud of Wynn," Crystal said. "He's such a loving and forgiving man."

Billy Ray turned to face Wynn. "I can't tell you how sorry--"

"No need," Wynn said. "We'll have lunch sometime and talk about it."

Billy Ray's face turned red. "That would be fine."

For the rest of the service, Billy Ray shifted positions and fidgeted with his bulletin. Now what? Not likely a coincidence, but I can't let Wynn bother me. If they're back next Sunday, we'll wait until they're seated and then sit some place else.

The Wednesday night Bible study, however, proved an even more difficult situation for Billy Ray. Everyone took an instant liking to Crystal, a graceful young woman whose silky brunette hair and slender features resembled that of a ballerina. Sally Mae and Crystal especially hit it off and seemed oblivious to the strain between Billy Ray and Wynn who sat across the table from each other. The subject of the study was from Luke 16:19-31 on the parable of the rich man who refused to help the poor man, Lazarus.

Lori read the passage and then summarized. "And so the poor man remained a poor man and when he died, was carried off to heaven. The rich man went to hell."

"So I guess it's better not to be rich," Mike concluded.

"Well," Lori answered, "I think it was Martin Luther King, Jr. who said that the rich man didn't go to hell because he was rich. The rich man went to hell because he didn't care."

"If we have a lot money and don't share it, then we're like the rich man who went to hell," Betty concluded.

"What does this say about the millions of poor people in the United States," Wynn said. "Are we liable for that?"

"I don't think God judges nations like that," Zeb said.

"I disagree," Sally Mae said. "Look at the judgment of the nations in Matthew 25. It was the nations who were judged for not clothing the naked or feeding the hungry."

"We discussed that passage in Matthew before and got nowhere," Mike objected. "God judges individuals, not nations."

Crystal looked at Matthew 25:32 in her Bible. "It seems clear to me. 'All nations will be gathered before him.'"

"I read it different from your interpretation," Mike joined in. "We are a nation of individuals each with an opportunity to become rich. In America, the poor are poor because of their own laziness."

"I would like to think our nation is more compassionate than that," Crystal said.

"So would I," Sally Mae said. "There's no question that God judges both individuals and nations. The policies that we support for the poor in our nation are certainly a matter of morality."

"Sally, you are just a bleeding heart liberal," Zeb said.

Sally Mae laughed. "Well, at least I'm not so hard-hearted that I can't bleed a little."

Lori turned the pages of her Bible. "Jesus talks quite a bit about the poor. Let's look at some of those passages."

The discussion continued enthusiastically with most of the class enjoying it. Wynn for a moment forgot why he was there and studied the passages. Crystal and Sally Mae stuck up for the poor and poked fun at the hard-hearted ones who softened up at the end of the discussion. Billy Ray remained silent.

Lori concluded the meeting with a prayer and then said, "Our next lesson is from Genesis 4:1-16, Cain and Abel. I also want to give you a heads up. My husband, Mark, wants to start coming to Bible study. Any objections? I know he's old--approaching forty."

Mike waved his hands in protest. "Forty! If we start letting old guys like this in, we'll have to change our name to the Geezer Class!"

"Is he going to participate or just sit there?" Betty asked.

"I'll tell him that he's on probation," Lori laughed with the others.

Billy Ray was not laughing. What's going on here? Mark's never been to Bible study. Why now? Have I overlooked something? How did he know where to find Hiram's body? Stay cool. I need to focus on what I'm doing now.

⅄

The next Sunday the congregation celebrated Communion. Billy Ray stood outside the large white doors waiting to see where Wynn and Crystal would sit. However, when Sally Mae saw Crystal, the two started chatting. Billy Ray tried to retrieve Sally Mae, but she ignored him. Then Rex and Celesta Barkley arrived, and Sally Mae took Celesta aside. Billy Ray looked blankly at Rex, remembering their counseling sessions.

"Celesta, Crystal and I are talking about going to the Monet exhibit in Fort Worth and then shopping afterwards. What's your schedule like on Thursday or would Friday be better?"

"Thursday's good. I'd like to keep Friday open for racquetball," Celesta said.

"Okay. I'll pick you gals up around ten Thursday morning," Sally Mae said.

"Hey, Sally Mae, instead of that, maybe we could meet you at your ranch. I'd like to see it," Crystal looked at Celesta who nodded in agreement.

"You'll love their ranch," Celesta said. "You should see what Sally Mae has done for the house and the landscaping."

Billy Ray's hopes of moving away from Wynn and Rex faded as Crystal motioned Sally Mae and Celesta to sit with them. The three men followed behind them.

Communion proceeded with the bread and the cups passed down the aisles. "The peace of Christ," Sally Mae said as she passed the cup tray to Crystal. Crystal gave the same greeting to Celesta and then Rex repeated it to Billy Ray.

Billy Ray mumbled, "The peace of Christ be with you," as he passed the tray to Wynn.

"And also with you," Wynn said.

Billy Ray's nerves were on edge. There is no peace with Sally Mae. She's forced me into a nest of vipers. I need a way out--an exit ramp to get back on my own pathway.

Chapter 44

At their ranch, Billy Ray sat across from Sally Mae at the dinner table. He had limited his conversation with her after she enlisted Lyle Richards to control his drinking.

"Sally Mae, uh, I have a favor to ask--if you don't mind," Billy Ray said.

"Well, well, he talks," Sally Mae said.

"I'm sorry. I realize I've behaved badly."

Sally Mae tossed her napkin onto the table. "So now that you want something, you're speaking. You know, I didn't get married to give up talking."

"It's been a difficult time for me. This Hiram thing ..."

"Yeah, I guess I should be more sympathetic."

"It's just this business of seeing Wynn every Sunday," Billy Ray said.

"So what is it you want?"

"I know it's a lot to ask, but could you talk to Wynn's girlfriend, Crystal?"

"And say what?" Sally Mae asked.

"That we can't be friends with them because it's so hard for me."

"Let me think now--whose problem is this? Is it Crystal's? Nope. Wynn's? Nope. Mine? Nope. Yours? Yep. So if you want something said, you do it. I'm not going to."

"Wouldn't you be willing to give up your friendship with Crystal--for my sake?"

"Nope--and I'm going to continue sitting next to her and Wynn at church," Sally Mae said.

222

"Why?"

"I think Wynn has been wonderfully forgiving of you, Billy Ray. I'm sad that you don't realize and accept that. It's just as important to accept forgiveness as it is to give it. Maybe God is trying to teach you a lesson."

"I'm just not able to--"

"Let me tell you something," Sally Mae broke in. "You need to think about this and stop your whining. People at church are inspired seeing you sit next to Wynn. Margaret Henshaw said that when we took Communion, it reminded her of "Places in the Heart." You should take pride in it and give thanks to God." Sally Mae stood up from the table. "I'm going for a moonlight stroll. You can come with me or not."

Billy Ray continued to sit, staring into the empty room. I didn't get married to be controlled by you, Sally Mae. Here's how it's going to be. You're either a helpmate or a nuisance. I've got no use for an attractive nuisance.

When Bible study came the following Wednesday evening. Sally Mae, Celesta, and Crystal sat together making plans for a second outing to a musical performance at the Granbury Opera House. As advertised, Mark was also there with his Bible. Lori laid out the familiar story of Cain and Abel from the fourth chapter of Genesis.

"So the two brothers made offerings to God, but God found more favor with Abel's offering," Lori began. "It's a sad story. Cain was angry, apparently feeling that God loved Abel more than him."

"Well, I can see why," Zeb said.

"I can't," Mike said. "God was in conversation with Cain the whole time. Cain was just jealous. There was no reason to think that God loved him less because of one offering."

"I've seen people at church do the same thing," Betty remarked. "One gets jealous because another gets praised."

Mark knew he had to say something. "Well, not to the point of killing each other."

"I'm interested in the brother's keeper question," Crystal said.

"Okay, let's look at that," Lori said. "After Cain killed Abel, God spoke to Cain: 'Where is your brother Abel?' Cain replied, 'I do not know; am I my brother's keeper?'"

Zeb took up playing the devil's advocate. "I agree with Cain! There has to be a line drawn. Am I responsible for everybody else? Isn't self-responsibility enough?"

"But, in this passage, self-responsibility includes responsibility for others," Celesta countered. "That's the whole point."

"Nah, you take responsibility for yourself. I'll take responsibility for me," Zeb said.

"You don't really believe that," Betty laughed at Zeb. "I've seen you donating clothing and food at the People Helping People store."

Mike nudged Zeb with his elbow. "Zeb, you are so busted!"

Billy Ray raised his head up. "Cain was an evil person. He was given the mark of Cain."

Wynn looked closely at the passage. "If I'm reading this correctly, Cain was given his mark *not* because he was evil, but for protection from those who wanted to pay him back."

"That's right," Sally Mae agreed. "Look at the passage. After Cain was banished, he was worried that someone might kill him for what he did. God said 'Not so! Whoever kills Cain will suffer a sevenfold vengeance.'"

Wynn continued the reading. "And the Lord put a mark on Cain, so that no one who came upon him would kill him."

"Wow, it *was* for protection," Mike said. "I never realized that. I thought it was a mark of evil."

"This passage gives a different view of God than some people have," Crystal concluded. "God cares about us even when our own evil gets us into trouble."

"Even when one brother kills the other." Wynn's eyes locked onto Billy Ray's.

The discussion continued until Lori summarized with a final thought. "I find it interesting that Cain was *not* given a punishment greater than he could bear. Instead Cain went on to build a city. After that he became the forefather of a distinguished family line including Jubal, who was 'the ancestor of all those who play the lyre and pipe.' There was joy in that family tradition despite its terrible beginning."

"So what God really wants is not vengeance, but restoration and redemption," Crystal said.

"Wow!" Wynn traced the passage with his fingers.

"Thank you, Crystal" Lori said. "You just gave us a great ending for this study."

Wynn waited until everyone was leaving and then approached Lori and Mark, "I wonder if you two would meet me at lunch tomorrow?"

Mark nodded in agreement and Lori replied, "Okay, let's meet at the Bistro on the Square at one o'clock. Most people leave by then, so we can find a quiet place to talk."

Mark touched Wynn's shoulder. "I'm not sure I have anything new to report."

"That's not why I want to meet," Wynn replied. "I've been doing a lot of thinking--and praying."

Lori rubbed her hands together. Why shouldn't he tell us now? I'm dying to hear what he has to say. --But, Crystal's waiting. Okay, it'll keep until tomorrow.

CHAPTER 45

The Bistro was a good choice for a private conversation. The location was right on the street side of the square. From the big window of the restaurant, they could see the stone court house with traffic driving by and cars parked alongside the curb.

"Thanks for meeting with me," Wynn turned to the waiter. "I want the check."

"You don't have to do that," Mark said.

"What you've done for me--and Crystal, too--can't be paid back with a lunch," Wynn said. "I had no idea what the church would mean to us."

"That Crystal is special," Mark said. "So what are you learning about Billy Ray?"

"I learned that anyone going to church with someone as wonderful as Sally Mae can't be all bad," Wynn said. "More importantly, I also gained a new perspective. I have to trust God to take care of Hiram. I was eaten up inside thinking about it--going over and over the shooting. As far as Billy Ray is concerned, I've lost my desire to pursue it."

Mark scooted his chair closer to Wynn's. "Let's think about this, Wynn. We may be on the verge of solving a murder here."

"I'm going to leave that with you," Wynn said. "I don't know what happened with Hiram, but I don't think Billy Ray is a murderer. I'm ready to move on. Lori, your Bible study has helped me, enormously. I can't spend the rest of my life obsessed with fantasies of vengeance."

"It's not a question of vengeance," Mark said. "There may be more killings than just one."

"What other killings?" Wynn asked.

"Uh, I can't say right now."

"I don't see how I'm helping. Unless you can be more specific, I don't think I'm doing any good for me or anyone else. I'm dropping it."

"So are you going to stop going to church and Bible study?" Lori asked.

Wynn reached over to Lori's hand. "No ma'am, just the opposite. Crystal and I want to join the church. We are doubly blessed by what we've found, and we hope you'll accept us as members."

Lori stood up and hugged Wynn. "I'm so happy to hear this! I would love to have you in our membership class. You can go now or after you've joined."

"We want to join now, and you can bet that we'll go to the classes," Wynn said.

"Wonderful, just wonderful," Lori squeezed Wynn's hand and sat back down.

Mark smiled for another reason. *Now that Wynn is joining the church, Billy Ray's paranoia will go out of sight. Wynn is helping more than he knows.*

Lori nodded toward the window. "Is that the sheriff's car parked outside? I think it's Billy Ray."

Wynn waved to the driver, and the car pulled back onto the street. "Well, I don't know. The windows are tinted."

Mark watched as the car sped to the corner. *Huh! If that was Billy Ray, I wonder what he thought about our meeting together. I wonder.*

λ

That following Friday evening, Sally Mae, Celesta, and Crystal attended a performance of "Ghost" at the Opera House. Billy Ray sat on his porch whittling on a block of wood with a bucket of beer chilling on ice. *Sally Mae didn't know about these beers I've been hiding in the barn. I can't let the tail wag the dog for too much longer. I need a plan--uh, what in the hell?!*

A trail of dust erupted as Wynn drove into the driveway with his new yellow jeep. He mounted the stairs of the porch and noticed the bucket. "Say, how about sharing some of that beer while the gals are at the theater?"

"Uh, why not? Pull up a chair." Oh God, now he's on my ranch! What's he up to?

"Man, that sunset is beautiful, isn't it," Wynn said.

"Yeah, good sunset." Billy threw his empty bottle out on the yard. "Did you enjoy lunch with Mark and Lori?"

"So it *was* you who stopped by," Wynn said.

"Were my ears burning?" Billy Ray opened another beer.

"I was discussing joining the church," Wynn said.

Billy Ray gagged on the beer and spit it out over the rail. "Well, uh, good for you."

"Crystal and I are really happy about it."

"Crystal's a hot babe...You gonna marry her or just shack up?"

Wynn lowered his beer. "Crystal's a fine woman."

"Yeah, yeah," Billy Ray's head began to sag. "So what are you really here for?"

"I was reading the Bible about making things right," Wynn said. "I think it's time we talked."

"So talk."

"I've stopped thinking about Hiram," Wynn said. "I know what happened was an accident or something. At this point, I just want to tell you--"

"Tell me what? That uh, that I'm your brother's keeper, or uh, ha! Your brother's killer? It had to be done, no choice--none at all, none, none."

"I want to let it go," Wynn said.

Billy Ray wiped the dribble off his face. "Then why are you here reminding me of the whole damn thing?"

"I want to tell you that my heart is broken over Hiram, but no matter what happened, I forgive you," Wynn said.

Billy Ray put down his bottle and looked hard at Wynn. "Get off my porch."

"What?"

"I said get the hell off my ranch and don't come back, you lying piece of cow dung!"

"I'm not lying. I came here to forgive you."

Billy Ray stood up and staggered toward Wynn. "You think, uh, you think you've got this whole thing figured out. Well, you don't! Now, get off my ranch and stay off."

"I'm going. I'm sorry. I didn't want it to end this way."

"OUT!" Billy Ray threw a bottle after him, and then collapsed back into his chair laughing. At least he left his beer. I'll finish it for him.

⌁

When Sally Mae came home from the Opera House, it was 11 p.m., and Billy Ray was asleep on the porch. "Shouldn't you be in bed?" Sally Mae stumbled over a bottle. "Oh no. Not again!"

"Yeah and I told that Wynn to get off my ranch and stay off. I, uh, I told him real good!"

"Well, I'm leaving too, Billy Ray. I'll be staying in town for a few days."

Billy Ray tried to get up, but fell back into his chair. "Aw, you'll be back."

"Don't count on it. You need help, Billy Ray, and I can't give it to you."

Billy Ray struggled to his feet and lunged awkwardly at Sally Mae. "Gonna lock up the sheriff and throw away the key!"

"Stay away from me!" Sally Mae dropped the clothes she was packing and ran out to her car.

"Go on, bitch. Stay away as long as you like! Say hello to Kyle Richards for me!"

The gravel flew up in the air as Sally Mae drove away.

Chapter 46

Billy Ray staggered to his bedroom and tripped over his own feet as he fell into bed. He woke up the next morning and started kicking furniture. Sally Mae's needle-point chair went sailing across the room and crashed into the wall. What am I going to do? I can't take it anymore. I've got to do something! O God, help your warrior. I need a plan--but what kind of a plan? I can't kill everybody, at least not at once. Calm down, Billy Ray, and think! Think. Maybe preparation, a contingency plan. Something for the future. Yes, I have that within my grasp.

Billy Ray walked out of the house to the barn. I'll call it the "Billy Ray Pre-burial Plan." No more killing on impulse. If there's a killing that needs doing--and I got one in mind--I'll be ready.

He climbed onto his excavator and bumped across the pasture until he came to a place covered with poison oak. Now, this is the perfect place for it, and I'm not allergic. Come to think about, Sally Mae's not either--not that that would make much difference, if she's the one that needs doing. Am I far enough away from the house? Yeah, yeah, pretty close to a mile. I'll make an extra large hole this time and conceal it with sagebrush. Hey, this is great, isn't it? Just great. It's wonderful how good you feel when you're prepared. I'll top it off with a refreshing shower and some Old Spice.

Billy Ray arrived at his office shaved and groomed for the day. His head hurt, so he took a Tylenol and chased it down with José's coffee. Tiffany came into his office.

"Boss, what about those street lights for our parking lot?" Tiffany asked.

Billy Ray tapped his pen on the desk. "What about them?"

"They're still out," Tiffany replied. "For our night shift, that parking lot is pitch black."

"If you're afraid of getting mugged, get them fixed. You can call maintenance just like I can."

"It might be done sooner if you called," Tiffany said, as she started back toward the door.

"Disguise your voice. Tell them it's me," Billy Ray laughed. "It's not that big a deal. The lights are only needed for a short time. The night shift is over at eleven when dispatch takes over. Anyway, José and I are covering it tonight so you have time to get them fixed tomorrow."

"Okay, I guess I'm stuck with the call," Tiffany sighed.

Billy Ray watched her leave. Nice curves, but a whiner. I've got nothing but whiners. Disrespectful whiners. That reminds me. I've need to check on Sally Mae; can't let her get ahead of me.

Billy Ray picked up the phone, punched in the speed dial for Sally Mae, and received a bland 'hello' at the other end. "Are you coming home tonight, Sally Mae?"

"Not for a few days. I need to do some thinking. By the way, the name's not Sally Mae any more, it's *Sally*."

"Sally, huh? Well, that's fine, Sally Mae--oh, I mean 'Sally.' I've got the night shift anyway. Let me know when you're coming home. I may have a little surprise for you."

Sally was glad to hear that Billy Ray was on the night shift. It would give her the time she needed to drive out to the ranch and get her things.

⅄

After lunch, José sat at his desk with a zip-lock bag in his hand. He took out the Lone Star button and examined it. It was the Texas star with a red ring around it, just like Billy Ray's. "Ah hell," José said aloud. "I'm tired of looking at it--need to get it off my desk."

José walked over to Billy Ray's office. "I have something to give you. I'm sorry I'm late in doing it."

"What are you talking about?"

"This thing," José placed the plastic bag on Billy Ray's desk.

Billy Ray stared at the Lone Star button. "Where did you find this?"

José remained standing. "In Hank Casey's grave. I don't know how it got there."

A knot formed in Billy Ray's throat. "I don't either."

"I trust you, Sheriff. I know you had nothing to do with Hank's murder, so I'm leaving it with you."

"You've kept this button all this time without saying a word to anyone?" Billy Ray asked. "I'm surprised you did that."

"No one knows except us. It's in your hands now." José walked to the door. "I don't want to see it again."

Don't worry. You won't. I have a wonderful pre-burial plan just for you--all paid up--but I can't be careless with the details. Okay, Sally Mae's not home, the parking lot will soon be dark, and I have the morphine. There won't be blood. He got up from his desk and flushed the button down the toilet.

♠

The days were growing shorter. Darkness came after six o'clock. The other deputies went home, and only Billy Ray and José remained. At seven, Billy Ray stood in the doorway of José's office. "José, I'm sorry. Sally Mae just called and I need to go home. Can you manage here?"

"No problem," José replied.

Billy Ray went out, but as soon as he entered the parking lot, he placed a call back to the office. "José, we've got a problem here. Can you meet me by my truck?"

"I'll be right there." José ran out into the parking lot and headed toward Billy Ray's truck. As he approached, Billy Ray stepped from behind, extended his metal club, and delivered a carefully placed blow to the base of his skull. José fell to the ground unconscious. "Good," Billy Ray said, "no blood."

Billy Ray shoved his club back into its shaft, and looked around for watchers. Seeing none, he knelt beside José and injected him with a syringe loaded with morphine. If my rabbit punch didn't kill you, that should do the trick. Only the best for you, José. Next comes the funeral procession with the dignity you deserve.

He loaded the body into the back of his pickup, looped a rope through José's belt and secured it on a hitch in the truck. Then he covered the body with a tarp and called to José as he drove to the ranch. "You like the ranch, don't you José? You've been there enough. Sally Mae may join you later when she finally comes home to stay. You'll make a charming couple."

Chapter 47

Sally drove out to the ranch to get her things. I have plenty of time. It's seven o'clock now, and Billy Ray won't be home until eleven. Hmm, just to be on the safe side, maybe I'd better call Celesta to let her know what I'm doing.

Sally gave a command to her car's blue tooth, "Call Celesta." The speaker answered, "No phone is available." Oh no, I left the phone at Plantation Inn. Well, I'm at the ranch gate now, and I don't want to go back. It won't take me long to get my stuff. I don't see his truck--should be okay.

Sally was about to go into the house, when she noticed lights moving in the pasture. Are those neighbor kids hunting wild pigs again? I'll need to call their parents. I better check first to make sure. It's too far to walk and too rough for the car. I'll take my golf cart; it's tough enough.

Sally approached the place where she had seen the lights. Hmm, I don't think it's the kids. A worker maybe, but at this hour? Then the small headlights of her golf cart fell on the back of the pickup with Billy Ray lifting up José's body.

Billy Ray released José who fell back into the truck with a thud. "Well-ll, hello, Sally Mae. So glad you can join us. Your timing is perfect. I'm sure José will welcome your company."

At first Sally was too stunned to move, but then she recoiled in horror when she saw the open grave by the truck. She swung the golf cart around and headed back toward the house. If only I had my cell phone!

Billy Ray laughed. "How far do you think you're going to get with that electric buggy? You're wasting my time, Sally Mae. It's all over."

Billy Ray casually climbed into the truck's cab and then moved quickly across a heavier patch of rocks to head her off at the house. The truck lurched up and down with a loud bang as one of his tires blew out. *Damn!* Billy Ray kept going with the bare rim scraping across the ground. He could still cut her off at the house and her car in the driveway.

Sally changed course and headed to the barn. She had a better angle than Billy Ray and got there first. With all her strength, she pulled open the large barn doors and then swung them closed again. There was a brace on the inside to keep the horses in. She fastened it. That's not going to stop him for long. What can I do now? I could go up into the loft, but what good would that do? There's a window to jump out of, but he can easily intercept me on the ground. The front loader! She looked in the cab. Damn, no key.

Billy Ray peered through a knot hole in the barn door. "I'm here, Sally Mae."

"It's *Sally*," she shouted as she threw cow dung at the knot hole.

Billy Ray wiped the dung from his eyes. "That's not nice. If you want the front loader, then come on out and I'll give you the key. --Let's see, how am I going to get in. Oh, I know. I have a sledge hammer in the truck."

As Billy Ray went back to the truck, Sally moved quickly. She took off her dress, stuck a shovel in the ground toward the back of barn, and draped her dress around it. The dress was barely visible but could still be seen. She then ran back to the front, grabbed a pitchfork and waited in the dark.

"I'll give you to the count of ten," Billy Ray said. "One, two--aw never mind." Billy Ray smashed open the doors with his sledge hammer. His eyes fell on the dress. "Hah! That's a pretty dress. I'll make it quick. Just one blow and …"

In one motion, a half naked Sally moved directly in front of Billy Ray and thrust the pitchfork deep into his left side. Billy Ray fell to the ground, blood running from his nostrils. He tried to speak. "I--I don't understand. How could you--uh--be--"

"Be what?" Sally knelt beside him.

"--two places at the same time? O God, it--it hurts."

Sally held his hand, then backed away as he struggled for his last breath. "I'm sorry for the pain."

Billy Ray was dead.

With tears running down her cheeks, she took the front loader keys from Billy Ray's pocket. She started the engine, swung the loader down to the ground, and scooped up Billy Ray. The front loader slowly bumped its way across the pasture with the scoop angled upwards so that the body would not be lost.

"Oh my darling quarterback," Sally whispered. "How I wish it could have been otherwise. I *can't* let people know how you died. Your reputation would be damaged and so would your foundation. You understand, don't you?"

Sally dropped Bill Ray in the hole he previously dug and said a prayer. "Lord, you know how to handle this. I don't. I don't understand at all why Billy Ray could not turn to you and come to faith. But, you know all things, and I commend Billy Ray to your keeping. Forgive me for the way I'm doing it."

For a moment, she thought she saw José looking at her, but dismissed it as her imagination. Sally scooped up the dirt around the grave and filled the hole. Maybe I can build a gazebo on top of this--something to commemorate his passing without people knowing about it. In the meantime, the crimson fall color of the poison oak is lovely. Now what am I going to do with José's body?

Sally went to the back of the truck and tenderly wiped the sweat from José's brow. Wait a minute! Sweat? Are you alive José? Really?

She saw movement from José's arms and legs. Yes! I need to take you to a hospital, but how am I going to explain all this? Sally drove the pickup to her car. "I don't think you'll remember much of this, José. Maybe that's just as well. Can you stand on your feet?" She staggered with him to her car and stretched him out on her back seat. "José, if you can hear me, I'll be right back."

She went into the house, took a quick shower, and dressed. As she drove José to the hospital, she talked out loud. "What am I going to say to the doctors? I've got to come up with something. Where should I say that I found you?"

Sally looked at him in her rearview mirror. "Can you hear me, José?"

"Uh, uh, ohh--Sheriff's parking lot."

"I can barely hear you, José. Sheriff's parking lot? Is that where I should say you were?"

"Yes." José drifted back to sleep.

Later, Sally explained to the hospital attendants that she found José in the parking lot. She apologized profusely for moving him. "I know I should have waited for the paramedics. I just didn't think."

⚓

Four days later, a much improved José sat up in his hospital bed, drinking orange juice. Sally was at his side. She was relieved that he remembered enough to back up the parking lot story. But then, she discovered that he remembered far more than that, including the front loader with her dumping Billy Ray.

"I'm glad it was Billy Ray in the hole and not you," José said.

"How am I going to explain his missing?" she asked.

"I took care of that--I hope," José replied. "I told Mark Travis that I remembered Billy Ray lying beside me in the parking lot. I made up a pretty good story of how he died and ..."

A knock came at the door. Mark Travis walked in accompanied by a tall man with a smooth Hollywood-style appearance, highlighted by an apparel of alligator shoes and a tailored dark suit. Mark could not resist the drama of the moment, "Meet Max Sanford, FBI!"

Sally turned white. FBI? This can't be good.

Max walked over to Sally. His deep bass voice filled the room. "You must be the wife. It's an honor meeting you, Mrs. Larson. Your husband was a hero in my book. He gave his life for what he believed."

"Uh, well, I'm so happy to hear you say that. Yes indeed, Billy Ray was well loved. Everyday I get checks in the mail for Billy Ray's Foundation. It's amazing."

Mark understood the importance of the foundation to Sally, and had taken that into consideration as he guided Max along with his investigation. "Thanks to Max," Mark announced, "we've pretty much wrapped this thing up!"

"Yes, I have," Max said, "There's no doubt in my investigation that this was a revenge killing by a drug cartel. The sheriff was involved in a number of drug busts, and it all points in that direction. I have just a few questions for José, and we'll be finished."

"To the best of my memory," José said.

"Fine," Max continued, "How many attackers do you remember?"

"Oh, at least three or four. One man was their lookout, and another was in the truck."

"A truck?"

"A big truck. There was also this giant of a man with large muscles. He grabbed Billy Ray and I heard something crack. I looked over to see Billy Ray on the ground--his neck was broken."

"You're sure?" Max asked.

"Yes, I passed out just after that."

"This large man you saw--do you remember any scars on his face?"

"Yes, he was badly scared."

"On the left side of his face?"

"Now that you mention it, yes."

"I know the man," Max said, "a chief enforcer for the cartel. We think he's somewhere in the metroplex. It all fits. We're closing in on him."

"I'm so grateful that Mark brought you in on this case," Sally said. "It gives me a sense of closure."

"Lori, you haven't said a word," Max said. "That's not like you."

Lori patted Max on the back. "I'm just amazed at your *incredible* detective work."

"Well, I owe Mark quite a bit. He's a great detective in his own right," Max said.

"Mark, what time do we meet with the media. I assume the Dallas and Fort Worth newspapers will be in on this."

"You bet, and the TV stations, too," Mark pulled out a notepad. "I have the schedule right here. I'll introduce you and let you make the report. The credit is yours."

"Once again I am in your debt," Max said. "Thank you, friend."

⊀

In the sunlight, Lori's eyes seemed to turn a shade of green as she drove Mark home. "So what do you think about my idea of pulling in Max? Do I get credit on this?"

"Absolutely! You get full credit. You got me off the hook! I mentioned the words 'drug cartel' and just like you predicted, Max came running. It was brilliant. You have no idea the pressure Rob and I were under--phone calls, people coming to office--demanding that we find Billy Ray's killer. Thank you for prompting me on the Max card. Perfect timing!"

"You're welcome. So now it's all in the hands of the FBI," Lori said, "and if people have any questions, they can call Max."

Mark reached over to Lori's hand. "You think you're pretty darned clever."

"Yes I do. Why don't I drive us to that new fancy restaurant on the square? Let's celebrate."

"Okay, but the celebration's not going to stop there."

"Really? What have you got in mind?"

Mark leaned over and whispered in Lori's ear, "I'll let you know when we get home."

END

About the Author: Personal Notes

 "The Granbury Murders" is my first *mystery* novel. I'm working on a sequel. Other books, including "Stepfathers: Struggles and Solutions," are from Westminster Press and Judson Press. Mystery writers often say that the most important role for them is the villain, and often fun to craft. A delusional egomaniac is not enough. (We elect those.) For a killer, it takes a special private world. With the divinely chosen Billy Ray, people are at best stepping stones and at worst obstacles in the way. I also enjoyed writing about Mark and Lori, and Sally Mae, the sexy TCU graduate who is a lot more than meets the eye. (I taught at TCU for the past 15 years in the Communication Dept.)

Okay, so I taught at Texas Christian University (TCU)--and at Tarleton University, Texas Tech University, and the University of Oklahoma (where I got my PhD in Communication). I also have a seminary degree from Louisville Presbyterian, and an MA in psychology from Eastern New Mexico University.

My professor role is part time, teaching mostly in the evenings. For my "day job," I'm a Presbyterian minister, serving 18 years in Granbury. I'm Dr. Somervill at TCU and Charlie in Granbury. I prefer Charles.